EYE
OF FAITH

BRENT LADD

A Cable Janson Adventure Thriller

Library of Congress Control Number: 2024918108

Paperback ISBN: 978-1-965092-48-4
Hardcover ISBN: 978-1-965092-49-1

    1. Main Category — Books › Mystery, Thriller & Suspense › Mystery › International Mystery & Crime
    2. Other Category — Books › Literature & Fiction › Action & Adventure › General
    3. Other Category — Books › Mystery, Thriller & Suspense › Thrillers & Suspense › Crime › General

Published by: AR PRESS
Roger L. Brooks, Publisher
roger@americanrealpublishing.com
americanrealpublishing.com

Dedicated to AJ, an inspiring young man with an inquisitive, intelligent mind and a heart as big as they come. A grandson who always keeps me on my toes—never stop, buddy.

THE AXUM EMPIRE 614 CE

A BUNA LUBBA RAN FOR THE back of the monastery, his sandals echoing off the worn stone floor. It was the first time he had run since he was a young man, and nearly every joint in his body protested. *May the Nine Saints give me strength*, he thought, as their judgmental faces painted on the wall flashed past. He prayed they would forgive him for not taking the time to remove his sandals.

It had taken almost eight days for word to reach him, and he could only hope there was still time.

A plan began to form in Lubba's mind as this new predicament forced him to focus beyond his daily routine. Religion was often like that—no change for hundreds of years and then upheaval. What the future brought was now in question for him and his beloved church. Doubt was a leader's Achilles heel, and he pushed those thoughts away.

Over the last sixty-two years, Lubba had seen his black hair go white and his shoulders slump. He had lost his wife many years ago to a sickness that swept through the region, leaving few standing. Somehow, he had endured, moving forward, day after day, building a regimen that was as efficient as it was comfortable. Now, all that was threatened.

His mind never slowed, always pushing him to do more and better. Today, he would need it to be at its very best. *Think!*

Tallow candles illuminated a collection of icons and relics displayed on the chapel's altar. The large carved stone pedestal bore the symbol of truth on its front—a swastika.

He looked over the pieces in front of him. Gold, silver, even once-precious iron. In the back, a stone carving of a goshawk caught his eye. It was a local bird of prey that loved to perch on the chapel's cross outside. Lubba reached for it, steadying his shaking hand as he pulled the carved stone from its perch. He had been present when the statue had been carved, made for a special purpose that only he knew. Now, it would have a second purpose.

The statue was slightly shorter than his forearm and made of red sandstone. Its solid square base supported carved legs perched on a branch. The torso was upright, with facial features including its distinctive hooked beak. Two wings were raised from the sides, connected to the torso with small wooden dowels hammered through holes in the wings and body. The wings were raised and had feathers carved in relief on the front, making the bird look angelic in its pose. The artist had neglected to carve any detail on the back, leaving it smooth to the touch.

"Perfect," Lubba voiced to himself as he looked over the stone effigy, his plan slowly solidifying.

He sat on the stone step in front of the altar and pulled out a sharp steel awl from his robe with his bony fingers. Using the sunlight from a small carved window, Lubba started to scratch out a hurried message on the backside of the bird, one letter and then another.

As an *Abuna,* or patriarch of the Ethiopian Orthodox Church in this area, Lubba was responsible for the worship and messaging his priests shared with their congregations. He was also responsible for the treasury. Every religion needed money to operate and grow—money that had to be collected, shared, used, and, most importantly, saved. The practice of hiding valuables in certain churches, known as *vault churches*, was common in the area. How and where funds were hidden within them was a closely guarded secret. *His* secret.

Lubba looked down at his work. The letters were uneven but clearly visible on the back of the statue. Two lines running from one wing, then across the torso, and ending on the other wing. It would have to do. He forced out the wooden dowels that held the two wings in place and separated them from the body.

Footsteps approached, and Lubba looked up.

A young man in a worn cotton *shamma*, or traditional white robe, paused when he saw Lubba sitting on a step in the small chapel with what looked like a broken sculpture. "Your Excellency, we must hurry."

Lubba smiled at the young, always eager priest. The white brimless kofia on Akan's head was askew, and sweat beaded across his forehead. "We must first find our path before we rush forward."

"Of course," Akan said as he lowered his head in respect.

He had just turned twenty-five only weeks ago. Lubba had assigned him as *Sebate*, or administrator. It was a great honor, and he was keen to prove his worth.

Akan's black eyes lifted, judging the level of scorn Lubba might be feeling at his rushed intrusion, but a kind face and a small smile returned. Akan relaxed and mirrored the sentiment.

Lubba stood and stepped to his friend. "I need three of our most trusted priests…go."

Akan took a second to process the request before running off to fulfill Lubba's wishes.

Lubba took the body of the goshawk and wrapped it in lamb's wool. He placed it inside his robe, then grabbed the two separated wings and ran from the chapel.

The trail to the village was obscured by dust. Riders. Nudel knew no one from the palace would be coming this soon. They had a dead king to deal with.

Nudel had been waiting and planning for this moment for some time now. At the first whispers from his spies of King Gersem's turn of health, he knew there would be a small window in which to act. As a faithful Beta Jew and *hakham*, or rabbi, to his people, it was Nudel's duty to help the faith grow, but living in an almost all-Christian empire had placed hardships of the highest levels in their direction. Those of his flock who would not convert to the new god, *Christ*, had been persecuted, even hunted down. Their numbers had dwindled, and to save the Jewish faith in this land, something bold was required.

As the dust settled, Nudel realized his mistake. Not riders but ten fighters jogging in his direction. Jewish foot soldiers. They were welcomed and given food, water, and a place to rest.

Since the advent of Christianity, local sentiment toward the Jews had changed, much like the smell of a fish left in the sun. *You would think we had killed their God, not the Romans*, Nudel thought.

The "Good Christians" had become hostile at times, forcing many of his followers to convert under extreme duress, even torture. As King Gersem grew older, his interest in a unified Christian Axum empire strengthened. Soldiers had sacked several synagogues, converting them into chapels with sacrilegious crosses on top. Nudel's pleas to meet with the king had been denied, and after many months of bent-knee prayer, it looked as though his God was finally listening.

He stroked his beard as he paced the temporary synagogue made from animal skins, poles, and ropes. At fifty-three, Nudel found his patience waning with every year that passed. Being a Nubian or Beta Jew was a source of pride, and they should be leading by example, not running and hiding.

Nudel's grand plans had all but fizzled over time. His people were still semi-migratory, and their numbers were on the decline. Some of his best and brightest had given up and converted to Christianity, now living in other villages or the capital. *A better and easier life should never take precedence over one's God*, he thought.

The king had died on Tuesday. Word had reached him on Wednesday. Now was the time to make his move before the new king could be crowned and respond. Nudel brushed the front of his white *abaya,* or cloak—a nervous habit he had picked up long ago. He looked up and made a decision, exiting the tent with renewed purpose and a determined stride.

The count was smaller than he had hoped for, but it was sufficient. The ten soldiers who had just arrived, plus his own, made twenty-three Jewish fighters ready to make their mark.

The goal was simple. Eliminate any resistance and garrison a land of their own. A sanctuary where they could grow and worship in peace. A place they could quickly conquer and, most importantly, defend. That meant the Simien mountain region to the northwest. But first, a stop at the nearest monastery. Rumors of newfound wealth and hidden diamonds had reached Nudel's ears, and his people needed that wealth for his plan to work.

The Axum Empire had flourished and expanded under King Gersem, adding lands to the south and increasing trade within its borders. It now consisted of a large section of Eastern Africa along the southern half of the Red Sea.

Since uniting under one religion and making Axum arguably the first Christian state in the world, King Gersem was intent on rebuilding a new Jerusalem here after the original city had been destroyed.

It was the king's desire to unite his people. The natural evolution would be to bring the Jews out of the Old Testament and into the New by tongue or blade.

Axum's riches and abundance of gold made many things possible. It had taken a front seat to everything—politics, trade, the church, commerce, and the royals. Little held sway over the production of wealth and the magnification of Christianity right up until the king's death.

Najashi stood in the ornate palace looking at the well-dressed corpse, for that is all it was. No longer a king to the empire, just another rotting carcass, something the burning incense did little to disguise.

Najashi's mortality flashed as he wondered about his place in this world. Would he be remembered or just another rotting body at the end of his days? He adjusted the tight crown on his head and scratched at his braided beard.

Najashi had been waiting for his coronation for what seemed like an eternity after the required week of mourning, but patience was a kingly trait. He would have to try it out, certain it would not suit him.

At twenty-eight and as the oldest nephew to King Gersem, Najashi was next in line, thanks to a female-only bearing queen. His broad forehead and wide black eyes were an almost exact match to his uncle's.

Najashi bowed his head as the procession exited the palace carrying the catafalque holding the king's corpse down the stone steps and into the streets. Outside, thousands had come to pay their respects and wail at the dead king's feet as he passed. Najashi followed at a respectable distance, letting the people get a good look at their next king. Some called out excitedly, but most were too distraught at the sight of Gersem's corpse to care about the emperor-to-be.

The procession crossed over the bridge on the River Jordan to the largest stele ever seen in the land. At twenty-four meters tall, the stone obelisk loomed ahead of the funeral march. It had been carved from granite and erected just a month ago, along with an extended burial chamber beneath. The practice was most likely carried down from a time when the land was known as Punt, an extension of ancient Egypt. But unlike in Egypt, there was no mummification of the body.

Najashi watched as the corpse was lowered into the tomb, then took a few minutes to speak to the people. The masses gathered to listen, each person hopeful the future of the empire would be bright.

Faez's tribe had first arrived from across the Red Sea many years ago. They were fleeing persecution in Arabia and were hopeful to find a place of safety across the narrow strip of ocean. Faez truly believed he was following Allah's will.

King Gersem had welcomed them into his lands. The king was, after all, a "Good Christian," something Faez knew little about. Years later, the Prophet Muhammad himself had written in the *Hadith*, an appendage to the Koran, explicitly prohibiting jihad against the Axum Christians because of the king's embrace.

Now, nearly twenty-five years since the crossing, there was peace and prosperity for Faez's small band of Muslims among the Christians. He placed that squarely on the king's shoulders or, rather, the dead king's shoulders.

Faez's mind turned to what might come next. He knew very little of the soon-to-be emperor, but from his experience, royalty could be much like a starling's song, changing their tune every few minutes.

Faez's village had more than fifty mud-brick homes, called *maskan*. There was a small square in the middle and a stout mosque next to it. The people were devout, performing their *salah*, or prayer, five times a day.

To Faez, it was paradise on earth, far from the persecution that had driven them here. May Allah forgive his pride. As a faithful Muslim and Grand Mufti of his people, Faez's responsibility was to help nurture the faith. Living in a Christian state required that growth be achieved through a growing the population, rather than conversion. The Jews had tried that, and it caused severe friction. Something Faez wanted nothing to do with.

The Arabs' lighter olive skin, in contrast to the Nubian inhabitants, had made them stand out in the land, but now it was time to stand out even more. Whispers had come to Faez about a planned revolt north of his village. Not something countrywide but a local skirmish designed behind the temporary loss of leadership in the state. With a little luck and Allah's blessing, Faez could make a statement the new king could not ignore, something that would continue to garner favor for his people.

He gathered every camel in the village and twenty trusted armed riders. These riders were seasoned fighters who had helped maintain peace in the area. A peace Faez was willing to fight and even die for.

Abuna Lubba exited through the thick wooden doors of the chapel and into the glaring sun. He squinted at the three priests Akan brought with him into the courtyard. They were wearing the more traditional *gabi*, the handmade cloth draped over their shoulders and wrapped around them. Two carried small knapsacks. Akan had chosen well.

Lubba decided to give it to them straight. "King Gersem has died, and the Jews are using his death to make war. Christianity here is at risk. The New Jerusalem is also at risk and we must do all within our power to preserve it."

The three young men looked horrified but stood their ground. This was not the type of thing a priest trained for.

"Not to worry, my faithful servants. I have a plan," Lubba said as he passed out the left wing to the first man. "Take this to the capital and see that an Abuna gets it."

The priest nodded, wondering what was so special about the stone wing.

Lubba handed the right wing to the second priest. "Go east and build a safe place to secure this. Stay there until I or another Abuna comes for you."

"How will you find me?"

"By your good works, my son," Lubba said.

"I will, my Abuna."

"Hurry now."

Both men ran off, each in their own direction.

Dust on the horizon grew as trouble approached. It was not lost on Lubba. He turned to the final priest. "Get to chapel Beite Amharic, burn the bridge, and seal the entrance. We can't have the Jews or anyone else finding its secret."

The priest nodded nervously.

"You can do this. I have faith in you," Lubba said with encouragement.

The priest hugged Lubba, then turned and sprinted away.

Lubba watched him disappear before turning to Akan. "Akan, my brother." Lubba pulled out the rest of the sheepskin-wrapped statue from his robe and handed it to him. "Take this and make a pilgrimage for only the most worthy, from Beite Amharic back to Saint Georges."

"Are you not coming with me?

"No, my son. This is where we part."

"I will not hear of it," Akan said.

Lubba took the man's right hand in his. "I'm sorry, Akan. Your journey is still ahead. Mine is here with the monastery. If God wills it, we will see each other again. If not, we will meet in paradise. But you must go now, or all will be lost."

"It is just treasure. We can find another," Akan said.

"It is the church's lifeblood, and we must protect it with our very lives."

Akan realized Lubba was right and shared an embrace before running away with tears streaming down his face.

Nudel kept his horse at a steady pace. It would do no good to outrun his foot soldiers. The army, if you could call it that, consisted of three camels, two horses, and nineteen foot soldiers. Each was armed with a sharpened spear, a small shield, and a sword. Six support staff followed behind, pulling hand carts filled with food, water, and a scroll of the Torah.

Some miles behind, women, children, the elderly, and everything they owned brought up the rear. Several overloaded carts were pulled by donkeys, and dust billowed west with the hot breeze.

The landscape was mostly flat, with a few tree-covered rolling hills. In the distance, a formidable mountain range touched the blue sky.

The first of the monastery's outbuildings came into view, and Nudel called out. "We are close. Divide up."

Half the soldiers moved to the right, the other half left.

Lubba stepped up to the front steps of the monastery, his monastery. Jewish warriors approached from two directions. He stood as tall as his aged shoulders would allow and cried out. "This is Christ's church. You heathens have no business here. Leave now or suffer the wrath of the king."

Nudel pulled his horse to a stop. "The king is no more. I, Abel Nudel, hakham to my people and rabbi to our God, am in charge here."

Nudel looked over the empty courtyard and the lone Abuna proudly standing on the steps of his church. "I will allow you to take your priests and leave, or we will do and take what we must. I know you have diamonds and treasure hidden somewhere."

"My God has no time for scared rabbits that flee at the first sign of danger," Lubba said as he held firm.

"Your God is false." Nudel nodded his head slightly to the right.

A nocked arrow from a warrior loosed. It impacted Lubba mid-chest. He fell from the steps awkwardly, his life's work and blood on display.

Nudel watched without emotion. "Go and find me those diamonds."

The command had every warrior charging forward, spears at the ready.

Lubba's last vision was of the demons of Satan prevailing. It was too much to bear, so he closed his eyes and let go.

The Jewish warriors destroyed everything not worth taking. Fires were lit, and priests were roughly gathered and pulled to the courtyard.

Akan watched from behind a nearby hagenia tree. He was too curious to just run straight off. His precious monastery was sacked, and many of the buildings were burning. The man who had been more than a father to him had been cast aside like camel dung from a sandal. His remaining brothers rounded up like goats. It was all so terrifying. Suddenly realizing his mistake in staying behind to watch, his body shook with horror. This was no way to fulfill his master's wishes. He quickly stuffed the stone statue Lubba had given him deep into his robe and grabbed his small satchel. As he turned to run, a man with a sword and raised spear stepped into his path. Akan froze.

Akan was marched and forced to his knees, joining his fellow priests in a simple straight line in the middle of the courtyard. Gold, silver, and more from the chapel's altar were piled on the ground in front of them. Akan looked down the row. Eight other brothers knelt beside him. That meant six had gotten away or had been killed already. He said a silent prayer for his fellow priests and then, just before finishing, added himself to the prayer.

Nudel stepped from his horse and looked the priests over. "Who is the treasurer for this monastery?"

Jittery glances popped in his direction from a few of the frightened men, but no one spoke.

"Your Abuna is dead. I will give you the same chance I gave him. Tell me what I want to know, and you can run from here with the sandals on your feet."

Faez encouraged his camel to pick up the pace with a flick of his *sjambok*, or camel whip. His acacia wood mahawi kept him locked in place as the animal began to gallop.

He smiled at the sound. Twenty-one camels and their riders were all bearing down on their enemy. It was marvelous.

Before them, a hazy view of a caravan of handcarts and donkeys appeared on the trail.

The fighters galloped up from behind, surprising the forward-looking drivers. Screams and panic started from the rear and grew as curved swords, called *scimitars*, dispatched any animal being used to haul belongings. Women and children ran while a few older men stayed to fight. They were cut down without a second thought.

Faez and his men paid little attention to any of it as his force swept through, disrupting the caravan, leaving it disabled and broken in their dust.

Up ahead, the cross at the top of the monastery came into view as it cleared the tree line. The monastery was on fire.

His chief warrior called over from his right. "Do you see it?"

"Yes. Allah be with us," Faez said.

His men began their ululation battle cry.

Akan felt himself shaking as Matar, the priest to his left, fell to the ground, his blood soaking the compact earth. Worst of all, Matar's lifeless eyes stared at him in confusion. He had been part of Akan's everyday life here in the monastery. Matar was a friendly priest with a childlike sense of humor, something he hid well around the older priests, but Akan had seen it and loved it. Now he was gone, and Akan was about to join Matar and the others lying dead beside him.

The blade of a very sharp sword moved to Akan's throat, and the words were repeated.

"Where is the treasure trove…the diamonds?" Nudel said as he glanced over at the paltry collection of relics his men had collected so far.

Akan's lips stuttered.

He remembered a time as a child when he and his two brothers had been accused of killing a neighbor's chicken. Akan's father had been furious.

They had been throwing rocks, and his little brother had accidentally hit the chicken. The three boys had made an oath to remain silent despite their father's intense interrogation and eventual punishment. They had all remained silent. It had taken a few days before Akan and his two brothers were able to sit again, but the bond between them was never stronger.

Today would be just another oath he would make between the Lord and his dead fellow priests. Akan lifted his chin and spoke. "Only the Abuna knew that…and you have killed him."

"Be done with him," Nudel said, his patience now gone. He turned to the chapel, confident he would discover the treasure's location, even if he had to tear the place down stone by stone.

The soldier moved his blade to sweep it across the throat of the young priest.

A war cry preceded thundering hooves, suddenly echoing from every direction as camels and riders crashed into the courtyard.

It was chaos, with scimitars swinging and cleaving any Jew in their path.

Jewish warriors tried to regroup and use their spears against the huge raging beasts.

Akan dropped to the ground after the Jewish soldier who was about to dispatch him took a hack to his neck and fell, gushing blood. Their fates had swapped.

Two camels and a few warriors from both sides fell during the brief battle, but once Nudel was surrounded, the rest of the Jewish fighters surrendered. It was over.

Nudel looked up with hatred at the lighter-skinned Arabs who surrounded him. After all his planning, he had failed his people and his God.

Faez stepped off his camel. "We will take you to the new king as a coronation present. Stopping an uprising in his kingdom should grant us additional favor and a long life in Axum."

His men cheered. Some of them started to tie up the prisoners. It was going to be a glorious day.

"Take the gold and silver as our payment," Faez said while pointing to the pile of precious relics nearby. He turned to the downed priest. "Christian brother."

"Yes?" Akan said, standing back up slowly, his knees still weak.

"Be sure, young priest, to spread the word of our actions today," Faez said.

Akan nodded his head in gratitude. "It will be done, Grand Mufti." Akan gave the Muslim leader a slight bow and left the monastery and his dead brothers behind. He needed to get word to the capital, but first, he had a promise to Abuna Lubba to fulfill. As Akan ran, he pressed his hand to the statue hidden under his robe, making sure it was secure. He would make a pilgrimage for only the most worthy of the church to follow to the greatest treasure he had ever seen.

CHAPTER ONE

NOBODY WANTED THE JOB, NOT even the locals. Cable didn't mind, he had done worse. Just a few months ago, he had waded through raw sewage to escape a bunch of armed hoodlums attempting to rob him in Mombasa. So, moving the overfilled latrine to a new location was relatively simple. Cover up the old smelly hole and dig a new one. Then move the canvas privacy tent over to the new hole.

At twenty-seven years old, Cable Janson had seen a few things. If he were to ever write up a CV, it would go something like:

- Grew up in Lakewood, east of Denver.
- Played lacrosse and studied martial arts. He eventually became a good student and even played saxophone in a local band named Rottweiler.
- Worked during the summers as an intern at the History Colorado Center and could speak French and Spanish by the time he was thirteen.
- Received a full ride to Harvard for modern and ancient linguistics and cross-disciplinary studies at the prestigious Radcliffe Institute.
- Consistently at the top of his class and destined for a high-level academic career.

It was at that point where the CV took a turn. After three years of hard studying, Cable decided to take a semester off. He bought a multi-destination global airline ticket and headed east.

He remembered the ad that had first caught his attention. *24,902 Miles Circumference, 7 Billion People, Over 6,000 Languages, 1,300 Destinations To More Than 190 Countries, One Ticket.*

He had traveled almost halfway around the globe before deciding the world held more interest and learning than an entire lifetime of college. That was the fork in Cable's path, and that was six years ago.

In spite of globalization's push forward, there were thousands of unique cultures and traditions still flourishing on Planet Earth and Cable was eager to imbibe. He'd seen a Malagasy tribal warfare dance next to a McDonald's in Nomad, Mauritius, and attended an Inuit *Quviasukvik*, a New Year celebration that takes place on Christmas Day in Ugashik, Alaska.

Cable had been beaten up in a street brawl in Prague, blessed by a monk in Bhutan, slept next to a camel in the Sahara, robbed twice in Istanbul, was inspired at the summit of Kilimanjaro, and all along the way, he'd gained many friends and expanded his considerable language skills and cultural knowledge.

Cable pulled off his tee shirt and tossed it aside. At six foot one and two hundred pounds, it was just another chance to get in a good workout. That was, however, once the old hole was covered over because man did it stink. Heat and feces never mixed well.

Cable adjusted the straw hat that helped keep the sun from cooking his brain. He looked out to the sea, wondering if cooler weather was in his future.

The twenty-six-kilometer-long island of Failaka was shaped like a slightly curved zucchini. It was just north of the equator in the Persian Gulf, and the slight breeze he felt was surely coming out of an oven, not off the nearby water. The mix of loam, clay, and rock made the work challenging, but progress soon showed, and Cable had to bend over to pull the dirt out of the deepening hole. He noticed the shovel still had the sticker on the handle from the store, Walmart. Even Kuwait City, just twenty kilometers across the water, had embraced the seduction of capitalism, a "blanding" plague that destroyed individualism and trapped many in a lifelong religious-like devotion to currency. Cable had seen America's unique towns and main streets give way to this cataclysm, making one town look just like the next. Its occupants were all chasing the same thing, destined to work and die in an unending chain.

The shovel hit hard with a twang and Cable let out a sigh, another rock. He used the blade to clear the loose soil away. The rock was flat, unnaturally flat. Cable reached down and brushed the last of the dirt off to get a better look. The flat stone had carved, unrecognizable letters on it. He stood and looked east.

The camp was a collection of tents and overhead tarps used for shade. Tables were lined up underneath. Some were used for eating, some held computers, and some displayed samples. The French-American-Kuwaiti-sponsored dig had discovered evidence of Christian occupation before the Muslims. It was a significant find so deep into the Moorish empire.

Beyond the camp was a cloud of dust identifying the actual dig that was going on. Stacked stone walls with many inner-connecting rooms stood out in the bright sun. Zuhal Injera, the Find Manager and a local hire out of Kuwait City, stood tall next to a group of researchers and students as they lifted a meter-tall, intact stone cross out of the dirt. Across from Zuhal was the Site Manager, Hilary Lavigne. She shared a triumphant smile with Zuhal that nearly knocked him over. He had longed for such attention, and even though it was over an artifact, he welcomed it.

Dr. Hilary Lavigne was a recent graduate from the prestigious Sorbonne Université in archeology. As a child, she had always been fascinated by history. She loved the stories even the simplest of artifacts could tell. She grew up on the outskirts of Lyon to a French father and an English mother, a bitter combination that carried the weight of historical rivals into their relationship. Hilary had taken the job in Kuwait, eager to prove herself and if she was honest, it was also to put even more distance between her and home life.

The cross was carried and set on a waiting table in the camp. Fala Aziz, the Excavation Director from Kuwait, stepped up to inspect it. She was in her mid-forties with dark eyes and pale features. Her hijab was light-brown, contrasting her darker pants and blouse, a mix of modern, practical, and traditional. To keep the sun off her head, she carried a small umbrella, which she lowered once under the shade of the tarp. As a devout Muslim, she had a passion for walking the true path but also for her country's past. Various religions played a strong role throughout its history, each worthy of at least a bold footnote.

"Incredible. Let's get it cleaned up, and Hilary, make an etching of it," Fala said with a hint of pride.

Hilary nodded and assigned two workers to start the cleaning process.

Cable walked up, speaking perfect Arabic. "Fala, I have found something you should look at."

"I thought you were digging the new latrine? Praise Allah, I hope it's not an unexploded bomb."

Failaka Island had a long, sordid history due to its strategic location near the confluence of the Tigris and Euphrates rivers with the sea. Starting with its early Mesopotamian settlements to Alexander the Great's interests and now the local Arab occupants, the remote island had been a home and a battlefield.

In 1990, the Iraqis invaded and removed all civilians from the island, mining the beaches and using the buildings as target practice. The Allies evicted the Iraqis a year later and established a temporary base on the island during the war.

After Operation Desert Storm, the mines were removed, but few Kuwaitis returned, leaving most of the island desolate and in disrepair.

Hilary followed Fala over to the other side of the camp where Cable had been digging. Over the last six weeks, despite their political differences, Hilary and Cable had become close friends. He looked up as the two women approached. Hilary's long brown hair moved with the breeze, and when she saw him looking her way, impossibly white teeth glowed back at him.

Fala, without meaning to, interrupted their moment. "So what have you got?"

Cable gestured down the hole. "Take a look."

Fala bent down and studied the inscriptions on the flat stone for a minute. "We hired you as an interpreter, not a digger." She stood slowly on tired knees. "But it appears you have many talents." She glanced at Hilary and Cable wondering if they picked up her double meaning at their burgeoning relationship. Fala dusted her hands off, the dirt here could be very powdery and worked its way into every crevasse. "I don't immediately recognize the symbols. I can tell you it's old, maybe Sumerian. We'll need to dig it up and get a better look at it. Do a little research…Sorry, but it looks like you will have to dig a new latrine somewhere else."

"*Bialtabe*," Cable said, which meant 'of course.'

"Ask Hilary to get some diggers on this right away."

Cable switched from Arabic to French in a single beat. But before he could get the words out, Hilary piped up.

"I'll get this roped off, and we can start digging."

The setting sun reflected off the Red Sea and illuminated the airborne dust, making it glow orange. The view of the camp beyond was hazy. The excavation had revealed a stone about the size of a common grave marker, only rounded on both ends. It had been broken, but both pieces were there and still fit together perfectly. As the dinner bell rang, workers secured the site for the day, covered the stone for the night, and headed for the camp's mess.

Twenty dusty and hot members of the tri-nation dig sat and enjoyed a simple meal of kebabs and rice. To the untrained ear, it was a mishmash of unrecognizable words, but the groups naturally separated themselves into their languages of choice—French, Arabic, and English. The excitement at having two incredible finds so close together was palpable and outshined their weary bones.

The Sumerian text on the stone reset their historical knowledge of the island back to around 2000 BCE. With a little bit of computer and satellite phone work, they had managed to decipher some of the words on the stone. It was a proclamation of some sort from the city-state of Ur. It would require an expert in ancient Sumerian from here on out.

Zuhal dabbed the lamb grease from his beard and stole a look at the French group sitting just down from him, more specifically, at Hilary. She was so full of life. The Arab women he was familiar with were noth-

17

ing like her. He couldn't decide if that kind of progress was good or bad, but some night, he hoped to get a sample of it.

At thirty-two and quite handsome, he had yet to marry, a mark against him back home, but his college education and work at the Sheikh Abdullah Al Salem Cultural Centre had been fulfilling. He was next in line to be a curator, and this dig would go a long way to that end. It was too bad there was no money in archeology.

Hilary caught him staring and gave him an uneasy smile. Zuhal turned back to his food. *Give her time*, he thought.

After dinner, Hilary and Cable took a stroll along the beach. The waves on this side of the island were ankle slappers that curled and died on soft sand.

Hilary spoke both French and English, compliments of her parents. When she was alone with Cable, they often bounced between the two languages. Tonight, for whatever reason, she was all English, and Cable was happy to conform. They moved along the water's edge, thankful for the cooler evening temperature.

A slight beeping had Hilary pulling her phone from her pocket. She glanced at the screen and put it back.

"You have a signal out here?"

"Says the man who doesn't carry a cell phone. Half a bar. Just the occasional text gets through. My mom's always looking to insert herself."

"That's what moms do. You're lucky you still have one in your life." Cable thought of his childhood for a moment. Losing his mother at such a young age had been devastating. He dismissed the thought and turned back to Hilary. *That was a long time ago.*

"Maybe," she said, without believing her words.

"Wow. Okay, subject change?" Cable playfully asked.

"Please."

He paused just a bit to fiddle with the prayer bracelet on his left wrist and smiled as he watched her deal with the uncomfortable moment. Even in the dim light, she was an extraordinary woman, intelligent, playful, and downright beautiful. Though she never considered herself so, she often dressed down and wore no makeup to prove it. Cable decided to give her a break and changed the subject.

"You've never really talked about your personal life. We always just seem to get stuck on work or politics. So, tonight, I'm going to tell you a bit about myself."

"Just what a girl wants to hear…a man talking about himself. And, by the way, it's hardly a subject change."

"Hear me out…and call it a shift."

"Okay," she said, a bit hopeful.

Cable took a deep breath. "Well, we both know you're pretty serious about your political agenda and opinions. Whereas I, on the other hand, am politically ambivalent. But do you know why that is?" He didn't wait for her to reply. "No, of course you don't. Growing up American, we currently have two very polarizing political parties. People seem to gravitate to one end or the other. The middle ground is dying faster than our middle class, and I believe…"

Hilary crossed her arms and shook her head.

Cable paused mid-sentence. "What?"

She just glared at him without comment.

"Would you rather hear about my eight years of Krav Maga training growing up or the six months I spent in China trying to convince a Sifu to let me study Pak Mei? What about my time in a Bhutan monastery, learning to forget all about fighting? Now that is a subject change."

"You are incorrigible. And for the record, you are not like any guy I have ever met before. But I thought we came out here for something more…interesting and tangible," she said.

Cable slowly closed his mouth, realizing his error. "You are so right." He placed his hand on Hilary's shoulder and pulled her close, real close, sliding his hand to the back of her neck. Their eyes met and locked for a second. Being this near without kissing felt slightly awkward and uncomfortable, but neither pulled back. The air around them charged with electricity as each detailed every pore and nuance of the other. Hilary's green eyes had small brown and yellow streaks. Her pale skin was flawless and smooth.

Cable's light-brown eyes were filled with gold flecks. He had the first signs of crow's feet starting to form from many days in the sun. His short beard was scraggly but fit him perfectly.

The intimacy was intoxicating and unnerving all at once.

Cable allowed the feeling to bloom, and Hilary did the same. They let the charge fuel them, and just when it felt like they could take no more, Cable pulled her to his lips and kissed her.

Hilary responded eagerly as lips brushed and parted, upping the voltage.

Eventually and slowly, they separated. It took a moment before Cable could speak. "I'd call that interesting and tangible," he said as he opened his eyes and watched Hilary's reaction.

It started with the edges of her lips, but soon, a smile that filled her whole face replied. "That's more like it, Lamoureux. I was thinking after our contract is up. I would like to show you Par..." Hilary stopped talking. Cable's eyes had shifted off to the left, focused on something other than her. She turned to see what was so important.

"Are you expecting company?" Cable asked.

A small black shadow moved across the water, leaving a white wake behind it.

"No."

"Stay here and out of sight."

Wassim Uday stood at the front of the boat, his black keffiyeh tied to his head flapping in the breeze. The sun had set, and the moon was just above the horizon, kicking off fractured reflections on the undulating water. He could make out the darkness of land ahead against the purple ocean. The text message had given him little time to prepare, but he had managed five capable men to assist him.

The craft slowed, slamming its bow into the wet sand.

Wassim jumped to shore. He was wearing all black with only one accessory, a locked and loaded AK-47. He stood nearly six feet tall and, at forty-two, was still a force of nature. His rugged looks were only betrayed by a collection of missing and blackened teeth. A lifetime of sweets and poor hygiene taking its toll.

He waved, and the others fanned out along the sand, each carrying the same weapon. The AK-47 was a gas-operated assault rifle that had found favor around the globe and was loved and feared by millions.

The antiquities black market in the Middle East had soared since the Gulf War, and a hoard of tomb raiders and collectors had taken their toll. The supply had dried up, but the demand was never higher. It required Wassim to adapt to the new normal, and tonight, he would cash in. Unarmed academics were no match for bullets.

The lights from the camp were just up ahead, and Wassim and his men began to circle the tents and close in.

"Professor Aziz," Cable called out as he ran to the camp, out of breath.

Fala Aziz stepped from her tent, wondering what the commotion was all about. She watched as Cable came into the gas lanternlight, a look of concern on his face.

"What is it?"

"A boat has landed just up the beach, and I'm not sure of their intent. Are you exp…"

A retort of gunfire finished Cable's sentence and answered his question.

Fala jerked at the sound of the shots and quickly ducked into her tent. She fumbled through the bottom of her bag and found an old pistol. Before exiting, she grabbed her satellite phone and slipped it under the bottom of the tent.

She emerged holding a Webley pistol in a shaking hand. Her eyes were big and darted about the camp, ready for anything.

Her Kuwaiti childhood had seen war, terrorism, and hatred. As a woman, she had been forced to the bottom of the pecking order and lived a life in fear. It wouldn't take much for her to be on the wrong side of any given male's whims with no recourse.

"I'm not sure that's a good idea, professor. Pistol versus machine guns," Cable said.

Fala looked down at the old pistol. It had been her grandfather's. He had collected it off a dead British officer during the battles over sand and oil prior to WWII. She handed it to Cable, and he tucked it into the back of his pants.

"Let's get everyone together. They are either going to rob or kill us, and there is not a lot we can do about it. We can start by not giving them a reason to kill us," Cable said.

Fala nodded and called out across the camp.

Soon, pointed gun barrels and then terrifying men dressed in black appeared in the sparse camp lighting. They surrounded the frightened workers, grouping them together. Cable stepped to the front and, in perfect Arabic, asked, "Who's in charge here?"

Wassim stepped forward. He had the look of a killer and pointed his rifle at Cable.

"What is it you want?" Cable asked, with no anxiety in his voice.

"I am but a simple collector and seller of goods. The kind of goods you possess. You let me take them…no one gets shot today. Agreed?" Wassim said.

Cable looked to Fala, who nodded. He translated the message into French. He decided to skip an English version.

"Everyone have a seat." Wassim gestured with the end of his assault rifle.

The group sat as four armed guards circled, keeping watch.

Wassim moved to the table where many artifacts were laid out. He perused them like a casual shopper in the produce aisle. The fifth man in the group followed along behind with a large canvas bag.

Wassim collected a few choice items. A bronze bowl, some intact pots, and a corroded dagger with a few jewels still in place on the hilt.

Cable looked over to Fala and he could see her rage rising with each piece taken. He placed a hand on her arm and whispered. "They're not worth your life."

Wassim placed his fingers on the cross they had pulled from the ancient church earlier that day.

It proved Christianity was here before the Muslims, and it was the main reason for the dig.

"What is this abomination?" He hefted it up and slammed it to the ground, destroying it.

A verbal gasp escaped Fala's mouth, and Cable squeezed her arm, employing her to stay calm.

The act was not lost on Wassim. He stepped back over to the group. "Where is the carved stone I was promised," Wassim called out.

The words "was promised" struck Cable as odd. Had someone betrayed the team? He looked around to see if anyone would answer.

When they didn't, he did a quick body count. Two team members were missing. Hilary and the Find Manager, Zuhal Injera. One of them was a conspirator.

Wassim moved closer and pointed his gun at Fala. "Where is the stone?"

"It's still in the pit. Cable pointed toward the new excavation. "Over that way."

"Come, you will show me," Wassim demanded.

The fifth guard set his filled canvas bag next to one of the other guards and followed behind, keeping his sights on Cable.

Cable discreetly made sure his shirt was covering the old pistol he had stuffed in the back of his pants. He led the thieves to the new dig site and pointed to the artifact they had spent the day carefully excavating.

Wassim pointed his light at the stone and nodded slowly. He smiled, showing off the three remaining teeth in front like a living jack-o-lantern.

There would never be a better time to use the pistol, Cable thought. The two men seemed enamored by the site of the carved relic, most likely already counting the money it would bring them. Cable instinctively reached for the gun and then stopped. No loss of life was worth an old stone, even gun-toting bandits. Besides, if the bandits wanted to kill them it would have been done by now. He pulled his hand back.

"This will do. Take him to the others and bring Omar back with you," Wassim said.

One of the guards systematically went through every tent, taking anything of value and making sure to collect any phones. He then had the hostages empty their pockets, grabbing up two more phones. Cable was shoved down beside his teammates. He could see moving flashlights over at the new dig site as three men collected and carried the artifact toward the waiting boat.

Once the armed man had ransacked the camp, the bandit grabbed the canvas bag with the artifacts and whispered something into the tallest guard's ear before departing.

This act made Cable nervous, and he slowly moved his right hand behind him until it rested on the butt of the gun.

The rest of the men moved off into the darkness for the beach.

The lone guard raised his AK and backed off several feet, but he did not fire. He just stayed put, waiting and pointing his weapon. The tension was substantial.

After a few minutes, a whistle in the distance sounded, and the tall guard turned and ran off.

The hostages finally released the breath they had been collectively holding.

Fala scrambled to her feet, sickened at their situation. "Everyone stay here, they are leaving."

Cable translated.

A shot followed a scream of "Traitor!" down by the water.

Hilary, Cable thought. Without delay, he pulled the pistol and sprinted into the darkness beyond.

Fala moved to the edge of the camp, willing her eyes to see into the night. She was angry and ready for anything.

Hilary had moved into the sea, keeping her head just above the water. She watched as several rifles fired into the air. The flashes were like a faulty fireworks show. It was hard to see what was going on, and after what seemed like forever, she slipped from the water for a closer look. Her team was circled up in camp, sitting on the ground. Several armed guards were watching them and three men were headed her way. She froze and dropped to the ground.

As they got closer, she recognized the one in front. It was Cable, and he was leading two armed men to the new artifact he had discovered.

The man she had started to care for was a traitor. She watched as he showed them the stone. He was speaking to them casually, but she didn't understand the words. Without a weapon, she was helpless to do anything but observe and hopefully report to the authorities. She tried to remember every detail of the other two men. Their faces just glowed from their flashlight's reflection off the stone.

Despite the fact she was wet from the ocean, she could feel herself perspiring, her nerves a jangled mess.

Cable and one other man suddenly turned and headed back to camp. That's when she saw the rifle pointed at him, and all the angst she was building against Cable melted away. He was being forced at gunpoint. She needed to do something to help.

After they passed her position, she moved back to the water's edge and turned right. She headed for the boat she had seen beached in the sand a few hundred meters down. As she approached, a figure sitting in the craft came into view in the pallid moonlight. It took a second before she recognized the form.

"Zuhal?" she hissed.

"Hilary." He stood suddenly, moving about the boat. It was an open-bow wooden fishing boat about seven meters long with a large outboard motor on the back.

"Praise Allah, you okay. I try break boat," he said, in broken French.

"That is a bad idea, Zahal. Think about it. Desperate armed men stuck with us on this island? We want them to leave."

"Yes, you are right." He stepped out of the boat and over to her. "Moonlight good to you," he said as he moved a tuft of hair from her face.

"Not now, Zuhal," Hilary said, pulling back from him.

"Yes now," he said as he pointed a pistol at her midsection.

"You?"

He only smiled back. Finally, he had his prize. "You make hostage."

Hilary could only see red at this betrayal. "Putain de mère. Traitor!" she screamed as she charged him without fear.

Cable ran for the ocean. A second shot rang out, off to his right. He saw the flash and changed his course. Next, a motor started and began to move away. By the time Cable hit the sand, the boat was powering off and out of range for the small pistol. He paused, gazing out at the men who had violated this peaceful place. That's when he noticed two bodies rolling in the small waves.

The Kuwaiti Police Agency stormed the beach like a military invasion as the pink glow of a new day began. Fala had used her satellite phone to immediately call them with the details, but the KPA had still taken six hours to arrive.

The thieves and murderers had gotten away with priceless artifacts and had taken one life, Hilary Lavigne. Zahul Injera had also been shot, but after his betrayal, the team no longer considered him one of them.

Raqib Nassar was the sergeant in charge, and it took very little time for him to get a general picture of what had happened. It wasn't the first time he had been to a dig site victimized by robbers. Police officers down by the water secured the two bodies. They tagged, bagged, and loaded them onto the boat.

The team had been separated and asked a thousand questions, repeated many times. Finally, they were allowed to just sit in the shade of a tarp as a group. Conversations were muted and few as the ferry boat that had brought the hopeful group of archeologists to Failaka Island pulled up. It would now take them back empty-handed, battered, and bruised.

Cable let guilt consume him, thinking about what he could have done differently to prevent Hilary's death. He flashed back to her vacant eyes staring up at him as he rolled her over in the shallow surf. It would haunt him for some time. Cable placed his bag on the bench as he loaded the ferry. His thoughts were lost and his next move was unsure. He glanced over as Fala sat next to him. Her look of despair was obvious. It was as if the heart and soul of the team had been extracted.

"Cable Janson?" The voice had a familiar and distinct accent.

Cable looked up from his thoughts.

Raqib Nassar stood holding his satellite phone out toward Cable. "I have an emergency call routed here for you."

Cable took the phone and put it to his ear. "Yes. I'm Cable Janson…I see…uh-huh…uh-huh…I understand. Okay, I will." Cable hung up and handed back the phone. His gaze set at a thousand miles out.

"Everything alright, Cable?" Fala asked, genuine concern in her voice.

"My father is dead…I guess I'm going home."

CHAPTER TWO

RAIN THREATENED BUT NEVER CAME. Instead, a cold wind howled across the grass pocked with white tombstones, taking every fallen leaf and meticulous hairstyle with it. The turnout was average, with friends of the family in attendance. The reality that Cable was the last in his family's line was not lost on him, but what to do about that information was. He managed a stoic pose, biding his time until he heard the final amen, then braced himself as a queue of black-clad well-wishers and condolence-givers filed past. Most he didn't know, but a few of his father's acquaintances brought back old memories, some good. He forced a smile and allowed the sorrow of others to be unloaded on him.

By 10 p.m., Cable was finally alone in the house he'd grown up in. It was a well-maintained three-story red brick home with three fireplaces and a gabled roof in Lakewood, Colorado. The home had been in the family for three generations, holding joy, love, happiness, and sorrow.

He loosened the tie on his rented suit and took a moment to peruse his father's liquor cabinet. A twenty-five-year-old bottle of Macallan caught his eye, and he poured himself a glass. The rich amber liquid had smoky notes of citrus and cinnamon, and it embraced and warmed his very core. It filled a void, if only for a short while.

It had been some time since Cable had touched alcohol. Working on an Arab-sponsored dig prohibited it. A couple of the guys had smuggled a few bottles in, but Cable respected the local beliefs and had not partaken.

The aged whiskey relaxed his mind. He picked up a framed photo and turned it over as he sat in his father's overstuffed leather chair. His recently shaved face held tension from the day. He tried to let it go. Holding on to feelings of resentment toward a dead person was a wasted effort.

Cable remembered watching his father sit in the same chair next to the fire, sharing stories from the past. It seemed important to him to pass on the family history to his son. Exploits of his grandfather and one of his favorites—the time his mother, Dolores, did her first solo flight in an unexpected storm. The plane had made it to the ground but would never fly again. Dolores would always pipe in at this point with her famous, *"I walked away in one piece, so it must have been a good landing."* Then his dad, August, would reply, *"It took me three years to pay off that plane."* Everyone would laugh. It was the most wonderful feeling. Those were the memories he needed to hang on to.

That had all stopped when Dolores died suddenly and unexpectedly on a Friday. Cable would never forget, it was the day of his sixth-grade graduation. His father had come to collect him before the ceremony. Cable had been put out until he saw the tears in his father's eyes.

August had sat Cable down on the concrete steps just outside the school's entrance and given him the news. It had taken Cable several hours to accept the words. *"Your mother won't be coming home, son."* He remembered watching his father's tears fall, making little dark star patterns on the impersonal cement.

August never fully recovered. His broken heart dictated his actions from then on, and the only way he was able to survive each day was to focus forward. He buried himself in work, and Cable suddenly took a back seat at the worst possible time in his life. No matter how hard he tried to get his father's attention, Cable had become nothing more than just a side note.

The night the policeman had brought Cable home—rather than booking him on vandalism and drunk and disorderly at the station—was a turning point for the young rebel. Cable realized right then and there that his father would never care whether he went to jail, college, or the moon. It was time to stop trying to connect and time to live his own life, for him and no one else.

Without realizing it, he had become his father, doubling down on activities and schooling. As a self-proclaimed overachiever, Cable garnered attention from his teachers and coaches but still failed at the one thing he most desired.

If you were to look back and analyze it, you might think that Cable had spent most of his youth trying to get his dad's attention and approval. But no matter how low or high he climbed, his father was lost to him. It took an around-the-world trip to finally break the grasp the man held over him. And if Cable was being honest, his desire to come home and have all those feelings resurface was extremely low.

He took another sip and let the subtle burn work its way down his throat. He considered lighting a fire, but that would require getting out of this chair, and he didn't have the energy.

Across from him was The Wall. That was the name he had given it as a child. It was the one space in the house dedicated to his ancestors. There were oil paintings, knick-knacks, and even a few museum-quality pieces that had been collected or purchased over the years. Each held a story of personal connection to someone in his family's past. Cable remembered spending hours as a boy using his fingers and imagination as he moved through the collection of carvings and trinkets. It looked exactly the same as it had before he left. He let his mind wander. The liquor loosened up his tightly held memories. He thought of Hilary and her tragic end. Zuhal and his treachery. Finally, he thought of his father. Killed while jogging in the park. Something normally so safe and harmless. Some unexpected early-season black ice, a slip and fall. It was only a six-foot drop, but he had landed squarely on his head.

Life was a lot like that. You'd be going along doing your thing, and suddenly, bam, everything changed.

His father lasted three days in the hospital before the brain swelling took him.

Cable lowered his head to the picture frame on his lap and slowly turned it over. His finger outlined the couple standing in a field with goofy smiles. It was a young August and Dolores. Both caught up in happier times.

Cable released a breath he had been holding. He tried to see them from a fresh perspective. They were just people doing what people do. Failing and succeeding their way through life. He realized now that he was alone, and it was up to him to carry on. It was up to him to forgive and ask forgiveness of them both. Forgive his mother for leaving him and his father for ignoring him. His eyes moistened as he burned their image into his mind.

"Love you guys." He stared at the picture for some time before setting it on the floor and heading off to bed.

The doorbell came early, or at least it seemed early. Cable found his father's robe and put it on before padding down the curved staircase, his hand sliding down the wrought iron railing. He swung the large stained-glass door open a bit too aggressively and followed with an accusatory, "What time is it?" thrown to the intruder.

Twenty-eight-year-old Dani Tran stepped back, not sure what to make of the man with the crazy bedhead hair, bad attitude, and a faded blue robe that was at least three sizes too small.

Dani was dressed in a scoop-necked navy summer dress with small white polka dots. She blurted out the first thing that came to her mind. "I'm sorry for your loss."

Cable stood there confused for a beat. "The wake was yesterday, you are a bit late."

"N-no, I'm not here for the wake—"

Cable interrupted, "Did you know my father?"

"No. I am here—" Dani tried again.

Cable continued. "Well, why are you here? What is it like six in the morning?"

Dani glanced at her watch. "It's one-forty-five."

"Wow, I guess I'm still on Kuwaiti time."

Now, Dani looked confused.

"Well, come on in. Let's get this over with. Do you need music, or are you going to sing while you strip?"

Dani stopped dead in her tracks. "Excuse me?"

Cable let his eyes focus a bit more. The beautiful Asian American woman in front of him was definitely stripper material. She had full lips and perfect skin, but she was dressed a bit too conservatively. Something was not right. She wore hardly any makeup, and her hair was simple. That was not stripper-like. He could see her face flush with anger and suddenly realized his mistake.

"Shoot. You're not the stripper, are you? I mean, you could be, but now that I really look at you, your hair and your...I'm so sorry. I'm meeting with the guys a little later today, and they said they had a surprise for me, and based on their past, I assumed..." Cable adjusted the tie on his robe. "Okay, I'm going to stop talking."

Dani's anger slowly subsided. This guy might be an idiot, but he was very good-looking. She cocked her head and patiently waited for him to recover.

"I apologize. Can we start over? Hi, I'm Cable."

"I'm Dani, and I'm here to appraise the artifacts."

Cable had no idea what she was talking about.

He closed the door behind her and stood for a moment, trying to collect his thoughts after making an idiot of himself. "What artifacts?"

"The insurance company retained me to determine the provenance and value of several pieces claimed in this policy." She held up some paperwork that looked official. "You see, August Janson had just finalized updating this policy before he...he passed."

"Well, the only artifacts I know of are in here." He led her to the study and The Wall.

Dani paused, looking the collection over.

"Some items have only personal value," Cable said as he stepped over to the cabinet and selected a polished shillelagh. "This was my great-grandfather's." Cable handed her the wood shaft with the hardened knot on one end.

She took the heirloom without interest. "What about my hair?"

"What?"

"At the door, you mentioned my hair."

"Oh, as I took a good look at your hair, I realized it was more corporate than…than what I initially thought."

She adjusted her hair reflexively. "I see." Her black eyes stared back, hiding all emotion. After a beat, she stepped to the collection and let her eyes scan some of the pieces. There were a few swords on one shelf and several sculptures on another. Pottery and wood carvings were scattered throughout. A flintlock and rolling block rifle were mounted on wood pegs above, and a few oil paintings of ancestors hung to the side.

"What did your father do, if you don't mind me asking?"

"He was a stock trader and, I guess a bit of a collector, as well."

"Very eclectic," Dani said.

"Yes, he was. Oh, you meant the collection. That's because half of these dust collectors are family hand-me-downs. My grandfather was the real collector. The problem was most of these pieces had meaning only to him, no monetary value."

"Well, at first glance, it is a bit overwhelming, but on second inspection I see a few pieces that are the reason I am here."

"Well, knock yourself out. I'll be in the kitchen." He started to leave, then turned back. "You want breakfast or something to drink?"

"No thanks, just had lunch." Dani pulled out her smartphone and began snapping a few pictures of the displayed items.

Cable watched for a few minutes, then wandered off to see if there was anything to eat besides wake leftovers.

After a while, Dani entered the kitchen. Cable was eating a bowl of cereal at the kitchen island. He seemed engrossed in his meal.

Cable looked up from his Frosted Flakes. "I'd forgotten how good these are."

"I hear, *They're Great!*" Dani said, imitating Tony the Tiger's slogan with her first smile of the day.

Cable finally relaxed after feeling like such a fool earlier. "So, did you change your mind on that drink?"

"What? No." She held up a carved chunk of stone that resembled a bird. "I was wondering what you know about this?"

Cable palmed the artifact and turned it in his hands. "Red sandstone, a carved bird with some kind of letters on the back." He waited for Dani to take the bait, but she was smarter than that.

"Thanks, Captain Obvious."

"My great-grandfather on my father's side brought it back from some war in Africa. I think my father said he took it or bought it from a church or something. Spoils of war, maybe it's a gray area. Things were a lot different in the 1930s." He stood and handed back the statue.

"Follow me." He led Dani back to The Wall. To the left, he pointed out a faded oil painting of a proud Italian gentleman in full uniform. "My great-grandad, Elio."

"Your great-grandfather fought in the Second Italo-Ethiopian War?"

"Wait." Cabled stopped, looking at Dani suspiciously. "How did you know that? What is it you do again?"

"I am a PhD graduate in archeology from Stanford with a minor in anthropology. I specialized in cultures that were influenced by the Egyptian kingdoms. That includes everything from the Romans to the Hittites to the Puntites. I work as an appraiser for PEAK Insurance, a company whose entire focus is rare and valuable artifacts. I don't do art, just 3D stuff like swords, pots, or statues." She held up the bird with the letters carved on it.

"So there is another career path beyond academia and tomb raiding for a PhD in archeology," Cable said with a dose of sarcasm.

Dani didn't find it funny.

"This statue is written in Ge'ez. So I'm guessing the Axum Empire, somewhere around 300 to 1000 CE. That's part of modern Ethiopia, used to be called Punt."

"Ethiopia. Fantastic country with the friendliest people you'll ever meet."

Dani ignored him. You're what, twenty-nine? So that would put your great-grandfather in his prime around the 1930s, and that would mean the Second Italo-Ethiopian War."

"Impressive. You should get a job moonlighting in a circus."

Dani ignored him again. "You've spent time in Ethiopia?"

"Six months. It was transformative."

Dani took a second look at the man. He had olive skin from time in the sun, with dark, pleasant features. His face was rugged but not hard, with a smile that was broad and infectious and kind, intelligent eyes. Dani wanted to know more. She had studied much about Ethiopian history but had never been there. Right now, however, she was on the clock for her employer.

"I always wondered what this bird had to say. Can you read the inscription?" Cable asked.

"Yes, but I'll need my computer to do it."

The garage door opened on silent rails. Cable was impressed by how clean the space was. Growing up, this part of the house was a hoarder's dream. Now, it was completely organized and mostly empty. A 1965 red Porsche 356 C coupe sat with its nose to the exit. Cable pulled the door open and admired the saddle leather interior before lowering himself inside and adjusting the seat back a couple of inches. The ignition was found on the left side. He inserted the key and started the engine. It sounded more like an old Volkswagen Beetle than a sports car, but it was hard to dislike the smooth, rounded lines and sleek stance of the car.

Cable rolled down both windows and let the cool night air in. The tall skyscrapers in the distance guided him east as he shifted through the four gears of the 95-horsepower car.

Street parking a small car is easier, except on a Saturday night. He was going to be late.

Cable looked up as the lasers and concert lights flashed and moved. The thumping bass rattled his core.

The Church has been a highlight of Denver's nightlife since 1996 when a Gothic-beamed Episcopal Church was converted for dance worshippers. It had evolved over the years, including a few remodels to match the changing times and music, making The Church the oldest and longest-continuously running club in the Golden Triangle neighborhood.

He pushed through the throng of partiers over to a private section that was reserved. Cable was wearing jeans and a brown button-up with rolled-up sleeves. A prayer bracelet hung on his left wrist, and brown loafers a size too tight, borrowed from his father's closet, smashed his feet. The bouncer eyed him as he slipped under the rope.

It took a second to recognize Parker. He had changed since his scarecrow days in high school. To his right sat Santé and to the left, Demola and Bryce. They all shared a good hug as Cable joined the group at a small coffee table surrounded by black, overstuffed chairs.

The DJ yelled out something and the music changed. The crowd roared their approval. Smartphones worked overtime, taking selfies and streaming video.

Dude, you look well. I mean, really well," Parker said, his hair perfectly coiffed and his fashion on-trend.

"Thanks, I hardly recognized you. Damn. 'Mr. Skin and Bones' filled in with real muscles," Cable replied.

"Been hitting the gym and juice," Parker said.

"That's not all he's hitting. Remember Alice More?" Santé said. He was the same as ever, big nose hidden behind big glasses.

"The cheerleader?" Cable asked, trying to recall.

"That's right, baby. Alice friggin' More." Parker gave a fist bump to Santé.

That got a laugh from everyone.

"Isn't she the one who gave her valedictorian speech pregnant?" Cable asked.

"That was just a rumor," Parker said.

A waitress wearing a tight blouse, short skirt, and knee-high boots brought the first round.

Parker plopped his Amex card down. "Start a tab."

"Good to see you guys haven't changed one bit. Except for Bryce. You can finally grow a beard, I see.

"Only took 'im five years of tryin'," Demola said. His cock-sure attitude and chin beard made him the hippest in the group.

"Can't say the same for you. So, how many languages do you speak now?" Demola asked.

"A bunch."

"Give us a sample," Bryce said.

"Yeah, tell us about your love life in…Swahili," Demola added.

Cable shook his head. *"Wewe ni Mjinga.* Which means 'you're an idiot' in any language."

They all laughed again.

"So, did you get your little surprise we sent you?"

Cable waited for more information.

"The stripper," Parker said with exaggerated force. "We figured you needed something besides a peasant girl to welcome you back to the world of the living."

The other three leaned forward, eager for details.

"First of all, peasant girls have a lot to offer, and second, the world beyond this place is…" He stopped mid-sentence. They would never understand. "But no, I didn't get the stripper."

"Ah, seriously? We sent a stripper to your house. 2356 Brentwood Street."

"I live at 2365 Brentwood Street. You sent a stripper to old lady Stubbs's house."

The mistake registered on Parker's face, but instead of making it a big deal, he decided to own it. "Yes. Yes, I did."

"I'm sure she loved it," Cable added.

There was another round of laughs.

Music thumped, dancers danced, and beer flowed as the night went on.

It was good to reconnect with friends from his past, but their lives were no longer Cable's. The more they chatted, the more Cable realized this. They talked careers, politics, investments, and new cars. They hovered over their smartphones like their lives depended on the information they contained. All things Cable had left behind.

As the night turned to early morning, the conversation slowed, and just being was good enough.

"So what's next for Cable Janson?" Demola asked after a brief pause in the conversation.

"Gonna stay a few weeks to get my father's affairs in order, then… not really sure."

"Must be nice. A man without a plan."

"How do you survive out there? You know, make money?" Bryce asked.

"I get by with a few odd jobs here and there. Just enough to get me to my next town or village. Money often creates more problems than it solves."

"Money is the root of all that is fun," Demola said.

"I'm not sure that's the quote," Cable said jokingly.

"No, just the truth."

Parker added, "I mean, look at you, bro. You don't even have a cell phone. How do you survive?"

"Oh, I've had a cell phone from time to time, usually a burner, depending on the country. I find that cell phones tend to separate more than they bind. I think we can improve the human condition by going out and shaking hands and meeting eye to eye, rather than posting selfies and voyeuristically hitting the 'heart' button on someone's posting."

Parker looked perplexed. "And you think one man can make a difference?"

"Always."

The boys all eyed each other, not sure what to make of Cable's nomadic lifestyle.

Cable just smiled.

CHAPTER THREE

C ABLE SKIPPED THE ELEVATOR AND took the steps two at a time. He wasn't late, just eager to get a little exercise, hoping to get on the other side of the hangover that caused his head to pound incessantly. The sun was up, and without a cloud in the sky, it was shaping up to be a perfect fall day in the Mile High City.

Cable glanced at the sign before he pushed through the door. Charles Brown, Attorney at Law. He wondered if the attorney had been teased for his name growing up.

"Cable, come in, have a seat." They shook hands. "Please call me Charlie."

Cable was sure of it now.

The tall, thin man brought a flash of memory from the funeral. Charlie had taken his time to talk to Cable about his fondness for his father, and he stood out over all the people there. The man had to be six-nine if he was an inch. Even once they sat down at his polished oak desk, he was still a foot taller than Cable. He had bushy eyebrows and short-cropped hair that was just thinning in the front.

For a single attorney's office, the layout was spacious and well-appointed. It had traditional hardwood furniture set against modern furnishings and art. One wall had a butter-yellow couch and the other a small bar.

"I'm real sorry about your father. He was well-respected and a personal friend."

"Yes, you mentioned that at the funeral. Thanks for your kind words."

"Yes, well." He cleared his throat and changed to the business at hand. "Your father was quite specific in his terms regarding the trust he left."

"I'm not interested in following his terms. Sell everything he left to me and give it all to charity."

"Oh, well, that's not exactly—"

Cable interrupted, "Is it not mine to do with what I want?"

"Technically, yes. He left *everything* to you, but we are talking about your family's legacy. Your father made some poor and some shrewd investments, and there is a surplus. It's not buy-an-island or retire money, but if invested well, it could be a nice cushion should a problem arise. And then, of course, the house," Charlie said, looking like he might be passing unexpected gas.

"Good, then maybe we can sell the house and divide that surplus among several charities," Cable added.

The attorney looked to Cable for some explanation, his fingers fidgeting nervously on the desktop.

"We were not close…after my mother died, we…drifted, if you must know. I have made my peace with it all, but forgiveness in humans is often transitory, and right now, I'm feeling incensed by the years and loss."

"I understand…" Charlie rifled through some papers on his desk and pulled out an envelope, handing it to Cable. "Perhaps this will help."

Cable recognized his father's handwriting. *For my son Cable.* He hesitated and finally, curiosity won out. He opened the envelope.

His eyes scanned the lines, and tears tried to form, but Cable held them back.

Charlie watched for some type of sign. After a few moments, he could not handle the silence. "Is everything okay?"

"Yes, fine. Please follow my father's instructions to the letter."

Fannie Müller stepped from her new-generation Defender and slammed the door shut. She hurried across the cobblestones and through the huge pivoting wood door of the old church. The 1,700-year-old stone structure had three large arches across the front and two square windows above, giving it a face of sorts. On the left side, above the roof, a single minaret tower stretched to the sky. It was once home to the Assyrian Christians but had long since been abandoned and sold, thanks to the growing local Muslim population.

Once inside, the space was more like a warehouse than a church. The pews were replaced by an acquisitions, storage, shipping, and packing business. Industrial LED lights hung from the arched roof and work tables connected to skate-wheel conveyors, allowing easy movement of heavy items from station to station.

Fannie moved past the two workers in blue overalls who were crating up a large stone effigy of a gargoyle, their incessant smoking causing a haze in the air. The back of the room held the storage portion of the operation and here, a collection of pieces waited to be placed.

Angled stone steps with aged wrought iron led up to the second floor, and she followed them. Her designer black slacks revealed practical low-heeled pumps of the same color that tapped as she ascended.

The second floor was a contrast to the worn stone-on-stone look of the floor below. Here, a hardwood floor and open-beam ceiling held a modern office. It had glass, steel, leather, and light wood accents. High-priced art hung on the walls, and several carved stone artifacts were on display.

An older man with graying hair and thick glasses looked up from the front desk.

"Is he in?" Fannie asked.

"I think he's on the roof. You want me to call him?"

"No, I'll go up, thanks," Fannie replied.

"Sure, Ms. Müller."

Fannie moved past the empty office on the right that used to occupy a very talented IT professional, though some might call her a hacker. Raven had joined their team several years ago through some connections of Fannie's in Belgium. Her dark bobbed hair and round glasses, set on a hawkish nose, seemed to mirror the intelligent bird's likeness.

Raven was a quiet person who spoke with action rather than words, and her omnipresent collection of knitted sweaters was straight from a 1970s librarian.

With the way things were in the world now, Raven had left Istanbul just over a year ago and relocated back to Antwerp along the coast, where she worked remotely.

Straight ahead was the main office, a spacious room with luxury appointments like a custom live-edge desk and high-back leather chairs. Fannie stepped through a door in the back.

The rear of the second floor held a generous apartment with a couch, TV, and small kitchen. There were two bedrooms and bathrooms beyond. To the right was a steel staircase mounted against the wall that led up to the roof. Light streamed down from above. The door was open.

Fannie went up the steps and onto the roof.

Stein Osman heard her coming before she cleared the stairs. He glanced over his shoulder as Fannie crossed the flat roof to the south side of the church. Her fire-red hair moved as she walked, set against smooth skin and green eyes. Serious green eyes. The kind that never stopped scanning. Through her sleeveless white blouse, her strong shoulders moved with purpose. You might peg her as a kickboxer.

"What's the news?" Stein said between puffs on an Ashton Estate cigar. He turned his head back to the view from beyond the church's roof.

The historic center of Istanbul was a labyrinth of narrow cobblestone streets and paths, with connected buildings erected over the last several millennia, creating a kaleidoscope of colors and a hodgepodge of architecture. Stein never tired of the view or the world-class people-watching.

"The stone was damaged, so I made a counteroffer," Fannie said.

"Did they accept?"

"No, and frankly, we are better off not dealing with them. They made the news again, and no one wants that kind of attention."

"You are probably right," Stein said after a slow inhale and exhale of his cigar.

"You know I'm right, but I could have told you all this over the phone."

Stein turned back to face Fannie, lowering his cigar and suddenly paying full attention.

She continued. "The item you asked me to be on the lookout for popped up on one of Raven's monitored sites."

Everything about Stein's demeanor changed. He pictured the hacker's bird-like looks, and a near smile followed. "After all these years... do we have the location?"

"No, just a name and IP address. She is tracing it now."

"Send a team as soon as they confirm the address."

"I think we need to hire locally. It looks to be in America." Fannie said, waiting for her boss to reply.

Stein Osman was in his midforties with a trimmed beard and balding head. His face was angular with small black eyes. Eyes that seemed to lack connection to anything—robot eyes. He was fit and always well-dressed. Today, he wore a dark blue custom button-up, Brunello Cucinelli slate gray slacks, and a Loro Plana black sport coat.

He smashed his half-finished cigar with his Christian Louboutin loafer and nodded.

"Okay, do it. America, huh? Didn't see that coming." Stein watched as Fannie picked up her phone and dialed.

"Luka. I have a job."

Cable sat at his father's desk, his world rocked. He fingered the envelope like it might hold the combination to Al Capone's vault. In his other hand, he held a black American Express card.

Attorney Charlie Brown had given him the card, insisting that his father wanted him to take it with him the next time he left the country *"because you never know."* To Cable, it seemed like a crutch. He placed it on the desk, vacillating on its usefulness. The afternoon sun streamed through the slats on the wood blinds. The dark wood-paneled walls soaked up much of the glow. A portrait of his mother smiled down in perpetuity from the right wall. There was a faint smell of sweet tobacco and aftershave.

Cable refocused on the envelope and pulled out the letter, allowing himself time to read it more thoroughly.

My dearest son Cable,

I am sorry to have to write these words and not say them to you in person. It seems life and death have placed a wall between us. Something I truly regret as I write this letter. I am so proud of what, and who you have become. You stand tall on your beliefs and principles. I am delighted to witness that.

Your family has a rich heritage and history. You are part of that and I am sure every day of your life, you are adding to this family's story.

It took a few years of you being gone to realize my error, and as I always have said, "An opportunity not taken is an opportunity lost." I won't make that mistake again. I would sell everything I have just to hold you in my arms and ask your forgiveness.

That will now never happen. My greatest loss.

As you move forward, I only ask that you please allow our family, our home, and our history to remain in your life as long as you can. For in doing this, we all stay a little bit alive.

I know in my heart great things will be part of your journey, just as I know in my heart how much I love you.

Dad

Cable leaned back in the office chair and closed his eyes, letting a single tear roll down his cheek. He had let his pride keep him from reconciling with August and his hubris from saving Hilary. Perhaps his friends were right. He was out of touch. Maybe it was time to stop roaming and start building. He let the conflicting thoughts fire back and forth in his mind until sleep took hold.

A knock at the door woke him from his slumber. His neck was stiff from sleeping in the chair. The sun was on its last glow of the day.

He stood and headed for the front door as the hammering repeated. As he swung it open, a familiar face smiled cautiously back.

"Hi?"

Cable was taken back at the sight of Dani. She was cast in the golden glow of the day's sunset. Her summer dress flowed gently in the evening breeze, and her shiny black hair was loosely curled and framed her face perfectly. In a word, stunning.

"Hi…did you forget something?" he asked.

Dani noticed the stubble on Cable's face and the bags under his eyes. New additions since she had last seen him. "Oh, no. I translated your statue, and I thought you might like to know what it says."

"Oh. Great, come on in. Sure, I'd love to know." Cable took a calming breath, realizing he had just come on a bit too weird. *Suave.* "I was just about to fix some dinner," he lied. "Are you hungry?"

"No, I have to get back."

Cable didn't buy it. "No problem, but you drove all the way out here to give me a message that you could have emailed, so please let me cook for you."

Dani looked down, then back up. Cable's smile was radiating. "Okay, but only if you let me help."

"Agreed."

The kitchen nook had good lighting and cushioned seating, with opened Chinese take-out boxes, paper plates, and cheap bamboo chopsticks decorating the zinc-covered tabletop. Dani and Cable sat enjoying their meal.

"Sorry about the whole cooking thing. I guess I need to go shopping."

"It's a shame. I was looking forward to spam musubi without the rice or seaweed."

"I think they just call that spam, and there was a can of green beans also in the cupboard don't forget."

"See. It would have been a complete meal," Dani said.

"I've eaten worse."

"Oh, yeah?"

"Aged camel is not as exotic as it sounds."

Dani put down her chopsticks. "It's not every day you meet a guy who's eaten old, I mean 'aged' camel."

"True that," Cable said as he picked up his 7 UP can and toasted Dani's orange Fanta.

After dinner, they cleared off the table. Cable brought the bird statue over and set it in front of Dani.

"Okay, so a little context," she said. "This is most likely a statue of a goshawk. It is a local bird of prey in Eastern Africa. I estimate it to be from somewhere between 200 and 600 CE and worth approximately $200,000.

"This sandstone bird with its faded markings and chipped head is worth over 200 grand?" Cable said in disbelief.

"Hey, don't insult the professional."

"Sorry. This sandstone bird with its faded markings and chipped head is worth over 200 grand!" he said with enthusiasm.

"That's better, and yes," Dani said.

"So, what's it say? Tie up your donkeys to this post. Dig here for the treasure?"

"I'll let you be the judge. The closest translation is this." She picked up her phone and read from it. "First line: 'A faithful pilgrimage begins. Second line: Pious and angels alike share.'"

Cable read it back aloud. "'A faithful pilgrimage begins. Pious and angels alike share.'

That is very cryptic."

"Or incomplete," Dani said.

"What do you mean?"

"Look at these slots on the side of the hawk." She handed the statue to Cable.

He inspected them. He also noticed the two dowel holes on each side. "Wings. Wings attached here and here."

"That's what I'm thinking, and if I'm not mistaken, there is more to the message on the back of those wings."

Just then, the lights in the house went out.

"Didn't pay your electricity bill?"

"That stuff should all be automated." Cable stood and cracked the wood shutter. The house next door was still aglow.

"Something's not right."

Dani picked up her phone and dialed 9-1-1. Nothing. "It's not going through."

A sudden memory of gunmen approaching in a boat off Failaka Island hit him. "Something's wrong. Come on."

Dani followed closely behind. "This isn't another of your 'do you need music to strip by' kinda things, is it?

"Definitely not." Cable led Dani up the stairs. A sudden knock on the door froze them. It repeated.

Cable moved back down the stairs and cracked the door.

A man with a flashlight blinded Cable. "Oh, sorry about that," he said as he lowered the beam. "I'm from Xcel Energy. We lost a transformer, and I need to get to the pole to fix it. Do you own that car?"

By this time, Dani had moved down the stairs and over to the door. "It's mine…a rental," she added, not sure why.

"Any chance I could get you to move it?"

"Sure." Dani moved past Cable, whispering in his ear. "Paranoid much?"

"Thanks," the man said. "I would also like access to your home to reset the subpanel before we restore power."

Cable looked out to the street. An Xcel truck was parked with amber lights flashing. It was the company that provided power throughout the Denver area.

Feeling a bit foolish for overreacting, he opened the door fully and gestured for the man to enter.

He watched as Dani jogged out to a white Toyota C-HR. She pulled away from the curb and moved behind the Xcel truck. He waited for her to reappear on the other side of the truck, but she didn't. That same uneasy feeling returned, and Cable spun back to his house, looking for the man who was supposedly resetting his subpanel. His eyes flicked across the nook table as he moved, and in an instant, he knew what was happening. A robbery. The goshawk statue was gone.

He sprinted for the front door and into the street just in time to see the energy truck quickly pull away. Dani's car was abandoned in the street, the driver's side door open.

As he ran to the empty car, two thoughts hit him. *Had she been in on the robbery, or had she been taken along with the artifact?*

Cable checked the Toyota, no keys. He looked up as the electric truck killed its flashing lights and turned right on West First, disappearing.

Cable sprinted for his father's Porsche.

CHAPTER FOUR

THE PORSCHE SQUEALED AROUND THE corner, threatening to fishtail. Cable counter-steered and regained control as he grew angrier with each passing second. He swiveled his head at every alley and intersection as he drove, not sure he was even traveling in the right direction. The city and its infrastructure were east, so he would head that way.

A flash of white caught his eye, and he slammed on the brakes and flipped a U-turn. The Xcel power truck was parked and abandoned on the curb of a narrow industrial street. A black van could be seen leaving in the distance.

They've changed cars, Cable thought as he gunned the sports car down the alley.

By the time Cable turned onto West Alameda Avenue, he had the van in sight. It was two blocks ahead in moderate traffic.

The van hit the onramp to the I-25 freeway, southbound. It was driving away from the city and the main airport.

Cable considered the van's possible destinations. He also reviewed Dani's motivations over the last two meetings. Was she a victim or perpetrator? At the very least, she would have taken her rental car as they left rather than leave evidence behind. He remembered thinking the same thing about Hilary at one point. Had those thoughts immobilized him and cost Hilary her life?

He processed all the facts. He had failed Hilary and perhaps his own family. He would not fail Dani.

For right now, he would give her the benefit of the doubt. If he was wrong, he would do everything in his power to bring her world down upon her with extreme callousness. For the first time in a long time, Cable wished he had a cellphone.

The van started shifting lanes. Cable was blocked by a semi-truck on his right, so he had to slow down to go around. The exit for the I-225 East came and went. He could just make out the darkness on the left that was Cherry Creek Park.

At the E-470 toll road, the van exited, and Cable knew his destination. The Centennial Airport, off South Peoria Street.

He lost sight of the van as it exited off the toll road, then spotted it again as the driver used a keycard to enter the security gate to the tarmac. They drove behind the Modern Aviation building as the old Porsche bounced and scrapped its way into the private terminal's parking area.

Modern Aviation was everything the name said it was. A stylized steel and glass building with simple landscaping, easy access, and a mini-terminal that looked more like a hotel lobby. The staff was knowledgeable and friendly, except for Whiley. Whiley was two pints shy of his suggested daily requirement of caffeine and he was cranky.

"Hey, you can't park there. After-hours parking is over there."

"I'm in a hurry."

"Aren't we all. Either move your car, or I'll make sure your flight is delayed and call the police for not following FAA regulations."

"You can do that?"

Whiley held up his radio like it was a weapon. "Try me."

"That's a great idea. Call the police. Get 'em here as quick as you can." Cable turned and ran for the terminal, ignoring the man's outburst.

"Hey, I'm not kidding," Whiley called out. He brought the radio to his mouth. "Be advised, passenger approaching, code sixteen."

A female voice retorted, "Give it a rest, Whiley. What? They didn't want to park in the far lot. You know the drill. Tag the car. We'll charge them an extra twenty bucks a day."

Whiley looked down at his radio. He hated this job, and dealing with entitled one-percenters with their private jets was the worst.

Cable ran past the ticket counter and the soft leather seating. A couple of passengers talked among themselves on a blue couch, but otherwise, the place was quiet. The back wall was all glass and looked out onto the private airstrip. The exit gate was clearly marked and locked. A petite woman in a light-brown uniform eyed him suspiciously.

Out on the tarmac, Cable saw the black van parked beside a Gulfstream G150. Dani was being guided up the loading ramp by two men. He couldn't tell if she was going willingly or not. One of the men he recognized from the house, although he was no longer wearing his Xcel Power Company uniform.

"How do I get outside?" he asked the woman in uniform.

She looked slightly confused at his abrupt, out-of-the-blue question.

Cable looked at her name tag. "Margie, how do I get outside?"

"You need a ticket."

"I'm supposed to be on that jet," he lied.

She stepped to her terminal and hit a few keys. "To Mexico City?"

"Yes."

"Name?" she asked.

Cable hesitated. The next few minutes might determine many things. If he came off like a crazy person, he would end up in a police car before ever getting out that door. If he called for the police, that jet would fly away, and he would be here all night answering questions without any physical evidence to back them up. Plus, the gate agent would need ID, and the only ID he had was his passport, something he always carried with him since first leaving the US. *Go with the truth.*

"Cable Janson."

She typed some more.

"No, sorry. You are not in here."

He glanced over his shoulder.

The door to the jet was closed, and it was powering up. Cable was out of time.

"Can you double-check that? My sister will kill me if I miss the flight." He wasn't sure what he expected her to find, but context was at the heart of every good lie.

Margie typed again. "Sorry. They are taxiing now, so there is no way I can get you on that plane."

Cable turned around. The sleek jet moved away from the building, heading for the runway. Dani was about to fly off into the night and there was nothing he could do about it. He moved to the back glass wall, feeling helpless and humbled. His hands found his pockets as he stood there, equivocating on calling the police. At least, that would be something. Maybe they could stop the jet before it left US airspace.

The hard edge of something unfamiliar to him grabbed his attention, and he pulled his hand from his pocket. The black American Express card. He made a decision and spun to the ticket agent.

"How fast can you get me to Mexico City?"

The Embraer Phenom 300 with extended tanks had a range of nearly 2,500 nautical miles, which turned out to be exactly what it cost to fly one-way solo to Mexico City.

Mexico was one country Cable had never been to. Though he spoke Spanish, it was more of a Castilian type. The locals would peg him as a visitor from Spain or Chile, both were countries he had spent time in.

The customs inspector eyed Cable suspiciously as he exited without a single piece of luggage, not even a toothbrush.

The jet he had been following was parked along with several others in the private airport apron. There was no sign of Dani or the man from the house.

Cable exited the terminal and looked left, then right. The air was crisp and cool like Denver, but the foul smell of unburned gas and diesel made him want to choke. A car had probably met them at the plane— Dani was in the wind. His valiant rescue attempt had come to an end. Frustration threatened to overwhelm, so Cable did what always worked. He pushed forward.

He needed a place to regroup and do some research, see what he could dig up. On the other side of the taxiway was a van with the word Hilton painted across it. Cable jogged across the busy street and climbed in.

He found a stiff-backed seat in the middle and watched as families and business professionals alike filed in and stuffed their luggage in the mounted rack. The van pulled from the curb and made its way onto the Cuarto Interior, a freeway that circled the city. The driver welcomed the riders to Mexico City in two languages with a smoker's rasp. He then began a well-practiced travel monologue.

"Originally the Aztec capital, Mexico City was conquered by the Spanish in 1521. Since then, we have grown to become the thirty-second-largest city in the world. It is a place you can find grandma's handmade tortillas and multiple Michelin Star restaurants. There is world-class shopping, multimillion-dollar homes, and the world's largest mega-slum. Mexico City has it all."

As the driver finished his words, the van bucked, then bucked again. The engine coughed and died. He pulled to the side of the highway amid horns and a screech. Smoke started to billow out of the hood.

"I'm so sorry, but as we say here, T-I-M. This Is Mexico."

The occupants groaned in unison.

"Please stay in your seats. I'll call for help immediately."

Cable didn't wait to hear the rest of the man's message. He pried open the sliding middle door and jumped out.

"Señor," the driver called out, but he could not leave his other passengers to chase one crazy gringo.

Cable jogged down the nearest off-ramp alongside a wall of moving cars. Mexico City had one of the worst traffic problems in the world, and walking was a good way to outpace most cars in the city, but that meant eating a mouthful of car fumes with every breath.

Cable found a little coffee shop called Churros Don Fede and ordered a traditional churro and a cappuccino. He was feeling jet lagged and needed a bit of a pick-me-up, but most of all, he was at a loss as to his next move.

He watched mindlessly out the café window as cars, bikes, and motorcycles jammed the street. It reminded him of a slightly more organized version of traffic in Mumbai or Vietnam. All that was missing was the odd motorcycle packed with a family of four, one pig, two chickens, and six trash bags piled high with the unknown. His mind filled in the temporary void with its need for order. *Next steps. Focus. A direction of travel and a plan*. He had no idea.

The sun moved behind the local hills, and Cable decided to stretch his legs a bit before hailing a cab. Any good cab driver would know his way to a decent hotel.

Local shopping was a good way to get a feel for the neighborhood, and walking always helped him think. Plus, he needed a few things, like a toothbrush.

The rows of small shops and open market stalls changed the oily quality of the air. He could smell fruit and spices, cooking meat, and body odor. Shoulders bumped shoulders as he moved along, purchasing a few needed items here and there.

Cable noticed a young boy, about twelve, selling Chiclets. The boy was about five feet tall with short brown hair and wide, large brown eyes. He wore a red tee shirt, worn jeans, and huaraches on his feet. A small open cardboard box filled with every flavor of packaged gum hung by a strap that looped around his neck to take some of the weight away. Cable thought it was odd that the boy needed a strap to support what was probably one pound in weight at the most. He watched as the boy flittered around tourists, begging for the sale, pushing his box close to them as he fired off his pitch, but something was off. The boy would spend easily a minute buzzing and pestering a patron, not taking no for an answer. Then, as if a switch was thrown, he would shift gears to another mark. It was a choreographed dance without the payoff of money at the end of it.

Cable watched the boy for a couple more minutes before getting his attention in Spanish. "I'll buy some Chiclets."

The boy seemed uninterested at first, then relented and presented Cable with his gum box.

"What's your name?" Cable asked in Spanish.

"Rene."

"I'm Cable. So, what kind of gum do you sell?"

"The best gum, señor Cable."

"What do you recommend, Rene?"

"Yellow fruit. You will like it." He held out a small pack of yellow-colored gum.

Cable held up a dollar bill. "Keep it. I've got no pesos."

He covertly lifted the gum box with his left hand as he handed over the dollar. The box was much too heavy for just gum.

Cable pulled back the dollar and took out his black American Express card. "Unless you *take* credit cards?"

The boy paused, realizing the implication. He started to back away.

"Relax. I'm not a cop. I'm nobody, really, and I don't care how you make your living. I find you smart, clever, and cunning. Something the world needs more of."

The boy stopped backing up, curiosity winning. "How did you know?"

"The straps. You are way too healthy and strong to need straps for that small box of gum. Plus, you are more interested in getting close to your marks than making a sale."

Rene looked down as guilt filled his face.

"High-powered RFID scanner?"

As Rene glanced back up to nod, something caught Rene's attention. "Look out, señor Cable!"

Cable turned just as metal and skull met. His eyes had no time to register the swinging crowbar. Arms suddenly supported him from two sides, and he was carried along in the crowd, dazed, like a buddy who'd had too much to drink. The people moving past didn't recognize his plight or didn't seem to care. He was suddenly moved right, and the light and crowds disappeared. Cable's last sensation was falling before his world slipped away.

Luka Meyer waited in the shadow of a large date palm. From across the street and down a ways, he could see the comings and goings of some very distraught individuals. Most of the men were in suits, and the women wore dresses of various colors. For a funeral in Egypt there was not the traditional dress-in-black like in the West.

The large stone home was set back from the street with a driveway that looped around a tall fountain in front. As the last of the family exited the house, including the maid, three cars started and drove away in a procession of sorts. They seemed to be in a hurry, as not one of them stopped at the intersection's stop sign before they all turned left and out of Luka's view.

Luka was five-ten with a wrestler's figure and big, meaty hands. His light-brown hair was shaved on the sides and combed across to the left. He had black pants and a simple black tee shirt. His dark green eyes were always scanning for trouble, today he sensed none.

He waited a good five minutes before bringing the radio to his mouth and pressing the transmit button.

"Go, go, go." He walked to the street and watched as an older Isuzu Elf turned the corner and pulled to the curb. It was a cab-over flatbed filled with gardening tools. Luka climbed into the passenger side of the cab, and the truck drove away.

It pulled up to the entrance of the target home and crept up to within three feet of the gate. The driver accelerated, and the reinforced bumper snapped the lock and knocked the gate off the track. Luka and the other passenger, Tarik, slid across the bench seat and out the door. The driver continued up to the house. Within a moment, Tarik and Luka had reset the gate on its track and rolled it to look locked and closed.

The driver backed the truck up to the front door, obscuring any street-side eyes. He removed a lawnmower and began zig-zagging in the front lawn, more interested in keeping an eye out than mowing. Luka picked the lock to the front door and, once opened, he went inside to defeat the alarm. In the family's hurry and grief, they had not even bothered to set it.

This was why he loved robbing homes during a family funeral. At the same time, that didn't mean they could tarry. In their usual efficiency, Tarik and Luka quickly separated and moved room by room.

The home was a combination of local hardwoods and stone walls. There were tall wood shutters on the windows, and linen seemed to be the color of choice for the furniture.

"Luka," Tarik called out. The Egyptian operator was of average height with rounded features and curly hair. He had an easy smile and hard, dark eyes. Luka hired him a couple of years back to help him obtain an ancient mask and headdress. It had gone flawlessly and the two had continued their collaboration since.

Tarik was born on hard streets and had a nose for things most people never noticed. He could sense danger or an easy mark long before most.

As a street-savvy operator, he could move in and out of places professionals would never dream of going.

Luka had spent time in the Special Operations forces in the German Army. His ability to plan and execute was first-rate.

Between them, they protected the what-could-go-wrong contingencies of an operation and could still pull it off flawlessly.

Luka followed the sound and found Tarik in a spacious room with couches and a bar. To his right, a couple sat naked and regal for all to see. Carved with exquisite detail, the King and Queen from the Hemba tribe in Africa each held ceremonial staffs to represent their power and authority. On a stand to the right was a Lubba divination board, a handheld, flat piece of wood with beads and metal pins used to connect to the ancestral realm. The last artifact was a pair of carved ceremonial pipes from the Katanga province.

Tarik flashed Luka his patented jackpot smile and collected up the pieces. He handed the King and Queen to Tarik and took the rest.

They loaded back into the truck and manually opened and closed the broken front gate before driving away.

It wasn't difficult to make real artifacts look like tourist collectibles. A little removable paint and some made-in-China stickers usually did the trick. For the more fragile pieces, careful packaging and DHL to a dead drop worked quite well. There was always the possibility of loss and damage, but the operating profit margin covered that.

By nightfall, Luka and Tarik would be back in Istanbul, each with cash in their pockets and the perfect city to spend it in.

Dani Tran felt lightheaded and dizzy. Her skull felt like it weighed a thousand pounds as she tried to focus on her surroundings but failed. There was movement, steady and rhythmic. She closed her eyes and tried again. Slowly, the interior of a small jet came into focus. She tried to raise her arm, but it was zip-tied to the seat, as were her legs. Her seatbelt was cranked like a crash might be imminent. Flashes of memory returned to her—being taken at gunpoint from her car, an argument among her captors over whether they should take her or leave her, and finally, an injection into her neck.

This was not the first time Dani had been taken against her will.

Dani remembered waking up on an old couch in a basement. Her hands had been tied behind her, and there was a chain attached to her ankle. Her sleepy eyes had followed the links to the padlock holding it to the metal beam supporting the floor above. A single lightbulb hung from the ceiling, illuminating only the very center of the room. Two plastic bottles of water sat on a faded end table.

"This is your new room and if you want to survive this, you'll be a good girl and do as I say."

As the drug in her system started to wear off and her new surroundings clarified, panic gripped her.

Dani was not an avid dater. She liked men but found most to be too immature or self-absorbed for her tastes. During the last semester of her undergraduate program, Dani finally started to loosen up a bit. It was, after all, college life. Her roommate had called it a "social transformation." Dani started going out drinking with friends and even had a couple of one-night stands, something she had never done before. *If my mom could see me now.*

Two weeks before, she had met with a teacher's aide to get a homework assignment clarified in her statistics class. She wasn't the first student to do this. Apparently, the professor had been somewhat obscure in his directions. The aide, Quinn, was a nice enough guy but not memorable.

The next week, she ran into Quinn in the hallway between classes. He had invited her for a coffee later that night. Not seeing the harm in it, Dani had agreed. To her surprise, Quinn was intelligent and even a bit funny. He came off as supremely confident, but something underneath it all was off. Dani couldn't put her finger on it, so she dismissed her initial judgment and decided just to be nice.

They chatted for close to an hour, at which point Dani made her excuses, thanked Quinn for the coffee, and headed for her car.

As she approached, the first wave of dizziness hit. Dani grabbed her door handle and hung on. As the wooziness passed, she noticed Quinn was standing right next to her. *Weird.*

"Everything okay?" he asked.

"Fine. I…I'm just a bit dizzy."

"Here, let me help you," Quinn said.

"No. I got it." But in reality, Dani didn't have it. In fact, she had no memory of what happened after that.

Now, here she was, locked in a basement by a serious creeper. She had become a statistic, the worst possible kind.

She started by refusing to eat, which is not the best choice if you want to keep your strength up. It had lasted five days, and Dani felt like her insides were consuming themselves. She was weak and just lay on the couch, unmoving. By the sixth day, Quinn was getting angry. He hit her and forced her to eat, but Dani fought back by vomiting everything up the minute he left the room.

After a little over a week had gone by, Dani woke one day in a down-town alley with no chains and no clothes. She found a trash bag and used it to make a bikini of sorts with torn edges and tied corners. She walked back to her dorm amid walk of shame jeers from neighbors, then inhaled two power bars and an apple. She took the longest shower in her life and passed out on her bed before she was able to get dressed and head to the police department.

The detective was nice enough but of little to no help. Dani had no idea where she had been held, and Quinn was in the wind. Apparently, he wanted a toy to play with, not a dead body. Her starvation tactic had worked.

"You are a very lucky girl," the detective had said, but Dani didn't feel very lucky.

They released a BOLO for Quinn and then sent Dani home. Her only consolation was the man had never raped her.

It took a few weeks, but Dani rebounded and finished out the semester. She transferred to Stanford for her graduate work and put a complete stop to her social transformation.

The jet bucked for a moment as it passed through some rough air. Dani looked forward. Two men sat by the bulkhead, chatting like it might be just another average day for them, which it was. The one on the right was taller and seemed to be in charge. He glanced back at his hostage and then just continued as if nothing had changed.

The Gulfstream G150 was just big enough to have a cockpit door, which was closed. It had seating for eight, and two of the rear-facing beige leather chairs could be completely reclined.

Dani glanced outside the oval window. Land. So they weren't flying over the ocean. *I guess that is some consolation*, she thought. The sun was just rising to the jet's left. That meant they were flying either north or south, depending on the time of day. She glanced at her wrist. Her Apple Watch had lost its charge.

She fought her restraints one more time. Nothing. She was just an unwilling passenger for now. Words interrupted her thoughts.

"You're lucky." The tall one said.

Dani didn't respond. She had heard that line before.

"We were going to throw you out of the jet over Saltillo, but for some reason, our employer on this gig wants to meet you." He turned back, unconcerned with Dani's reply, so she didn't give him one.

An hour later, the jet started its descent.

The man on the left looked back at Dani. "We are getting ready to land, so make sure you buckle up." He turned back and laughed at his joke.

The Gulfstream touched down and started to taxi. The tall man stepped back and double-checked Dani's bindings. Her hands were turning white from the zip ties.

"Mac and I make this trip once a week. Usually with more girls... sometimes a young boy. Never had an academic and an old statue, but I suppose it's all the same. The money certainly is." He chuckled a bit at the thought of getting paid the same for one girl as they usually did for five.

"Our network is pretty well established, as is our routine, so sit back and enjoy the trip. We'll have you halfway around the world and sold off in no time." He placed his hand on Dani's shoulder. It was like having a hot poker hit your skin, and Dani thrashed in repulsion.

"You're slavers. The lowest form of scum on this planet."

"We're capitalists. Hard cash for services rendered. Be happy I didn't sample the goods." Dani almost threw up at the words. A haunted past suddenly threatened to overwhelm her.

The man stuck a needle into Dani's neck for the second time in twenty-four hours, and she slumped, her panic temporarily abated.

CHAPTER FIVE

C ABLE OPENED HIS EYES. IT was getting dark out. He leaned up and rubbed his head. There was a nice goose egg above his temple, and he could feel it throb. As he looked around, a picture came into view. He was in a side alley just down from the shops. Dented garbage cans to his left expulsed a carrion stench that was years in the making. He stood on shaky feet and instinctively reached for his passport. It was gone, along with the black American Express card Charlie Brown had given him.

He shuffled out of the ally. The street was quieter now, and he angled to the right, not sure of his next move. Cable had been robbed before, and he'd gotten through it. He could do it again.

"Señor Cable."

Cable turned to see the young street urchin, Rene, walking in his direction. He still carried his Chiclets gum box, but his attention was now on a street taco he was eating. The crowd had thinned, and several shops had closed up for the night.

"Hey, Rene."

"I wondered what happened to you. The Samaritas took you down hard. They have a way of smash-and-grab that is next-level."

Cable pulled his pockets inside out. "Lucky me. They even got my toothbrush."

"Yes, lucky you. Last week, they crowbarred a guy too hard, and he didn't make it."

Cable rubbed his head. "Seems like a lot for a wallet and ID."

"You have no idea. We are right next to the Neza-Chalco-Ixta."

Cable looked confused.

"The mega-slum." Rene pointed to his left. "The people there will kill you for fun."

"Well, I can tell you it wasn't fun."

"You are funny," Rene said.

"So are you, my friend."

Rene paused for a moment, thinking. "Come on. I'll buy you a taco."

Cable smiled. "A taco it is."

The next street corner had two competing taco stands, one serving birria tacos and the other al pastor.

Rene was eager to show off as a host. "I always have a hard time deciding when I come here, so you must eat two of each."

Cable watched as the spiced charred pork with pineapple slices was carved from the spit straight into the tortilla. At the birria taco stand, a corn tortilla was dipped in au jus and seasoned oil, then grilled with cheese and shredded seasoned beef.

The tacos were fantastic, as was the fresh-made watermelon juice.

Cable thanked Rene for the food and his compassion.

"Where will you go?" Rene asked.

"I guess the embassy. Gotta get my passport back."

"That is far from here. Come, sleep at my place, and you can start fresh in the morning."

Cable considered the words. They made sense. "Lead on."

Rene seemed excited to have a gringo that spoke fluent Spanish all to himself. He talked endlessly about his business, the routes he used, and how the city was changing. Nothing seemed to be off limits. He was a very grown-up twelve-year-old. Living on the streets can do that.

The mega-slum was just that, massive. Homes built on top of homes, all crushed together and made from leftovers and found items. There was no end in sight. A quarter moon was just enough to give the place some serious creep factor. Some shacks had lights, others had flames, some were dark. Figures in the shadows lurked and watched as Rene and Cable walked along the narrow dirt paths, moving up the hill.

The Neza-Chalco-Ixta mega-slum holds over four million residents, accounting for 10 percent of Mexico City's population. The drug of choice is methamphetamine, and it is rampant. Gangs control much of the downtrodden infrastructure, but to Rene, it was home.

He called out to a couple of friends and made a few detours to avoid others.

After a time, Rene climbed up a steep pathway to a small corrugated shack on the side of a hill. Stilts rose from the downhill side, giving the structure a not-long-for-this-hillside look. The steel exterior had long since rusted, and the two small windows were cracked and broken. Rene pulled on the rope handle and opened the door with a creak.

They stepped inside, and Rene hit a switch to a single bare lightbulb.

The room was small but functional. There was a single bed on one wall, a small hot plate and sink for a kitchen, and two worn metal chairs that looked like they were from a sixties diner. The table in between was a weathered wooden cable spool, and the floor was cracked concrete sur-rounded by walls that were a lesser rusted version of the outside.

Having been to the slums in South Africa, Cable wasn't shocked or even put off. The space was simple, clean, and had a roof.

"The baño is behind that wall," Rene said, pointing to a piece of faded plywood in the corner. "You can have the bed."

"Not a chance. It's your house. I'll take the floor."

"If you want, but the bed is more comfortable." As he spoke the words, he stepped over to the small kitchen counter. He pulled on a hidden handle, and it slid back from the wall, revealing a steel rung ladder leading down. Rene climbed down out of sight without another word.

Cable hesitated for just a second before following the young boy.

Below the spartan shack was a contrast in living beyond black and white—hardwood floors, wood-paneled walls, and recessed lighting. There were flat screens on several walls, one of them showing a grid of security images outside. A serious computing station was to the left, and a luxury kitchen to the right. Two doors led off to bedrooms with full baths. A leather couch with an entertainment center occupied the middle of the room.

"Okay, maybe I won't sleep on the floor," Cable said in awe as he looked around.

Rene set his Chiclets box down and pulled his jacked up RFID scanner out of a hidden slot below. He plugged it into his computer, and the monitors responded by lighting up and starting the download of stolen credit card and ID information.

"So, do you use these cards yourself?" Cable asked.

"No. I just sell the information off. Much safer that way."

Cable nodded in understanding. "You must be pretty good on computers."

"I am the best, Señor Cable," the boy bragged.

Cable walked over to the computer. "Think you can help me find a kidnapped girl?"

Rene stopped typing. He turned to look at Cable to see if he was serious.

He was.

"Perhaps, but it will cost you."

"Will you accept a verbal agreement to pay you when I can?" Cable asked.

Rene paused and considered the words. "What details do you have?"

Cable grabbed a chair from the kitchen and joined Rene. "Her name is Dani Tran, twenty-six, maybe twenty-eight, if I had to guess. I don't know where she lives, but she works for PEAK Insurance."

Rene typed and scrolled for a bit. "Nothing here...you sure she works for that company?"

"That's what she said."

"Ha, women."

"Really? From a twelve-year-old?"

"Fact of life. The sooner you learn it, the better off you are."

"Well, I disagree. Women are the glue that binds this world. You must have just had a bad one. Who was she, out of curiosity?"

"My mother."

Silence filled the room for a minute as Rene typed.

"Dani Tran doesn't work for PEAK Insurance."

Cable's faith in Dani's innocence started to fade.

"You sure she was kidnapped?" Rene asked.

"Pretty sure. Certain things just don't add up. She was taken from my house and put on a Gulfstream 150 at The Centennial Airport out of Denver. They flew to a private hangar at the main airport here in Mexico City last night...and oh, the tail number on the jet was N904XE."

"Now that is something I can use," Rene said. He banged on his keyboard for some time, muttering along the way.

"Okay, Gulfstream 150 tail number N904XE is leased by a firm out of San Diego. I hacked their records, and they have a chartered flight that matches your information. It looks like the jet is still here in Mexico. Its next fight is tomorrow morning, from Cancun to Salt Lake...nope."

"What?"

"The charter is for the Carston family. The company that paid for the charter from Denver is here...FC Holdings. Looks like a shell company. Not much here...oh."

"What is it?"

Rene angled his screen in Cable's direction. It had a picture of a freighter plying the open ocean. "FC Holdings has a cargo ship, the *Peridot*, and it's loading in Veracruz as we speak."

"A cargo ship. Yes, that could be it. I need to get to Veracruz."

Rene pulled the screen back in his direction. "That will really cost you...and I might need you to drive."

Dani slowly opened her eyes. She felt even groggier than the last time. The drugs they were giving her were powerful. The sound of a large jet taking off thundered nearby. She was still at the airport. It was dark but not night. A few pinpricks of sunlight shafted into the room like laser swords. She tried to move but couldn't. She was strapped to a small metal bed frame. She wiggled some more. The frame was bolted to the floor. She was going nowhere.

Her eyes slowly focused, and she identified her surroundings. A small plane hangar. It was wide and not too tall, made from steel, with a few rust spots showing. The floor was concrete, and the space was mostly empty except for eight other beds just like hers. Every one of them was occupied.

"Hello?" she asked.

"Shh, keep it down, or they'll sedate you again," came a voice to the left.

"Who are you?" Dani whispered.

"Jennifer."

"I'm Dani…I'm from Austin."

"Sacramento."

Another voice piped up. "We're all from the Sacramento area."

"What's going on here?" Dani asked, afraid of the answer.

A strong voice from the darkness boomed, "Human trafficking, for those of you too stupid to realize it. Now shut up, or I'll do as the lady said and tranq you all again." He waited for a moment, making sure they had stopped talking.

The room fell silent except for the roar of another jet taking off.

"That's better because I would much rather hydrate and feed you all before the next part of your vacation to an exotic land."

Dani watched as one-by-one the girls were untied and taken to a bathroom. They were given a bottle of water and a sandwich, then re-tied to their bed frame.

When it was her turn, she watched for any chance of an escape, but her captors were very practiced and focused. The bathroom had no door or window, and an armed guard was always just out of reach.

Once she was tied back up, Dani felt the effects of something she had eaten or drank, and her eyes started to flutter. She got a glimpse of the hangar door sliding open and a cargo van backing in before she slumped back into darkness.

As much as Stein loved the old church he operated from, he could never get used to the musty smell in the chapel-turned-warehouse. He had tried ozone generators and fans, but after 1,700 years, the stone building was infused with its history and moisture. Luckily, he had none of those issues upstairs.

He watched as Deniz Reis, who went by the street name of RezDez, inspected his latest acquisitions. The skinny African-Turkish wannabe rapper wore a black hoodie and a beanie holding shoulder-length dreads. He used a small magnifier that hung on a gold chain around his neck to inspect details of the recently acquired African artifacts.

Gangster rap blasted from his earbuds as he sang along with the explicit lyrics. It was a weird routine of dancing, singing, and inspecting, all to the beat of some very edgy music. The whole play, as Stein had coined it, always amused him. He set the King and Queen carving down, picked up the Lubba divination board, and eyeballed it.

"Might wanna give my dead mom a call with this," RezDez said a bit too loud.

Finally, the music stopped, mid-chorus. It was time for business.

"Okay, you are looking at some first-rate stuff here. The patina is close to a thousand years old. That's hard to fake. I'll authenticate these pieces and apply a valuation, then send you all the documentation." RezDez put his speaker and laptop into his backpack as he spoke. "As usual, if you're going black market on these pieces, take 40-60 percent off the price. I'll email you the documents by EOD. You can Venmo me payment. Cash, please. I'm not taking Bitcoin right now. It's in the toilet."

"Out of curiosity, what are we talking about here?"

"I have to do a few comparisons, but you are looking at an open market somewhere between $400 and $600K. That's for all five pieces."

"They do make a nice collection," Stein said.

"I wouldn't say no to a shelf with these in my house. You'll definitely get more selling them as a collection than selling them individually. Of course, you have to find the right buyer for that."

That was exactly what Stein was thinking, and he had just such a buyer in mind. He reached forward and completed their business with a handshake.

He watched as RezDez popped his earbuds back in and danced his way out of the church.

"So what did RezDez have to say?" Fannie asked as she stepped down the metal staircase.

"We should be able to clear $200K on this deal."

Fannie nodded with satisfaction.

"Where do we stand on my prize?" he asked.

"Your prize should be leaving port within the hour. That means thirteen or fourteen days from now, we'll have possession, depending on the weather."

"That's a long time to wait."

"The wait is what draws no attention to us," Fannie said.

Stein nodded in agreement. "What have you found out about the girl?"

"I think you made the right call. She is exactly what we need. Vulnerable with top-notch skillsets."

The drive to Veracruz was normally six hours with traffic. At 2 a.m. and breaking every traffic speed law, Cable and Rene had made it in four.

Rene kept a brand new V8 Jeep Wrangler in a paid parking structure at the bottom of the hill. It had been tricked out with 37-inch tires on black rims and a lift that required Rene to use a box to climb in. He had taken his prize vehicle out a couple of times for a spin but was just learning how to drive it. With the seat all the way forward, he could reach the pedals, but driving around a block or two was quite different from a high-speed road trip to the coast.

Cable had weaved in and out of the myriad of trucks that connect container ship deliveries to the city of over twenty-two million. A few near misses had Rene, who was not used to such speeds, ducking for cover.

"This is my newest baby, so please be careful."

"I take it you are just learning to drive?"

"Yes, I have a friend who got me a valid license, but driving on the computer is not the same."

"*Gran Turismo?*"

"*Need for Speed,*" Rene replied as Cable sped around a box truck.

"The secret to driving is looking ahead. Point your car where you want it to go, steer accordingly."

Cable swerved, just missing a semi changing lanes unexpectedly. "If you start to feel the car slip, you need to counter-steer. It is a bit counterintuitive, but it will save you. If you get a chance, go to an empty parking lot on a rainy day and give it a try."

Rene was too busy holding on to listen.

Veracruz was once a tourist destination along Mexico's eastern coast, but as the country's main port to the Atlantic, it had become more industrialized over the years. The tourists moved south to Cancun and Playa Del Carmen.

The 140 freeway died at Avenida Miguel Alemán, and Cable followed the road to the docks. Across from the Mexico Naval Museum was the *Peridot*, painted green like her namesake. She was a medium-sized container ship with a single onboard crane for smaller ports. The raised super-structure was at the rear of the ship, giving the bridge a view of all the containers stacked on the deck.

Cable pulled the Jeep to a stop and looked past the chain-link fence at the green and black ship. A huge land-based crane placed a steel container on the nearly full deck.

"She's almost loaded," Cable said as he scanned the manned guard gate to the left.

"What are the chances Dani's on that ship? Rene asked.

"Fifty-fifty, if I'm lucky."

"I lost quite a bit of cash to those odds once."

"Noted." Cable turned back from the ship. "Thank you, Rene. You might have just saved a life."

"Or cost you yours. That would make it hard for you to pay your debt to me."

"Yes, it would," Cable said.

They shook hands, and Cable left the vehicle and his newest friend behind.

He could hear the Jeep roar to life and have trouble turning before lurching away and into the night.

Cable jogged over to the fence and walked the perimeter, heading away from the guarded entrance. He found a spot where the retaining wires had worn loose from the poles holding the chain-link. He pulled at the bottom of the fence, creating just enough space to slide under.

Keeping to the shadows, he moved closer to the ship. A huge rope tied the bow of the vessel to the pier. No one seemed interested in his presence, so Cable slipped onto the rope and shimmied aboard.

He didn't know how much time he had to search the ship before it left port, but his desire for a long sea voyage was minimal.

A few years back he had paid for passage on a freighter from Cape Town to Madagascar. The seas had been unusually heavy as a storm moved through the Mozambique Channel. The ship had nearly capsized twice, and Cable had spent most of the trip puking in his berth. Never again, he had promised himself.

Once on board, Cable moved along the narrow space between the rows of forty-foot steel containers. They were stacked five high on the deck and easily that again in the holds below. This would take some time. If Dani was in one of these containers he might never find her.

Dani woke to a loud banging. She pulled herself to her feet and looked around. Her head pounded like it might explode. Her surroundings had changed once again. She was in a shipping container with bunk beds attached to the walls. The door was open, and light from outside streamed in. She moved to investigate. The banging grew louder as she did. Outside was not outside, but rather somewhere in a ship's hold. The lighting was artificial. There were containers stacked on either side rising into the air. Beyond the container's door was a caged area about twenty by ten. There was a toilet and a sink out in the open and two picnic tables in the middle. She realized she was no longer with eight other girls. Now, there were closer to twenty, mostly blondes, but there was one redhead and several brunettes.

The banging came from a man on the other side of the cage. He was hitting what looked like an old hubcap with a hammer. Once all the girls had exited the container, he stopped.

"Ladies!" Listen up." He put down the hubcap and hammer on a folding table just on the other side of the cage. "Welcome to your world for the next fourteen days."

Dani noticed a distinct southern accent.

"Please keep any complaints you may have to yourself, as management is not interested." This made him laugh.

"If you behave, you will be allowed to roam and do as you like within the confines of your cage. If you cause any problems, you will be locked into a dark container with three bowls. One water, the other dog food, and the third empty...I'm sure you can guess. So don't cause any problems and we will get along fine. My brother and I are responsible for your health and safety."

Another man appeared. He was younger than the man speaking, but not by much. It was clear they were related, as each had the same teardrop-shaped face with a broad forehead and bushy eyebrows. The older one continued. "We take our job here seriously. Remember, you girls are valuable, so we monitor you 24/7 because we want you to be the best versions of yourself when we arrive."

The second brother took over the indoctrination. "Should any of you try to hurt yourself or one of the other girls, we will sedate you for the whole trip with an IV and a colostomy bag. That is not how you want to spend your time here, I assure you."

The first brother added, "There is no chance for escape. If, by some miracle, you got out of your cage, you would find yourselves on the high seas with nowhere to run. So, sit back, relax, read a book, you might learn something."

The first brother tossed several magazines and paperback books into the cage, then the two men left.

Dani looked around and realized she was by far the oldest in the group. She estimated the youngest to be around thirteen. A thin girl with wispy blonde hair was off in a corner, crying. Dani stepped over to console her.

Cable found an exterior hatch on the starboard side of the ship, away from the active loading. He spun the wheel. The six dog levers released, and he pulled the door open.

Inside was a steel hallway to the left and a staircase going up and down in front of him. He heard footsteps from above and chose down. After six rows of stairs, he exited at CH5.

The time he spent not throwing up on his last cargo ship cruise had been slightly augmented by a few tours of the infrastructure. CH stood for Cargo Hull, and 5 meant the lowest level, or fifth deck. He skirted the narrow walkway between the stacked containers and the double-skinned outer hull. Up ahead lay the large sealed-off refrigerated section. The walkway became a tunnel, lit by small cage lights along the ceiling. As Cable exited the tunnel to the other side, he noticed something different in the stacking style of the containers. They formed a U-shape instead of the usual side-by-side rows.

He moved around the U and slowed as he came to the end of the stack.

Inside the U were two single containers lying parallel. One had its doors open, and the other was closed. Beyond the containers was fencing, much like an enclosed baseball backstop. There were two picnic tables in the middle, and several forlorn-looking women meandered and sat about. A locked gate was in the front, and a small construction trailer was just across from it.

It took a few seconds, but Cable found what he was looking for. Dani. There was no longer any doubt in his mind. She had been taken.

He wanted to run for her and make up for his failure back at his house, but caution was required here. He squatted down and started to move closer.

"That's far enough," said a voice with a southern accent.

Cable turned to see a man holding an automatic pistol, pointing at his midsection.

Another man appeared from the right. He looked eerily similar to the first man.

"What'a we got here?" he asked.

Cable stood with his hands slightly raised to his sides. "You took something that doesn't belong to you."

"Sorry, you've got the wrong guys. We're not in the taking business. We're transporters."

The other one added, "Yeah, like the movie. Only with a ship."

"Then you won't mind if I collect my friend and be on our way," Cable said.

"Oh, we'll mind. Just so happens we can use a feller like you."

The door slammed, and the cogs locked. Cable listened as a chain rattled around the lever, locking him in.

They had escorted him to the forward bow, somewhere below the waterline. He could feel the shift as the ship pulled from the dock and began its tow to open water.

The tiny space looked to be an old paint storage room, the floor-to-ceiling shelves long emptied. A small cage light by the door was his only source of light, and Cable prayed they would leave it on as footsteps receded outside. Most concerning was the six inches of smelly water sloshing around on the floor.

On the left wall was a small steel worktable coated with a lifetime of spilled paints and scratches. It was the only horizontal area that was dry. On the table were three buckets and a sign. One bucket was empty, the other was filled with water, and the third was filled with what looked like dry dog food. A small sign lay nearby: *14 days make it last.*

Cable slumped. He had just gone from bad to worse. Then the light went out, slamming him into darkness.

CHAPTER SIX

THE SMALL CAGE LIGHT POWERED up, causing Cable to avert his eyes. After fourteen days of total darkness, he was a mess. His hair and beard were matted, and his clothes were filthy. He had managed to stretch his food for ten days and his water up until a day ago. The biggest toll, however, was on his mind. The four-by-five-foot steel table had become his only livable surface in his midnight world. The seawater on the floor was filled with diesel and oil. That table had been his chair, workout room, sanctuary, and bed. At first, he had prayed for light, then a bath, food, water, sanity, and finally, death. None of them came.

He was pulled from the room and pushed along a corridor. His legs were weak, and his shoulders slumped.

"Man, you stink," one of the guards said.

Cable had no reply. He was just hanging on.

Hands pushed him up against a steel wall, and a high-pressure hose blasted him with seawater. He cowered from the pain, unable to do anything but endure.

Cable was taken into the ship and down to the fifth level. He was placed into the cage, and the gate locked behind him.

"Thought you might like some real food before your next adventure," the guard said as he pointed to some food laid out on the picnic table in the middle.

"Not sure I can handle another of your adventures," Cable muttered as he sat down. He picked up a sandwich and took a bite. It was magical and delicious. The best sandwich he had ever eaten. A quick inspection revealed two pieces of packaged ham and a slice of cheese, nothing more, but after dog food for ten days and then nothing for four, it was five stars. He ate the rest of it like it was a competitive eating contest, feeling his body start to revive with every mouthful.

It was at that moment Cable realized the girls were missing. The doors to both containers were closed. He finished off his sandwich and guzzled two bottles of water, then shuffled over to inspect the containers. They were both locked. He tapped with his knuckles and called out in a hoarse voice. "Hello? Dani, are you in there?"

No reply.

He banged harder and yelled louder. Same result.

He turned and headed back to the table and sat. He was feeling dizzy. No, not dizzy…drugged. Before the thought could be properly processed, Cable sank to the floor.

The smell was familiar. Jasmine and citrus. It pulled Cable from the void into a light and cheery world. A world with fine linens and exotic hardwoods. He was still moving and swaying. A boat, but this dream was far beyond the horrors of his previous blacked-out, cargo ship, steel storage room world.

As he sat up, Cable noticed a small placard next to the bed he was lying in. *Cable, feel free to clean up and change clothes. I am anxious to meet you. Welcome aboard, Fannie.*

Cable scratched at his unruly beard. He looked around. The well-appointed berth was part of a larger, more luxurious vessel. He could feel the subtle hum of the engines and the gentle sway of being underway.

The head had everything he needed to shower, trim his beard, and feel a bit more like himself. The closet held several wardrobe choices, and he selected jeans, a yellow short-sleeved shirt, and a pair of boat shoes. He did a final mirror check—haunted, sunken eyes stared back. He shook it off before leaving the room and heading out into the unknown.

The yacht was named the *Arinna*, after the ancient Hittite sun goddess. She was a 110-foot K-584, produced by CPN shipyard and made for serious expeditions. Hard military lines gave her more of an old-school battleship look than the ultra-modern yachts of the day. *Arinna* was built for a distance, not necessarily speed, with a range of over 6,000 nm per fill-up. A narrow carpeted hallway led to a small lighted staircase heading up. The stairs ended at a modern salon with an open floor plan.

"Ah, you're awake and looking much better. Come on in, and let's get acquainted."

Cable glanced over to a woman in her midthirties with a casual disregard for his circumstances. Her creamy skin, set against fiery red hair and green eyes, stood out.

Sitting across from her was Dani. She had on khaki shorts and a light-blue short-sleeved shirt. Her olive skin, black eyes, and shiny black hair were in contrast to their host.

Out the windows, blue water and sky in every direction.

"I'll stand if you don't mind." Cable was still suffering some PTSD from his last boat cruise.

"Of course. First of all, hi. My name is Fannie, and I'd like to start by apologizing. Using a known and trusted human trafficking network might have got you here undetected, but I'm sure it was not the most pleasant of experiences." She turned and smiled at Cable with false eyes, then turned back to Dani.

Cable gave no reaction, but he noted her South African accent. He looked at Dani. "You okay?"

She nodded slightly before Fannie continued.

"And you, Cable, we weren't expecting you at all. It took a bit of negotiation to get you here. So, welcome."

"This is a joke, right?" Cable said flatly.

Fannie ignored him. "I mean, who could believe you would chase Dani halfway around the globe? Are you two related or dating, or is there something I have missed?"

"Nothing like that," Dani spoke for the first time. "Thank you, Cable, for your efforts."

Cable looked over to Dani, and their eyes locked for just a beat.

"Sure, anytime."

"Wow. Okay. So we've got a burgeoning romance. Good for you two."

"First of all," Cable started. "There is no burgeoning romance and if there was, we don't need a narrator added to the mix. Now, you mentioned halfway around the world. Where are we, and what do you want?"

"We are just north of Aveiro…"

Portugal, Cable thought to himself.

"You two made the transfer over late last night from the *Peridot*… oh, I almost forgot…"

Fannie was wearing a lime-green bikini with a matching sarong. Her casualness was off-putting as she reached down and retrieved a small clutch that Dani recognized immediately.

"Your purse and wallet. For now, I will hold on to your phone. I'm sure you understand."

Dani grabbed her purse back a bit too aggressively, her mind still spinning at the thought that she had been in Denver just a short time ago.

"And it is not what I want. It is what my employer wants." Fannie stepped over to a polished cabinet and reached inside.

Cable decided to exit the back door and see if he could launch the tender, clearly visible on the rear deck.

Fannie pulled out the goshawk statue, and Cable stopped mid-stride. "That's mine."

"True, and soon you can have it back. I am only interested in the secret it holds."

"A faithful pilgrimage begins. Pious and angels alike share," Cable recited from memory, holding his hand out for her to give it back.

"Impressive. The ancient language of Ge'ez is not exactly on the required reading list."

Cable looked to Dani. "It was part of my thesis on Punt and the empires that followed," she said. "I even put together a translator app of sorts for a couple of the dead languages in that specific area and era."

"Well, it looks like we were right in collecting both of you. That is slightly different from the version we had. Which puts us in a bit of a pickle. We could sure use your help," Fannie said.

"So, you kidnapped, stole, and transported us here just to ask for our help? Next time, try calling or texting," Cable said, the anger in his voice rising. "You're crazy if you think we would help you do anything."

Fannie was unfazed. "My employer ran across an ancient Axum Empire scroll. He was naturally curious when he saw this painting."

She pressed a button, and a flat panel screen rose up out of a cabinet. An image from antiquities popped up. A profile of a bearded man dressed in a white robe sitting in a yellow and brown cheetah-spotted chair. He had the traditional orange circle around his head. His feet sat on a rug with unknown letters, and his hands held a large crystal. There was a multicolored, patterned border surrounding him and a small swastika in the bottom right corner. Above the swastika was a depiction of Cable's grandfather's statue, only it had outstretched wings.

Cable paused and looked at the screen. The image was intriguing. He stepped forward, letting his eyes cover every detail. "This circle usually signifies a saint. So this man must be a well-known priest. The swastika is used by several ancient religions as a mark of truth or luck. Hitler pretty much killed that concept in the modern era." He looked even closer at an image above the small swastika. "If I'm not mistaken, that looks a lot like my statue, only with wings."

Dani joined him taking a closer look, as well. "Yes, it does. I've seen paintings like this before in other manuscripts and scrolls. I would have to say, ancient Eastern Africa." She pointed to the sandstone goshawk. "It is extremely rare to match up two seemingly disparate pieces from so long ago. I personally have never experienced it until now...that is, if this is real."

"Oh, it is very real, Doctor." Fannie pointed to the object in the priest's hand. "What is your opinion of the stone the saint is holding?"

The screen zoomed in closer.

Dani and Cable studied the crystal-like rock for some time.

"Some kind of gemstone, maybe a raw diamond?" Dani said, completely guessing.

Cable was less onboard. "That could be anything from a quartz seer-stone to a glob of melted sand, like Libyan desert glass."

"It is above a box which could represent a vault," Dani added.

"Yes, I'm sure you're right."

"Okay, we've helped you. Can we go now?" Cable said.

"Actually, you have helped, but you have told us nothing we didn't already know. Just confirmed it."

Fannie flicked the screen to another image. "This is from the next part of the scroll."

Cable looked at the stylized writing. He thought it looked similar to the scratched symbols on the back of his statue.

Dani looked closer. She also recognized them but said nothing.

"Can you translate them?"

"With access to a computer and time," Dani said.

"I see. Well, you two have been most resourceful. Make yourselves at home on the *Arinna* and we will drop you at our next port of call." Fannie turned off the screen and left the room.

Dani and Cable stared at Fannie as she left, both a bit taken back.

Cable stepped to Dani and placed his hand on her shoulder. "Sure you're alright?"

"A bit shaken, but I'll be okay. *Arinna* is a Hittite sun goddess."

"Is that important?" Cable asked.

"No, but if we do get off this ship, it might lend some fact to our far-fetched story," Dani said.

"This whole thing is out of a B-movie."

"Did you really do what she said?"

"What?"

"Chase after me all this way?"

"Once a stalker…"

"Be serious."

Cable looked at his toes for a moment, remembering Hilary. "I lost someone I cared about once by not acting, and I promised myself I would never let that happen again. So, in a way, my actions were…" The words got too hard for Cable to continue.

Dani tried to take some of the pressure off. "Well, I'm flattered. No one has ever gone to such extremes for me before."

"Their loss," Cable said with a burgeoning smile.

Dani reached up and gave Cable a simple kiss. "Thank you."

The kiss sent nerve endings firing and chemical compounds releasing. Cable was overwhelmed and speechless. He locked eyes with Dani.

They were black pools that matched her hair perfectly, but somehow, they seemed to draw you in and captivate you. They were all-consuming and intelligent, like they could sense the truth.

After a beat, he shook it off and recovered. "Sure. Come on, let's get outta here." Cable led Dani out the back slider and onto the stern. An eighteen-foot open-bow runabout was sitting there in blocks. It was the ship's tender, and it was big enough to find land. Cable did a quick inspection of the craft before his heart sank.

"It's locked up."

"Guess we're gonna stay a bit longer."

Cable barely nodded as he stared out at the empty blue horizon.

"Let me buy you a drink," Dani offered.

Cable followed Dani back to the galley to raid the wine cabinet.

They found a bottle of Pasaeli Rosé, a corkscrew, and a couple of glasses. Cable poured, and they took their time enjoying the caramel-pink fruity wine with a hint of strawberries and raspberries and, quite frankly, a magnificent view.

Fannie entered a small office on the second floor. She opened up her computer screen and Stein Osman's face appeared.

Fannie recognized her partner's office background. "Did you get all that?"

"Every word," he said, adjusting the headroom in his picture.

"So, what do you want to do?"

"Have the girl translate the page. Maybe we'll learn more. Then, follow the plan. We can't have them following us or calling the police." He clicked on his keyboard for a few seconds. "The information you requested came in, and I've just forwarded it. Our contact is standing by with the drones you requested. Just let him know if you need any other hardware," Stein said.

"Good to know," Fannie said.

"How much longer?"

"We'll be in Gothenburg tomorrow morning," Fannie replied.

"Okay, safe journey."

"Talk soon."

They both clicked off.

Fannie gathered up her laptop, notepad, and pen. She headed back to the salon, letting her mind process her next steps. It was funny how life had guided her to this place.

Several years ago, a mutual acquaintance had introduced her to a man at a security conference in London. The man was Stein Osman.

If you were to stand back and judge them based on their appearance, you would see very little in common. Fannie had an angled face with thick red hair, green eyes, and down-turned pouting lips. Stein's face was more teardrop-shaped, with a balding head and dark features. His up-turned thin lips were barely visible through a close-cropped beard. A sort of Jekyll and Hyde on the outside.

When it came to business, however, they had seen eye to eye from day one.

The black market antiquities business in the Middle East had boomed during the allied occupation and war in Iraq. Museums had been looted and collectors robbed. Out of that crisis, demand for goods grew until 2015, when the supply started to dry up. The business in general fell apart, and providers and middlemen faded away as fast as they had arrived. Collectors, however, were still out there, demanding more and paying higher prices than ever before.

Stein had ridden the illicit trade-of-antiquities wave into prosperity, but he also saw the changes coming and evolved accordingly. He transformed his business model and its name, Cronus Logistics, giving him a more legitimate look to the outside world. Raven was hired to focus on keyword searches that revealed new artifacts, recently discovered artifacts, or unknown artifacts that might show up in an estate sale or even an attic. They were easy pickings for someone who knew what they were doing. Dig sites were notoriously unprotected, and a family that had just lost a key loved one, for example, was never focused on home security. All he needed was a team that could go get them.

That's where Fannie came in.

After a promising career start in the Special Operations Group of the South African National Defense Force, Fannie tendered her resignation and left the esteemed branch. Her upward movement had been stopped dead by a jealous, misogynistic general. Fannie had no time or patience to fight it. With her skills, she figured she could do better on her own in the private sector. Little did she know how vindictive and far-reaching the general's connections spread. Every interview was a polite "no thank you." She had watched as her savings dropped week by week, unable to procure anything to her liking.

Fannie took a chance and bought a plane ticket to a security conference in London with the last of her savings. The first time she met Stein Osman, it was as if they completed each other's business language. He needed her skills, and she needed his.

Crossing the line into the illicit side of operations had been easy for her. All the same rules applied. Get in, get out, and don't get caught. She had used her skills to recruit a small but talented team that kept the flow of product constant for Cronus Logistics.

From this simple but ingenious business model, Cronus Logistics had risen to become the premier antiquities black marketer in the Middle East. Best of all, it was the least known antiquities black marketer to the authorities, and Fannie worked hard to keep it that way.

Operating out of an old church in Istanbul, a city where East meets West, gave them easy access to ports and clients around the globe. Stein stayed nimble and was always pushing to improve the way things were done. His connections and clever ability to coordinate the shipping of goods made delivery assured. Fannie's ability to obtain the artifacts, leaving no trace back to them, created a steady cash flow.

Business, after all, was not a static beast. It was constantly evolving. For example, in the last five years, his Chinese clients had grown to consume nearly 60 percent of his business. Commerce he would have lost if not ready for this shift.

Fannie was proud of the operation they had built and her pivotal role in it. The money was exceptional, and it allowed her to rebuild her savings a thousand times over. It also gave her a chance at revenge.

Four years ago, she had watched with glee as the news channels carried the story of a disgraced general in the Special Operations Branch of the South African National Defense Force. Leaked photos and inappropriate emails had sealed his fate. Public opinion gave him a verdict of guilty, and whatever came out in the courts after that didn't matter. His ability to live in this world as a sexist egomaniac was over.

That was the moment Fannie knew she would ride side-by-side with Stein to the end. Intertwined partners, each doing what they did best, but not lovers. No man could hold her heart.

Eighteen months ago, things changed. A scroll from the Axum Empire crossed Stein's desk. He had taken a particular interest in one of the paintings inside. A saint holding what looked like a giant diamond. Rather than have the scroll valued and resell it, Stein kept the scroll and poured resources into getting it translated. He even had a couple of experts weigh in on the mystery diamond. Over time, he had become more convinced and obsessed with its authenticity and the truth of the story it held.

Fannie tried to convince him to stay focused on their booming business, but Stein was no ordinary partner. He convinced Fannie of just the opposite, and the two were now both consumed with the scroll's message.

They had expanded their search, looking for anything that might lead them to the next step. Several trips to Ethiopia had resulted in nothing but a frustrating vacation.

It took a young archeologist working as an appraiser to turn their luck. She posted a picture of the goshawk statue to a fellow academic for confirmation of her valuation. That had led to a hit on Fannie's keyword search.

Stein and Fannie were convinced the goshawk statue matched the one pictured in the scroll, except this one was missing its wings.

Once Fannie had the statue in her possession, she knew Stein had been right all along. The words on the back proved it. There was a message, and they needed to find the two missing wings to complete it.

Cronus Logistics put everything on hold while Raven scoured and hacked the globe for any mention of statue wings, stone wings, goshawk wings, Coptic wings, etc. Several hits amounted to nothing. It was a very specific and obscure search. One, however, looked very promising and that's where the *Arinna* was motoring now.

Fannie stepped into the salon and slid the computer next to Dani.

"We would very much like you to translate the scroll."

"Who's we?" Cable asked.

"My partner is a very private person, so let's just say *I* would like you to translate the scroll."

"And if *I* refuse?" Dani asked.

"There is an easy way. Where you translate the scroll, and we drop you off at our next stop."

A man holding an assault rifle entered the salon and stood by the back slider.

"Or a hard way. Where we make you translate the scroll." Fannie hooked a thumb at the guard. "Then he dumps your body in the ocean when you are done, but not before dismembering your friend here to ensure your best efforts." She gazed at Cable with a deadly hunger.

"How do we know we can trust you?" Cable asked, unfazed by her glare.

"Trust is a strong word. You can believe what I say. I make a business out of backing up my words. Also, I currently have no reason to kill you, so let's not go there, okay?"

Dani grabbed the laptop and opened the screen. A secure search engine named Swisscows popped up.

Fannie pointed to the very small camera in the ceiling. "Remember, we will be watching, so let's not do anything stupid."

Cable popped open a second bottle of wine and poured both glasses. He noticed a freighter passing to starboard and wondered if he could swim to it. *Not a chance.*

The sun had moved to the horizon, casting an orange glare off the water. Dani had her translation page open and was following the painstaking steps to translate ancient Ge'ez in between sips from her glass.

Cable watched the process, taking it all in. "Did you notice most of the wines onboard are Turkish? I think the owner might be Turkish or lives in Turkey."

"Or they just like Turkish wine," Dani answered.

"Maybe…if that's a thing." Cable looked around. "This yacht is not cheap, so someone with real do-re-mi has a hard-on for whatever it is they are looking for. I'm thinking hidden treasure, rare minerals, or maybe lost knowledge. What's your take?"

"Aliens," Dani said with a smirk. "Write this down." She slid the notepad over to Cable.

She then proceeded to vocalize a series of letters. When she was done, she pulled the notepad back over so they could both see it.

Dani's eyes scanned the words. "Treasure. They are definitely going for treasure."

CHAPTER SEVEN

THE SUN HAD LONG SINCE set, giving the ocean an oily appearance. Every now and then, Cable saw lit ships pass on either side of the boat. None were close enough to flag down. They had worked through dinner and into the night. A couple of armed men had helped themselves to coffee or other food and then left again. The translation process was laborious and, honestly, a one-woman job, but Dani was adamant Cable learn the basics of her program.

Cable finally stood and stretched. He left Dani and headed for the galley.

"What's your opinion on peanut butter and jelly?"

"What's the jelly?" Dani asked.

Cable perused the cupboard. "Orange marmalade."

"Hard pass."

Cable moved to the fridge. "Oh, found some wild blueberry preserves."

"Count me in."

Cable made the sandwiches and a pot of coffee. Once back at the table, they ate and worked.

"I thought for a while you were in on the theft of my statue."

Dani stopped chewing and looked over. "Me?"

"Yes. You made quite the distraction while they grabbed it and disappeared into the night. I tried to look you up and you're not on the PEAK Insurance website. I had my doubts."

"I work freelance for PEAK, and while you were being robbed, I was being held at gunpoint, drugged, and kidnapped."

"I know that now," Cable said.

"So?"

"So, I hope you're not as picky about your rescuers as you are about your jelly. I also know that—" Cable stopped mid-sentence as Fannie entered the room.

Dani was just about finished chewing when she paused. "I think I have it."

Fannie crossed to the table. A row of letters was broken by vertical lines, designating words.

"*'A pilgrimage for the worthy to unimaginable wealth. A Sokar, now as three, marks the...'*" Dani paused reading. "The next word doesn't translate exactly. It basically means, 'beginning of a path or start of a journey.'"

Fannie moved closer and repeated the words. "A pilgrimage for the worthy to unimaginable wealth. A Sokar, now as three, marks the beginning of your journey."

"Sure," Dani said.

"And that's it?" Fannie asked.

"No. The next part is a declaration to a priest who helped save the church."

"What about before it?"

"That was a brief genealogy of the church leaders. There were some very difficult names to translate, and I'm not sure I succeeded."

Fannie nodded. "What do you make of *'a Sokar now as three?'*"

"A Sokar was the god of seeking truth from the Punt region, just south of ancient Egypt."

"A half-man, half-hawk kinda thing. Specifically, a goshawk," Cable said.

"*'Seeking truth.'* That sounds like a pilgrimage for the worthy," Fannie said.

"There are a lot of statues and paintings that depict Sokar, so the chance that it refers to my goshawk statue is extremely slight," Cable added.

"Yes, but how many of those statues have wings?"

Dani did a quick search. "Very few."

"It mentions *'now as three.'* That statue is clearly missing its wings, based on the painting. That would account for *three*. A statue of a god now broken into three pieces."

"It's certainly possible," Dani said. "Just like it is possible there will be more to the message when the statue is complete. It is also possible that this is not the statue and that there will be no more to the message. You are taking one plus one and coming up with six."

Cable pointed to the picture on the screen. "You also have to consider the painting of the saint holding the unknown rock. That rock could be Libyan desert glass. Something that would have been extremely valuable back then, *'to unimaginable wealth,'* but not so much now. I bought a chunk about that same size in the Sahara for a hundred bucks. Context is required."

"True," said Fannie. "But I disagree with your theory. I do, however, thank you for your efforts." She collected her laptop. "We will make port tomorrow, and you will be free to leave, as promised."

Dani and Cable shared an uneasy look as Fannie left the salon. They sat at the table a bit longer in reticence before Dani downed the last of her wine and broke the silence. "I'm going to bed. I'm exhausted."

They locked eyes for just a second before Cable replied, "Right behind you." He collected the empty wine glasses and set them in the sink as he watched Dani leave. She was truly a remarkable woman. Smart, funny, and just enough drive. Even as kidnappees, they made a good team.

Cable stepped out on the stern of the yacht. The wind was cool and refreshing in the night. Stars by the billions covered the sky from horizon to horizon. It always was a great reminder for Cable just how insignificant he was in the big picture. He was in no big hurry to go back to his berth. Closed doors and small rooms still carried scars for him. A light in the room a floor above turned on and he decided to investigate. Cable crept up the ladder to an open seating area with a canopy roof.

It led to another slider with a view to an open floorplan beyond. There was an office and a large bed, all surrounded by polished hardwoods and glass windows.

Cable crawled behind the closest overstuffed chair and peeked into the room. Fannie and two men were in an animated conversation over something on her laptop. Cable couldn't make out the conversation, but he could see a large, long room with a checkerboard floor on the computer screen. Fannie changed the image to a floor plan of the room.

An armed man stood back by the wall. He suddenly moved toward the rear slider. Cable ducked and froze. The man opened the slider, and the conversation floated out of the room.

"Thank you, Marcos. It was getting a bit stuffy in here with all the testosterone," Fannie said.

Once the guard returned, Cable relaxed and leaned closer to listen. He could just make out the screen on the computer. The floor plan zoomed into a closer section with a display cabinet.

"The cabinet is protected by cameras and an alarm. The guard, if there is one, usually positions himself here or here." Fannie moved, and her body suddenly blocked Cable's view of the screen.

"Once you are in the room and have confirmed the wing's location, we'll occupy the guard's attention. You will take care of the rest."

They've found one of the wings and are going after it, Cable deduced.

"Remember, speed and misdirection are essential," said an unfamiliar voice with a German accent through the speaker of the computer.

Cable waited for Fannie to move her body, as it was still blocking his view of the screen.

Eventually, she did. The image on the screen was now of the exterior of a public-looking building with a neoclassical warm brick façade and a large bronze fountain in front. The writing on the building was hard to make out, but Cable was able to extrapolate most of the words. The Gothenburg Museum. They were heading to Sweden.

Cable stayed a bit longer, but the conversation moved off topic. He crawled back down the ladder and slipped into the salon. A guard was waiting for him inside.

"What were you doing out there?"

"Taking in some air. It is a nice night out," Cable said.

The guard stared him down for a beat before leaving to finish his rounds.

Stein clicked off his monitor that was showing the two guests on his yacht. Fannie had been right. You get more from the carrot than the stick, but that didn't mean the stick wasn't needed. The translated message was more complete than the one he had previously paid for.

Dani Tran knew her stuff.

Firing up one of his favorite cigars, he silently read the words one more time. He compared them to the original translation he had first paid for.

A pilgrimage for the worthy to unimaginable wealth. A Sokar, now as three, marks the beginning.

Dani was a real find. Her translation took him to the next level. A message leading to one of the ancient world's great mysteries was slowly unraveling. A mystery only he and Fannie truly understood.

The words called to him and pushed him forward. He would not be denied. He now had proof that the starting point to a pilgrimage of unimaginable wealth was contained in the entire goshawk statue, but to complete the message, he needed both wings to go with the statue.

He opened the floor plan of the Gothenburg Museum in Sweden. It was a giant rectangle with multiple floors holding some of northern Europe's most precious art. Rembrandt, Carl Larsson, Picasso, and Van Gogh. One particular room was of interest to him, the sculpture hall. It had a black-and-white tiled floor with tall white alcove walls. High arched windows ran along one side while the other was filled with hanging pieces and displayed carved art from many epochs.

Stein zoomed in to a more detailed view of the open room in the shape of a rectangle. He moved his mouse over to an outline of a cabinet against one wall. According to his contact, the next piece of the puzzle was there. He knew Fannie had a plan, but he never involved himself in her operations. He was only interested in her results, so he clicked off the screen and leaned back, sucking in the fragrant, sweet smoke of his cigar. His mind ran with the possibilities. He was getting close.

Cable woke. Something was off. The yacht. It was not moving. A flash of fear for Dani coursed through his body. He jumped from his bed and exited his berth, then opened the door next to him. Dani was sleeping soundly. She looked peaceful. He relaxed. Two bottles of wine had been enough to push him past his internal wake-up clock. He rousted Dani gently.

"Dani."

"Hmm. What is it?"

"The yacht is not moving." He pulled her curtain aside, and the sun blasted the small room. Cable squinted past it to see they were docked in a harbor.

"I think we are in Sweden."

Dani sat up.

"We need to get dressed and get out of here." It was at that point he realized he was wearing nothing but boxers. "I'll be right back."

Cable got dressed and filled Dani in on the details he had overheard last night.

"We should go to the police."

"I agree. Or to the museum and warn them."

"I think the police," Dani repeated.

"Okay."

The kidnappers had taken her phone, but Dani still had her wallet.

Cable still had empty pockets.

They ran down the gangplank, not looking back. Gothenburg is Sweden's largest port city on the North Sea. Ships and boats sat floating in every direction Cable looked. The long dock finally emptied out onto a dry dock filled with trailered boats. They walked through a parking lot with a sign that read Alvsborg, which meant nothing to either of them.

Saltholmsgatan was a two-lane road just beyond that, leading into the city. It took some time, but eventually a cab passed by, and they flagged it down.

Swedish was not a language Cable knew, but most Swedes spoke English as well.

"Take us to the Gothenburg Museum," Dani called out.

"The Gothenburg Museum. Very nice, you will like there." The driver had a strong Russian accent. It seemed no country's cabbies were made of locals. He started the meter and drove away.

Cable turned to Dani with concern. "I thought we were going to the closest police station?"

"Sorry. I started to think about that. If we go to the police right now, it will take at least an hour to convince them we are not crazy Americans pulling a prank. The police have public safety concerns, not artifact concerns, and we might be too late. The museum will surely have security and their primary concern is protecting their artifacts and art." Dani paused for just a beat. "I say go to the source."

Cable nodded. He understood Dani's logic, he just wished they could have discussed it together before making that decision.

The cab pulled to the curb, and Dani used her credit card to pay the fare. They ran past the bronze sculpture of Poseidon and up the steps to a large, beige brick building with tall, narrow arches. Once inside, they spotted the ticket office off to the right and a security station to the left.

Dani ran to the station where a guard in a security vest stood. She opened her wallet and showed him her ID.

"I am Doctor Tran, and I am an appraiser for PEAK Insurance. I need to speak with your head of security. It is quite urgent."

The guard stared at her ID and then looked her over before picking up the phone and calling.

Cable leaned over and whispered in Dani's ear. "Give me some money. I'm going to see if I can spot them. Maybe even stop 'em."

"They won't take dollars here." Dani handed Cable her credit card. "Be careful."

She drummed her fingers on the reception desk while the man slowly spoke words into the phone that had no meaning to her.

Cable purchased his ticket. "Thank you. Do you know where the room with the checkerboard floor is located?"

"Checkerboard?" The ticket lady in a white uniform looked puzzled.

"Black-and-white tiles on the floor."

"Oh, yes. That is our sculpture hall on the fourth floor."

Cable nodded his thanks and hurried off.

The museum was built on a hill, giving the architect a chance to mix styles. On the ground floor was a castle-like stone façade that housed the public entry and acted as a visible foundation for the tall brick building above it. Steps on both ends of the structure led up to the tall arches where a small protected courtyard lay. Here, you could rest, look back, and view the plaza below or take shelter from the rain.

Fannie, Tarik, and another man marched up the steps and found a bench to call home. They sat casually looking down at the people below who filled the plaza. The courtyard was a popular place to meet others for lunch, but on a fall morning at 9 a.m., it was empty.

Fannie spoke into a hidden mic, "Check status?"

A voice returned. "I'm entering the room."

Fannie opened a briefcase she had carried and launched a specialized drone about the size of a dinner plate. It quickly lifted off and disappeared from sight near the ceiling. The drone carried a small sonic resonance cannon capable of firing a sound wave destructive enough to shatter glass.

Fannie turned to Tarik. "Get the rope ready." Now, all she had to do was wait.

Cable walked quickly whenever someone was around and ran when they weren't. He took the stairs two at a time. As he moved up the levels, he noticed that each floor was either light or dark wood, with no tile floors. There were also no windows. All the rooms were climate-controlled, and the lighting was very specific to the art.

The stairs to the sculpture hall emptied in the center of the room.

Large black-and-white floor tiles stretched in both directions. Tall white walls and natural light poured in from a row of high windows on one wall. Cable looked around. The windows started a good twelve feet up, and the ceiling was at least twenty-five feet up. Most of the pieces here looked more modern. Visitors milled about, taking their time enjoying the experience. Nothing seemed out of place.

He moved through the room, his eyes darting from person to person, looking for anything suspicious. He tried desperately to remember the faces of the men he had seen last night talking to Fannie.

"Right this way, *fröken*," the guard said.

He led Dani through a back entrance and down a hallway lined with doors. At the fourth door on the right, he tapped and opened it after a muted "*stiga på.*"

Dani stepped into a functional office with light wood tones. Freja Lubell. a midforties woman with long blonde hair tied up in a bun, sat at her desk looking at her computer. She wore a white shirt, blue slacks, and a frown. She was a no-nonsense woman with a hard-wired suspicious streak earned over time.

"You wanted to see me?" Freja said without looking up.

Dani stepped closer to the desk. The escort guard left the room.

"I am curious. Where is the man you came with?" She spun her computer to show Dani a security camera image of her and Cable standing in the lobby. He was wearing a blue long-sleeved shirt and a goofy look. Dani almost smiled, except for the scowl on the woman across from her.

"Cable went on ahead to try and stop...let me start over. I am Doctor—"

"I know who you are."

"Okay." Dani glanced at the woman's nameplate on her desk. "Freja. We have a credible threat to one of your artifacts. They are planning to steal it, and we think it will happen today."

"That is a lot of pronouns. You will have to be more specific."

"A stone wing from the Axum Empire."

"I am unfamiliar with that piece." She spun her computer back around and typed for a few moments. "Ah, is this what you are referring to?" She spun her screen back again.

Dani was slightly taken aback. The image of the missing right wing from Cable's goshawk was right in front of her.

"Well?"

"Yes. That looks like it," Dani said.

Freja pulled a radio from her desk and spoke rapid Swedish into it. "Code sixteen in the sculpture hall. I repeat code sixteen, the sculpture hall." She set the radio down and stared at Dani, switching back to perfect English. "I have sent two guards to check it out. Now, I suggest you start from the beginning."

Dani swallowed hard, wondering where to begin.

Luka Meyer held his phone up like he was taking pictures. In reality, he had released two micro-drones about the size of a quarter. His phone individually controlled each one of them to do a specific task, which was to land on the two security cameras in the room. The micro-drones were extremely quiet, like an air conditioning vent at ten feet. By the time they were in the air and heading up for their targets, they could no longer be seen or heard.

Luka wore jeans, a black long-sleeved shirt, and a gold and brown vest. He fit perfectly into the art crowd that was roaming the museum. He tipped his head to the two security guards rushing into the room and watched as they ran over to a large glass display case and inspected it before getting on their radios. Next, they spread out and started looking around the room. Luka was unfazed.

Cable almost ran toward the two security officers to warn them as they entered the room. Instead, he decided to hang back and watch. He needed to ID the perpetrators first. He decided to check out the display case for himself and stepped up to the stanchions that kept visitors from leaving handprints on the glass. Several patrons leaned over to get a better view. The case beyond held a collection of smaller sculptures, each with a description and known history. Near the back of the case was a carved stone wing that matched the style and tone of his goshawk. *One of the missing wings.*

As the micro-drones landed on the cameras, they broadcasted a signal just strong enough to distort the picture. It would last for three minutes before the drones would self-destruct and fall to the floor in pieces.

Once the drones were both in place, Luka's internal clock started ticking. He moved slowly without a care in the world.

He spoke into a bone mic just above a whisper. "We're blind here. Twenty seconds to target. Pigeon in the nest."

"Copy that," came a reply in his earpiece.

Twenty-one seconds later, the corner window shattered, sending glass shards into the room.

Some patrons screamed, some ran. The two guards hurried over to investigate and make sure everyone was safe. One man was cut on his arm, but nothing serious. The guards quickly took charge trying to get patrons back from the glass.

One of the guards spoke on his radio. "We've had a window shatter in the sculpture hall. We need a cleanup crew."

Luka moved away from the chaos, closing the distance to the case. He put his phone away and palmed a brass window punch. He listened as a voice counted down in his ear. "Three, two, one."

He stepped past the stanchion at the display case and pressed the punch into the glass. It shattered into a thousand shards. At the same time, the window right next to the one in the corner shattered as well. This time it sent glass all over the two guards trying to make the area safe.

Cable and the people next to him jumped as the display case shattered. He turned as the second window followed suit. By the time he turned back to see what was happening, the wing was no longer there. An alarm in the building sounded. Cable instinctively backed away from the case and all the glass. He called out to the two guards who were running his way. "Someone is stealing your wing!" he said while pointing at the broken case.

Instead of investigating, the guards grabbed Cable and restrained him.

Then the corner window at the opposite end of the room shattered. This was too much and patrons ran for their lives. The guards tried to stop anyone running, but in their attempt, Cable broke free and joined the throng in their mass exodus.

As soon as Luka had the wing, he stuffed it into his shirt and walked toward the guards in a casual way, as if he might want to help out. When the crazy American started calling out, the guards rushed past to intervene. When the window in the opposite corner exploded, he stepped up to the first broken window just as a rope flew through it and landed at his feet. He clipped himself in and spoke up. *"Exfil."*

Luka was pulled up and out the window in seconds.

"I'm just telling you what I know. I don't have all the details—" A museum-wide alarm interrupted Dani's words.

The alarm sent Freja into action mode. She stood and grabbed her radio. "Code 99. Lock down the museum. No one in or out." She turned to Dani. "You stay right here."

Dani nodded her head, suddenly scared, as Freja ran from her office.

Fannie hit the self-destruct on her drone as Luka dropped from the window. Small melted plastic pieces fell to the ground. Tarik collected the rope and stuffed it into a backpack. The four of them walked casually away from the museum long before the sirens arrived.

Cable stayed in the middle of the crowd which was mostly panicked as they headed for the exit. When he came down the stairs that led to the lobby, he could see the guards locking the exit doors and trying to get control over the angry, trapped patrons. He noticed a female security officer exit a side door and try to take charge of the anarchy. Before the door completely closed, Cable slipped inside. He hurried down a long hallway with many doors, hoping for a back exit.

"Sergeant. Listen carefully," Freja said as she rushed to the security desk. "There is a person in my office who is in on the robbery. Send someone right now to keep an eye on her. We need the police to check out a yacht called the *Arinna*, supposedly docked at Alvsborg. Also, there is a man in the museum, an American. He is six feet, late twenties, brown curly hair, wearing a blue shirt and brown pants. Find him."

A quick nod and the sergeant ran off, issuing orders into his radio, hoping he remembered everything his boss just rattled off.

Dani stood and paced the room. She noticed the picture of the goshawk wing on the computer and stepped over to get a better look. The wing was triangle-shaped with feather relief. There was no writing to be seen. The site was in Swedish, so she had no chance to navigate it, but there was a small arrow to the right of the picture. She clicked it. The back of the wing slid into view. It was smooth with no feather detail, but there were obvious symbols carved in the soft stone.

She grabbed a pen and paper and then quickly copied the symbols before resetting the screen back to the original page. Grabbing the paper, she peeked out the office door. To the left, it was empty. To the right, a person was walking quickly away. It was Cable.

"Cable," Dani hissed.

He turned and ran back to her.

"We've got about ten seconds to find a way out of here."

"What are you talking about?" Dani said.

"I think they wanted me to see them."

Dani still looked confused.

"Last night. Their little planning meeting on the yacht. We're the patsies for this robbery. They played us."

The light came on for Dani. "Oh no. I just told them all about us."

"It's alright. Come on."

They dashed down the hall and hung a left at the end. An employee exit was clearly marked ahead, but it required a keycard to access. They were trapped.

CHAPTER EIGHT

THE GUARD OPENED HIS BOSS'S office to find it empty. No sign of the girl. He called it in on the comms, making sure every guard and arriving police officer would be looking for the two coconspirators, Cable and Dani.

Freja was mad, mostly at herself for leaving her office in such a hurry. She could have slowed down and waited for a guard to replace her and keep hold of the one accomplice she was sure had been sent as a distraction.

Cable pulled Dani into a door right next to the exit and left it open just a crack so he could see out. The room was small and dark, but he could smell the cleaning supplies.

"You okay?" Cable whispered.

Dani was crouched next to him, trying to calm her racing heart. "What happened?"

"These guys are good. By the time I realized what they were up to, it was over."

"The carved wing?"

"Gone, and they're looking to us like we might be in on it."

Dani processed the words as fear ratcheted up. "That's why they let us go."

Cable peeked out, then turned back to Dani. "Let it be known I always give my dates a good time."

"This is the worst date I have ever been on. We're going to end up in jail."

"You're welcome?"

"You're an idiot."

"Ever been in jail?"

"Of course not," Dani said.

"It's not that bad, three meals a day. Lots of time to think." Cable looked back at Dani. His calm demeanor was not helping. "We probably should have gone to the police."

"Are you blaming me?"

"Absolutely not. Just an after-action report. You know, for next time," Cable said.

"I think we should turn ourselves in."

"Shh."

The door to the outside opened and a guard came rushing past.

"Keep up," Cable said as he dashed for the closing door.

Dani was right on his heels,

"Hey, hold up! Stop right there!" The guard noticed the two fugitives and turned on a dime, running back in their direction.

Cable caught the door just before it closed and pulled it open. Once Dani was through, he forced it to close as fast as he could. He then held up the lever on the outside, preventing it from opening.

They were in a back alley entrance to the museum and could hear the guard banging and yelling on the other side of the door.

"If I release this lever, he will be on us in seconds. See if you can find something we can jam in here," Cable said.

Dani came back with a chunk of broken brick that Cable wedged into the latch.

Once Dani and Cable were out in the plaza, they mingled with pedestrians and began to feel less panicked. They moved along the tree-lined sidewalk amid shops and restaurants.

Dani was the first to speak. "We need to get to a cash machine. We've got about three hours before we are on the police radar, and they can track us when we use my credit card."

"Who are you, special agent Tran?"

"I watch a lot of cop shows."

Just then, two police cars, with their sirens blasting, drove past. Cable pulled Dani close to him and put his arm on her shoulder. Just another romantic couple strolling the plaza.

"Over there." Cable pointed to an ATM.

Dani withdrew her daily limit and they continued to move away from the museum. She used her card to get them a few supplies, two backpacks, and a change of clothes. They ditched their museum clothes for something more active. Dani wore navy leggings with a cranberry fitted tank and a matching fleece pullover. Cable put on black joggers, a long-sleeve green tee shirt, and a black lightweight parka.

Their last purchase was a cellphone and a small laptop. Dani downloaded the Styr & Ställ app on their phone and transferred some money into it. "I've been to Stockholm before, and Sweden has bike rentals in every major city. This app is all you need to get one." She showed Cable.

They used the app to find an automated rental station and grabbed two bikes.

By the time they hit the road, it had started to drizzle. Dani followed her phone to a nearby coffee shop with Internet. They ordered breakfast and two coffees. She spent some time in between bites getting her computer connected and running.

"Here." She handed Cable the pen and paper she had stuffed into her pocket before their mad dash to freedom.

"What is this?" Cable opened it up and answered his own question. "It looks like the same writing that's on my statue."

"It is," Dani said without looking up.

"From the wing?"

Dani nodded, still focused on setting up her computer.

"How did you?"

"Don't ask."

"Right or left?"

"What?" She paused to look up.

"The right wing or the left."

Dani pictured it in her mind. "The right wing if you face the front."

"So it's the first part of the message."

Dani did the visualization in her head. "Right. I mean, correct." She opened a page to her translation program and took a bite of pastry.

Cable smiled. "There is a lot more to Dani Tran than meets the eye, and let me tell you, that part is pretty nice too."

"For a fugitive, you say the nicest things. Okay, write this down. F-R-O."

Dani slowly and painstakingly translated the message.

Once they were done, Cable had an idea. He borrowed the laptop and did a quick search. "You inspired me with your bike rental idea. How are you at long-distance rides?"

"Okay. I have a road bike back home that gets used occasionally."

"Good, because I just signed us up for a EuroVelo trail tour from here to Oslo."

"EuroVelo?" Dani asked.

"Bike paths all over Europe. There's one that passes through this city up to Oslo, Norway."

"What is that? Like three days of riding? And how do we get across the border?"

"Two days."

Dani nodded her head, not sure if it sounded like fun or not.

"Norway has a loophole that allows bicyclists to enter the country without a visa, passport, or anything."

"No visa. No passport. No problem if you're on a bike. Hmm," Dani said. "Okay, I like it."

"But we need to get a move on. Our tour begins in twenty minutes."

Dani nearly choked on her coffee.

Dani was already tired by the time they got to their starting point. The city bikes were exchanged for road bikes with helmets, and a follow van collected their backpacks. The group consisted of eight other riders from various countries around the globe.

Dani was grateful for the casual pace that was set as they headed north along the Tagenevagen before connecting to the Ellesbovagen. They huffed and puffed as they watched the city fade away into rolling, lush green countryside. The bike path roughly paralleled the E6 freeway north, occasionally crossing it. A strong reminder of just how slow they were moving.

Tanumshede came into view as the sun touched the horizon, casting everything in an orange hue. The small municipality was quaint and homey, with a vintage main street that welcomed tourists and locals alike. Pitched roofs in a variety of colors with traditional Scandinavian designs were everywhere.

The follow van pulled ahead and turned left over a single-lane bridge across a slow-moving stream. It stopped at a rustic red barn conversion nestled in the trees. The outside was weathered and original. Only the modern windows told the story of three levels of an updated modern home inside.

Dani peeled herself off her bike and hobbled into the barn. Cable wasn't much better off as he silently followed her.

"Welcome to Det Gamla Hus," Lars, the follow van driver, said as they stepped inside. It was an open floor plan with the best of old and new. A large picnic table was the centerpiece of a modern kitchen, and a casual, comfy living room with a roaring fireplace was just beyond. A wooden beam staircase on the right led up to the bedrooms and baths. They had a traditional Swedish dinner of meatballs with lingonberry sauce, hasselback potatoes, and a simple salad. For dessert, apple pie and a glass of Akvavit.

After dinner, a 'get-to-know-me' session took place in the living room, as each shared something about themselves. Cable opted for the truth and got a big laugh. Eventually, the conversation topics splintered and slowed. One-by-one, couples retired for the night.

Dani started up the stairs. Everything hurt. She watched as Cable unlocked their room.

"One key? I don't think so."

"You may remember we were a late add to the tour. We were lucky they had room for us at all. Don't worry, I'll take the floor," Cable said.

He opened the room, and as Dani walked in, she began to laugh.

"Children's bunk beds?"

"Maybe I don't have to take the floor. Top or bottom?"

Dani tried to picture lying down and looking up at Cable above her. "Top, please." She'd take a view of the ceiling instead.

Cable tossed his backpack on the bottom bunk and tried to sit. "My ass is killing me."

"Maybe we should fake an injury and ride in the follow van tomorrow."

"That's a solid plan."

They each took turns in the bathroom, then turned out the lights and crawled into their bunks.

After a moment, Dani leaned over and looked down at Cable. He was lying on his back with his feet hanging over the end of the short mattress.

"If you really want the top bunk I can switch with you."

"No. I'm good," Cable said.

"We have been so busy jumping from one fire into the next that I never really got a proper chance to thank you for trying to save me."

"You're welcome. Honestly, I just kinda reacted. And things went from there."

"Well, I'm glad you did."

Cable didn't reply.

"If we make it out of Sweden, what then."

"When we make it to Oslo, I say we go right to the embassy and try to get things straightened out."

"Makes sense. I can't believe how badly we were manipulated by Fannie and her gang."

"Yeah, that, more than anything else, has got me angry. I'm half-willing to take our clues and try to beat them to whatever it is they are after," Cable said.

"I get that, but they have guns and things."

"Together, we are much smarter than they are. We could do this."

Dani hesitantly nodded.

Cable recited the message they had translated so far. "'From the house made of one. A faithful pilgrimage begins.' Something, something. Then, 'Wealth for the church and all. Pious and angels alike share.' Something, something…"

Cable paused. "We just have to find the other wing and translate the something, something."

"If it was that easy, it would already be done," Dani said.

"Not necessarily. This treasure, or whatever it is, has been lost to history. Not because it was so cleverly hidden but because the clues were so separated. Think about it. My grandfather had one of the main clues in his study, all the way from Ethiopia. That, under any normal circumstance, is a message lost to time. But here we are with two-thirds of the message translated and a path forward, some seventeen centuries later."

"It is pretty amazing," Dani said.

"Yeah, it is."

A moment of silence followed, and Dani rolled back into her bed.

"Cable?"

"Yes."

"Goodnight."

"Goodnight, Dani."

Crossing the Norway border on the EuroVelo trail was everything Cable had hoped it would be. It was the nine additional hours of saddle time that had pushed him to his limit. If only the bucolic scenery could make up for his cramping muscles. The group rode into downtown Oslo without incident. After a fabulous Italian dinner at the Olivia Aker Brygge on the water, Cable and Dani said goodbye to their new friends and their bicycles. It was bittersweet.

They walked uptown to the Anker Hotel and passed out in their individual twin beds almost as fast as their heads hit the pillows.

Cable woke to the sound of light clicking. He looked over to see Dani on her laptop. She was wearing a sports bra and panties. Her stomach was toned and flat. The sun was glaring through a small crack in the curtains, helping to pull his focus away. "Good morning," he said flatly as he struggled to sit up. He was wearing boxer shorts and bedhead hair.

"Yes, it is. I have ordered room service and Advil."

"Brilliant. Hand me the phone, would ya?"

Dani did so without looking.

Cable dialed the embassy and started the passport replacement process. After some back-and-forth, he hung up. "I have to show up in person this morning, but if they confirm my existence as a real person, I should have a replacement within forty-eight hours."

"Our government, hard at work," Dani said.

"Thankfully. It helps that we have an embassy in Oslo, not a consulate."

Dani suddenly stopped typing and looked over. "Did you bring up the kidnapping thing?"

"No."

"Why not?"

"What do we gain by telling them?"

Dani thought for a few minutes without an answer. "Gain? Maybe a free plane ride home?"

"True, and maybe we can ID our kidnappers and help put a stop to Fannie and her band of thugs."

"And stop the human trafficking transportation service," Dani added.

"For sure, but I feel like we should do all that from the States, not here. I don't know who we can trust or who might be in league with one or both of those operations. It is very possible that we could get sent back to Sweden to face charges."

"Makes sense. Back to the States, then do everything in our power to pass what we know on to the authorities," Dani concluded.

"Hopefully, we can straighten things out with the police in Sweden from there as well. I'd like to go back there someday."

"Just no bicycles."

"For sure," Cable said.

They looked at each other with matching goofy smiles. Dani's eyes wandered down to Cable's firm chest and narrow waist. A small tattoo sat over his heart. She let her gaze linger before looking away. "Is that a star or compass?"

"Both. The North Star with compass points."

Dani waited for more. She turned her whole body away from her computer and faced Cable.

He couldn't help but notice how her sports bra clung to her, but his past memories pushed the thought aside. "When I was little, my mother was my rock. Always pushing me to do more and better. Guiding me down a path I didn't even understand yet. She had a real love of the stars. I can remember lying in the grass next to her on a summer's night as she pointed out constellations. The North Star was the first one I could pick out."

The fond memory lasted on his face for just a second. "My father," he continued, "that's a story for another time, but when she died, he kept my mother's ashes on the mantel. A tribute of sorts, I suppose. When I turned eighteen, I scooped out a few of the ashes and had this made with 'em so she would always be with me. Right where she belongs, close to my heart, my guiding star."

"How did she die?"

Cable hesitated.

"Never mind. It's none of my business."

"No. It's okay. When you're little, you don't understand things like depression. Life is a gift that you constantly need to unwrap. That's your focus. Your parents are infallible. The fact that my mother would have days where she didn't connect…well, seemed normal to me. It's all I knew. When she took her life…it was like getting t-boned in an inter-section, unexpected and violent. At least to me. I blamed myself for a long time, then blamed others. It took maturity to understand it all and perhaps come to terms with the scars."

"I'm sorry."

Cable nodded and put on his tee shirt, feeling suddenly vulnerable. "What about your parents?"

"Still living in the same house I grew up in back in Austin."

"You're lucky."

"I tell myself that every week, except Christmas."

Cable looked at her curiously.

"I spend a whole week at their home every Christmas. Love my par-ents, just can't live with them."

"I get that…so how did you get hooked on getting your PhD in ar-cheology from Stanford?" Cable asked.

"My father was a military man. Did his twenty years, then started a construction business when he got out. Tran-sit Construction."

"Clever."

"Every summer, he would take a month off, and we would go somewhere. Usually to our houseboat on Toledo Bend Reservoir, but one summer, we went to Israel and Egypt. We saw all the holy sites and did the pyramid thing. I was fifteen years old and will never forget the majesty of physical history standing before me, holding on to the centuries and defying time itself. The story a simple carving in a rock three millennia ago could tell. Or the idea of uncovering something no one has seen in thousands of years. It spoke to me."

"But didn't you say your specialty was in cultures that were influenced by the Egyptian kingdoms?" Cable asked.

"Good memory. Everyone does ancient Egypt or Mesoamerica. I wanted to focus on the effect Egypt had on its neighbors. What many call the lesser kingdoms."

"Like Ethiopia?"

"Like Punt, then D'mt, the Axum Empire, followed by several rotating dynasties, and finally Ethiopia, yes."

Dani's computer dinged, and she looked back at the screen with focus for a moment. "What's your thought on taking a small detour on the way back to the States."

"Bad idea. Why, what are you thinking?"

Dani hesitated. "I might just know where the other wing is."

"Translation?" The tense excitement was barely hidden in his voice.

Fannie had rarely seen Stein like this. As they got closer to the answer to their mystery, he became more consumed.

Once they had obtained the first wing, high-definition photos of the symbols on the back were taken and sent out to be translated. They had weighed anchor and left Sweden behind, not sure of their next destination but sure they wanted nothing to do with the authorities in Sweden.

The *Arinna* spent most of the day steaming south before a reply popped up on Fannie's email.

"I just got it. Sending now. The translation seems a bit rough to me." She watched Stein's expression on the screen as he read through it. His face rarely gave away his emotions, but this time was different. His brows bounced up and down as he read, like a jack-in-the-box.

"'From one mansion. A faithful pilgrimage begins. Wealth for the church's own. Pious angels like and share,'" he recited. "Still quite cryptic, I'll admit, but there is always room for interpretation when it comes to long-dead languages. Maybe we should bail out Dani and have her translate a version for us."

"Except she isn't in jail," Fannie said.

"What?"

"The cops couldn't find them. Somehow, they got away. There is an arrest warrant out, but no sign of them," Fannie said. "Should I get Raven involved?"

Stein thought for a moment. "Yes, let's put our best hacker on her trail. Make it a priority. Guess I was wrong to use them as a pawn. Clearly, they are bishop material."

Fannie nodded at the chess references. "You can never get every decision right."

"Where are you now?"

"Just leaving the English channel. We should be in the Med by tomorrow."

"Okay, talk then."

They both hung up.

Fannie let her mind process the situation. How had a seemingly unprepared and unskilled couple who were implicated in a major robbery of a national museum just disappeared?

She had seen this once or twice in her career. Nonprofessionals did things that were not in the playbook. Usually, that meant they were easy to find and collect. But now and then, they did something so out of the box that they were impossible to predict or find. Luckily, modern technology made it almost impossible to hide for very long. She was sure the Swedish police would have them soon. If not, Raven would locate them soon enough, and her men in play could pop over and pick them up. She needed to get Luka and Tarik to shore, somewhere near an airport.

She picked up a wall phone and pushed five.

"Captain," a voice answered on the third ring.

"We need to do a quick offload."

"Understand, La Rochelle is only about forty minutes out."

"Perfect. Make sure the jet is waiting."

"Okay, I hope you're happy," Cable announced as he stormed into the room. He seemed upbeat and ready to go. After two days of lying low, the walls in the hotel room had shrunk significantly. He held up his replacement passport.

"About what?" Dani had opened the curtains, and the sun filled the room through two disparate windows. She was sitting cross-legged on her bed, working on her computer.

"You're no longer rooming with an undocumented alien. I explained our situation to my attorney. He agrees we should deal with everything back in the States. He suggested the sooner, the better."

"You have an attorney?"

"Just recently. He sent my replacement credit card to the embassy. I am now legal and have access to money." He flicked the card in her direction.

"Whoa, a man of means. Not like the usual guys I room with on the lam." Dani picked up the black American Express card. "It says CTJ Enterprise. A business account with no personal name?"

"He was kind enough to set that up before I left. It gives me a certain degree of anonymity, and from here on, I'm buying."

"Good, because the tickets I have on hold need to be purchased within the next hour or we lose them, and I was hesitant to use my credit card. I'm sure the Swedish police are trying to electronically find us by now.

"Use my card and see if you can upgrade to business class."

"Since we're what, now a business?" Dani said playfully.

"A partnership."

Dani looked at him suspiciously.

"More like a brain trust. I say we check out your lead. Get in, get out, and get back home."

"Agreed, but before I become a partner, I want to know what the T stands for?"

"T?"

"CTJ Enterprise? Cable…Janson?"

"Timothy."

Dani smiled

"What?"

"You're a good man, Cable Timothy Janson."

Cable accepted the compliment with grace. "Thanks, I guess."

Dani Tran stood and stepped closer as she spoke. She was wearing an Athleta crop top with matching leggings.

"You chased halfway across the planet to save me, and then, when we got ourselves even deeper in trouble…you stayed. I mean, you could've just left me at the museum. There have been multiple opportunities for you to make a perfectly valid excuse and bugger off, but you are still here trying to help."

"Just a sucker for a brunette in pink."

Dani shook her head. "It's electric fuchsia."

"Exactly."

Luka and Tarik pressed the button for the fifth floor. Luka pulled his ball cap low over his eyes, well aware there was a camera in the corner. The Anker Hotel was a tall, modern glass and steel building in the heart of Oslo. Luka was feeling short-tempered after having to fly back to nearly the same place he had just left the day before.

They listened to a bland version of Abba's *Take a Chance on Me* as the lift began its accent.

Raven had worked hard to track Dani's credit card to the hotel in Oslo, while Tarik and Luka had flown back across Europe in the company jet. With a little digging, they were able to locate the room number and floor layout of the hotel. Raven had reserved rooms on either side of the target and prepaid for everything. A simple dead drop was planned once Tarik and Luka cleared customs, and a rental car in their fictitious names was waiting curbside.

Luka loved working with true professionals. Though he had never met Raven, the hacker Cronus Logistics employed, she had yet to disappoint.

Once on the fifth floor, the two men separated. Luka took the room on the right, and Tarik delayed slightly, looking lost, before moving to the room on the left.

As soon as Luka entered, he knew he was in the wrong room. He spun about and left, heading down the hall to join Tarik. As he reached for the door handle, it opened in front of him.

"May I help you?" Tarik said, acting surprised.

"Bite me," Luka threw back as he entered the room.

Tarek couldn't help but chuckle as the door closed behind them.

Luka went right to the passthrough that connected the two rooms and opened the first door. He dropped to his knees and began picking the lock on the second door.

It was not so easy to get an electronic door code and a counterfeit keycard. That only happened in the movies. Hotel security had significantly improved over the last few years.

What was easy was renting an adjoining room and picking the deadbolt to the passthrough door.

After a few moments, a quiet click was heard. Luka stood and pulled out his Walther PPQ. They had collected their guns from an intermediary on their way from the airport.

Tarik pulled out a subcompact as well and followed to the right as Luka pushed through the doorway on the left.

They were too late. How late was anyone's guess, but Luka figured not by much. The room still held remnants of occupation and the smell that goes with it. He put his gun away and scanned the two messy beds. "Not sleeping together." He checked the trash cans.

Tarik looked through some receipts left on the desktop.

"Nothing here," Luka said.

"I have some receipts for clothes, a couple of restaurants, and two suitcases."

"What kind of clothes?"

Tarik picked up on the meaning behind Luka's question. "Warm weather clothes. Where did you say they were picked up in the United States?"

"The girl was collected in Denver," Luka said.

"Not sure they are heading back there."

Luka nodded in understanding. He dialed his phone, and on the second ring, Fannie answered.

"Status?"

"Empty nest. Might be heading south for the winter."

"Understood."

CHAPTER NINE

A KNOCK ON THE DOOR WAS followed by an intrusion before Freja could say 'Come in.' She looked up from her desk to see a short woman in a white collared shirt and a black suit enter her office. She had short blond hair and dark eyes. She used bangs to help shorten a long face that had very little makeup.

"Hej, I'm Juni Eklund, CIO Interpol." She flashed her badge.

"Please have a seat. I'm Freja Lubell. What's a Criminal Intelligence Officer from Interpol want with the museum's head of security?"

"The LEO asked me to take a look at this heist. I just need a couple of questions answered if you can."

"Okay, but isn't it odd for our local enforcement office to involve Interpol in a local crime?"

"I specialize in the black market, illicit trade of art and antiquities. White-collar stuff. I'm following up on your recent incident. There is strong evidence that the heist was carried out by an international team."

"Americans, for sure."

Juni looked up at the woman for more information. When none came, she continued. "What can you tell me about the woman you had in your office on the day of the robbery?" Juni slid a photo of Dani standing next to Cable, taken by her own lobby's security camera.

"She was an American named Dani Tran. Claimed to be an artifact appraiser working with PEAK Insurance. Her accomplice was a man named Cable Janson. She also claimed they were kidnapped along with his personal artifact and forced to translate it. According to her story, they overheard their kidnappers planning to steal an artifact here in the museum and felt it was their civic duty to warn me."

"Do you believe her?" Juni asked.

"Absolutely not. They were nothing more than a distraction team for the heist. Possibly the brains behind it, if you ask me."

"Well, I am asking you, so good to know. Tell me about the artifact."

"It's a carved wing from the Axum Empire. Honestly, there were much more valuable pieces in that case. Here, take a look." She rotated her screen to show Juni an image of the carved wing.

"Quite unremarkable," Juni said as she looked at the screen.

"My thoughts exactly. Why go to so much trouble to steal this?"

Juni leaned back in the chair. "My only thought would be if they had a specific buyer in place. Do you have any other angles on the piece?"

"Hmm…" Freja looked closer and saw the arrow at the side of the picture. She clicked it. An image of the back of the wing appeared.

Juni bent forward and took a look. There were carvings on the back of the otherwise smooth wing.

"What can you tell me about these symbols?"

"Hang on a second." Freja picked up her phone and dialed an extension. "Hej, It's Freja. Can you come to my office right away? Thank you." After she hung up, she gave Juni an uncomfortable smile.

Juni slid a business card across the desk. "Can you email me those photos?"

"Of course."

"What about the artifact Ms. Tran said was taken along with her?"

"We were just getting to that when the alarm went off."

"So, no idea what it was?"

"None."

"Did she say where she was taken from?"

"Didn't get to that either."

The door creaked open, and an older man with thick glasses and thinning hair entered. He wore a red-and-white pin-striped short-sleeved shirt and brown pants that had seen better days.

Freja made the introductions.

"Doctor Ram, thanks for coming," Juni said. "What can you tell us about these symbols?"

He moved closer to the screen and took a good minute to look them over.

"Hand-carved Ge'ez letters," he finally said.

"Do you know what it says?" Juni asked.

"We did a translation when the wing first arrived here, but because Ge'ez is a very old and very dead language, and the symbols on the wing are honestly poorly done or maybe carved in a hurry, the results were… well, see for yourself." He gestured to Freja's computer. "May I?"

She nodded and moved out of her seat, and Dr. Ram sat in her chair.

He logged into his account and navigated through several layers.

"How did the wing come to the museum?"

"It was donated as part of a collection from a wealthy estate in Stockholm," Doctor Ram said as he typed. Finally, he found what he was looking for. "Here."

Juni pulled out her phone and took a picture of the words.

From one house

Wealth for the church

Doctor Ram looked up, smiling, then realized he was still sitting in Freja's chair. He quickly pulled himself up.

Freja replaced him almost instantly.

"That means nothing," Juni said.

"True, it is somewhat incomplete," Doctor Ram said. "That's why I have always thought there was more to the message."

"What do you mean?" Juni asked.

"This wing originally belonged to a body."

"Like an angel?"

Doctor Ram raised his palms. "Angel, bird, insect."

Juni nodded slowly. "Thank you both for your time today." She stood and left the room.

The bright yellow Citroën C4 compact moved north along the A-66, out of Seville. Dani watched multistory buildings become single-family homes as they started their three-hour journey. Before long, small ranches became open countryside. At one point, they passed the Rio Guadiemer, and Cable asked Dani for some water. She dug in the back seat for a second before producing two bottles.

Sometime later, they turned south on the N-435, a narrow two-lane road with rolling hills dotted with oak. Cable slowed the vehicle slightly due to the winding road and rolled down the windows. The autumn sun was out and it was a perfect day for cruising or hammocking.

Cable broke the silence. "So, what should I expect from your friend?"

"Celeste? She and I went to grad school together and majored in the same program. She specialized in the Muslim influence in Europe during the Middle Ages. Did you know at one point Islam spread from Spain to Sumatra? They controlled most of the Mediterranean Sea and Indian Ocean. Celeste has been working over here for the last four years to help preserve what's left of that history."

"Sounds like she picked a niche that will keep her busy for a long time, but I was referring to her personality."

"Oh. Fun, focused, and friendly."

"Three *f*'s, really?"

"If the shoe fits."

Cable turned left on the West HU-8105. They moved up in elevation through a canyon. The road was now just wide enough for two small cars to pass.

"It's strange to me how an Axum figurine from the sixth century ended up in such divergent places. It just proves that time is the great manipulator. Given enough of it…everything can change."

"The roller coaster of life."

Cable nodded as he upshifted on a small straightaway.

"Archeology is a lot like that. Discoveries and knowledge come in fits and starts. When I sent out my request for information on the wing, I used several archeology blogs I'm connected with. In truth, we are a small and very connected group of colleagues. The sharing of information is what moves the needle forward on history, but because it is also a business, there are always those who keep things close."

"Wouldn't want to miss out on a grant or a big sale to a museum because someone else stole your hypothesis?" Cable asked.

"Something like that," Dani said. "I don't know what we are heading into, but it's the only lead that I got a hit on."

"And your friend?"

"Celeste. I trust her. We were roomies for two semesters."

"Just two?" Cable asked. "What happened?"

"Boyfriend. Thought she found the man of her dreams."

"They don't exist."

"A cynic who speaks the truth."

"As a member, we are pretty flawed," Cable said.

"Aren't we all?"

Juni leaned back and rubbed her neck. The tension headache was trying to decide whether it was transitory or staying for the night. The letters on the screen seemed to blur. She blinked her eyes until they found focus and continued scrolling. She was well aware of the mountainous stack of files that sat on her desk labeled 'current unsolved cases.'

The illicit antiquities trade crimes were, at best, difficult to solve and prosecute. The world's laws varied widely, from none at all to basic fines and jail time. Since there was rarely any violence associated with the trade, it always took a back burner to the more violent crimes at Interpol. That left Juni and her team of eight to cover the entire globe and save and protect inanimate objects whose only value was determined by the passage of time.

She had gone over everything she had on the wing heist at the Gothenburg Museum. Getting a jump on a fresh case was the best way to solve it. Like any criminal investigation, the clock was your enemy.

The wing definitely belonged to something else. Probably an angel. Angels were always being carved and drawn over the centuries. That meant there was more to the message. It was the only angle that made sense. Who would go to all the effort to steal one of the least valuable items in the display case? That had to be it. A carved message. She wrote the word down on a piece of paper, then added the translation Dr. Ram had provided.

From one house
Wealth for the church

The tip of her pen tapped absently on the paper as she reread the words. She stood and went to the pinup board in her office. Along the left side was a collection of suspected names of black marketers under the heading of 'professionals.' This group was certainly professional. She scanned the list, willing a name to pop out. It didn't.

Interpol rarely sent agents across borders to investigate crimes. They used their National Central Bureaus located in their member countries. The NCBs kept track of things in their territory and passed pertinent evidence and information up the chain to Interpol's headquarters in Lyon, France. That information was stored in a central database, which could be accessed and used by agencies around the world. In truth, the main focus of Interpol had little to do with criminal investigation. That responsibility was in the hands of the local police. The exception was when a crime crossed borders or had multiple suspects from different countries. That was when people like Juni got involved. In truth, the evidence she was working with could go either way. Maybe she should just let the local police handle it. For some reason, her mind flashed to the Interpol motto: *Connecting police for a safer world.* It seemed too soft to Juni, but if those connections brought down a criminal, then she was all for it.

Her phone buzzed, and she looked down at the screen.

Byron wanted to meet for dinner at eight. She checked her watch, fifteen minutes until eight.

Juni had struggled back and forth with their relationship. Byron was an amazing man. He had the personality, stability, and career. The problem was Juni. She was emotionally adrift if she was being honest with herself. Commitment to a point? Fine. Commitment like Byron wanted? Not ready. At the back end of thirty-eight, she wondered if she would ever be ready. Maybe that kind of relationship wasn't in the cards for her, ever. She let out a heavy sigh, picked up her phone, and texted. *Can't tonight, sorry.*

With Byron out of her mind, she turned back to the main points of the case. Professional operation. Looking to complete the figurine's message. Someone with money.

All three made sense. She sat back down and pulled up an image of the wing.

Her office was small but efficient, with a sturdy wood desk and plain white walls. One of them held several plaques for a job well done. It was located inside the national police headquarters in Stockholm. She had transferred here from the Paris office in 2018, when two seventeenth-century crowns had been stolen from the Strangnas Cathedral, just outside of Stockholm—another case that had yet to be solved. Once an artifact was sold to a private collector, it was nearly impossible to find. It typically took a careless collector showing off or their death to loosen their grasp on illicit art or artifacts.

A tap on her door had little effect on her focus. "Come."

Juni's boss poked his head in. "Hey."

She looked up with expectant raised eyebrows.

"Go home. You work here, not live here."

"I'm just finishing up," she lied.

"You know I have a policy of being the last man out the door. You're starting to make me look bad, and that pisses me off," he tried to look mad. In reality, the two had a solid working relationship. He bossed her, and she ignored him.

"Well, we can't have that." Juni shut her computer down and grabbed her purse and coat.

They walked past the cybercrime division and Juni spied several young guns hopped up on energy drinks and plastered to their screens. Some of the divisions here ran 24/7.

"That's why I run the white-collar crimes unit," the boss said, pointing.

"Regular hours?"

"Regular hours and regular cops. Those cyberpunks are a whole new breed."

They took the elevator down to the lobby and exited the front door. They said their goodbyes and Juni turned left, her boss, right.

As she rounded the corner, Juni paused and waited. After a couple minutes, she spun back and headed for the lobby.

The officer at the duty desk looked up. "Forget something?"

Juni held up her phone like she got a text. "Crime never sleeps."

She pressed the elevator button for the seventh floor and waited patiently for the doors to open. As she walked passed the cybercrimes unit, she stepped into the open bullpen-style office. Juni grabbed an empty chair and rolled it with her over to a young man with a neon yellow beanie and a collection of chains around his neck.

She sat down, and the man-child pulled the headphones from his ears.

"Sup, Juni?"

"Hey, Squirrel. I have a favor to ask."

Melvyn Castro, or Squirrel, as he preferred to be called, had gotten his avatar by doing just that—squirreling his way into electronic places no one else could get to. He turned to Juni and leaned back in his chair.

"Is this one of those jobs where I go in and shoot everybody in the room, then scale the highest wall, blow the window to the penthouse, kill the bad guy, and save the girl?"

"No. This is much more simple."

"Too bad. What'cha got? I was getting bored chasing e-ghosts trying to nibble on the NBN."

The National Banking Network connected all the Swedish banks on one secure system.

"I need you to do a search for this credit card number, and while you're at it, see if anyone else has searched for it. Also, see what you can find on emails attached to either of these two." She handed him a piece of paper with the names 'Dani Tran and Cable Janson,' along with additional information.

"Interesting. Give me a bit, and I'll see what I can find."

"Thanks, Squirrel. You're the best," Juni said.

"I know."

"And modest."

Squirrel gave Juni a genuine smile.

"This isn't another wild goose chase, is it?" Luka asked as he climbed into the passenger seat of the gold Lancia Montecarlo.

Tarik hit the gas, and they left the private terminal behind.

"Could be. That's all part of the job," Fannie said through the speaker of his phone.

Luka looked over to Tarik.

He just shrugged.

"True. Okay, what have you got?"

Fannie cleared her throat. "A hit on a blog that mentions our missing wing."

Luka sat up straighter. "You've got my attention."

"Dani Tran reached out to several archaeology blog sites. She requested specific information on a goshawk sculpture or wing sculpture from the sixth century, Axum Empire."

"Dani needs to learn to stay off public Wi-Fi," Luka said.

"She's leaving a trail a blind man could follow. Anyway, she got pinged back by Dr. Celeste Navarro. A former student in her grad school. Navarro has dual citizenship in Spain and the US. Her father was a diplomat before he died—"

Luka cleared his throat, interrupting. "I'm okay with the background. What's the current situation?"

"Gotcha." Fannie was a fan of details, but Luka was right. It was time to cut to it. "She's working with a UNESCO-funded project in Spain right now. Raven has her cell phone pinging out of a small town called La Granda de Rio Tinto. There's an old monastery there. More details to follow."

Luka put his hand over the phone's microphone and turned to Tarik. "Rio Tinto."

Tarik grabbed his smartphone and inputted the name for directions.

"Any hits on Dani or her boyfriend?" Luka asked.

"Nothing yet. We had a ping on the phone she used to call Celeste. It was a burner. Then nothing."

"Probably tossed it."

"That's our guess as well. If they are traveling, they're using an alias or covering their tracks by paying cash. Getting customs information on passports under their names is nearly impossible.

"Yeah, that's not so easy to do anymore."

"And trying to crack into every airline and ship that comes and goes out of Oslo would be pointless."

"All that spycraft seems unlikely for those two. Most likely, they have holed up somewhere, scared out of their minds," Luka said.

"I agree. I'll let you know if we get any hits, but the reality is they're in the wind for now. If, by chance, they are planning to meet up with Celeste, keep your eyes open. You can do a two-fer, but keep in mind that the priority is the second wing."

"Not a problem. We can handle the librarian. She'll spill her secrets."

"No backlash."

"There never is."

Tarik pulled onto the freeway and accelerated north.

"And Luka?" Fannie asked.

"Yes?"

"It's time to stop playing nice."

"I couldn't agree with you more."

The Citroën downshifted as they rose in elevation. The trees thickened along the winding road. At one point, Cable and Dani cleared a small rise and had their first view of La Granda de Rio Tinto, a sprawling town of just over 1,800 situated in a small valley. To the left was a hilltop with the ancient monastery, Almonaster la Real, overlooking the valley.

Cable followed their smartphone's directions through the narrow streets lined with white stucco and red-tiled roofs.

He pulled off the road into a small field and got out. Most of their stiffness from their two-day bike marathon was gone, but a five-hour flight and a three-hour road trip was the opposite of a cure.

They shuffled up a concrete incline toward the ancient church. An old bullring, still occasionally used, sat to the right. The date on the plaque said 1891.

Dani led the way past the ring to the ancient stone façade beyond.

It was a mix of styles, part fortress, part church, and part mosque. The stone was heavily weathered, making it look like it might tumble down at any minute.

The main entrance was a double-arched Neo-Mudéjar doorway that faced east. To the left was a castle turret with balistraria for archers to shoot through. On the right stood a square Muslim minaret, converted to a bell tower, with tall arched windows and a wooden cross mounted on top.

The temperature dropped several degrees as they entered the old monastery. The ceiling was supported by four rows of arched columns, each showing its age.

Cable was speechless as he looked around at the incongruent elements that made up this unique and magnificent church.

"Hello?" Dani's voice echoed around the room's pristine silence.

Footsteps to the left grabbed her attention.

"OMG. Dani Tran. Seeing you brings back so many memories. How are you?"

"Celeste. So good to see you."

Cable watched as the friends embraced and did a quick female size-up. It had been a minute.

"Sorry you had to drive all the way out here, but this is my office for the next two months. Plus, if truth be told, I'm so excited to see you," Celeste said.

She was slightly shorter and rounder than Dani, with trademark Hispanic features. Celeste had a bobbed haircut and large framed glasses that hung on a chain around her neck. Denim overalls and a cream tee seemed to suit her casual style.

"I see you've picked up an accent since you moved here."

"It's not too often I get to use English," Celeste admitted.

Dani smiled and introduced everyone. Cable let them play catch-up for a while. Eventually, the conversation turned to the purpose of their visit, and he tuned back in.

"Welcome to Almonaster la Real, the last of the rural mosques in Spain."

"Mosque, that makes sense. It seems to be a mixture of two religions."

"You have a good eye, Cable," Celeste said.

"The foundation of this church is Roman. In fact, the cornerstones still have the original Roman cement. After that, it was a Christian chapel, partially torn down and rebuilt as a mosque in the ninth century, and finally, it was reconfigured as a Catholic chapel in the sixteenth century. Let me show you a few highlights."

Celeste took them on a short tour, ending at the Visigoth altar with its original adornments of peacocks in relief.

After the tour, she led them back past a chain with a sign that read No Pasar.

In a small room beyond the chapel, Celeste had a desk and laptop set up. Paperwork and files were strewn around the room, as were empty Monster energy drinks and to-go coffee cups.

"You may know that Spain has a sordid history. It was colonized by Greeks, Carthaginians, Romans, and even the Germanic tribes. Around the seventh century, Islam took over until the late 1300s, when the Christians returned. Legend has it that the Apostle James brought Christianity to the peninsula, which makes him the patron saint of Spain."

"So you have lots of overlapping rules," Cable added.

"Right. Since the 1400s, when the Catholic church became the dominant religion, almost all the mosques have been converted back to churches. So there is a lot of lost information. Back then, one religion considered the other heretical and destroyed much of their writings and history. Even things of great value were melted down and repurposed."

"So, slim pickings," Dani said as she looked at a faded mural on the right wall.

"Very."

"In the last five years or so, Spain has really embraced its Muslim heritage, and many of the mosques that remain are now protected."

"That's where you come in?" Cable asked.

"I am just part of a team entrusted in that cause. There are quite a few of us all over Spain doing the work."

"Sounds very fulfilling," Dani said.

"Yes, quite so." Celeste moved behind her desk. "When you reached out to me about a wing, your timing could not have been more perfect. I was organizing inventory lists, so I had access to a database I don't normally work with. Three wings popped up, and one fit your description. Unfortunately, it was destroyed in a fire during the Napoleonic French invasion."

"So how does that help us?" Dani asked, a bit disappointed.

"Because a drawing was made of the wing by the abbesses there. According to Sister Maria of the Convent of Saint Norberto, the wing was left there for safekeeping 'by a traveler from the South.'" She read the words off her computer screen.

Cable and Dani shared a glance.

"It was kept along with several other religious artifacts, including the finger of Saint Leticia. Sister Maria was quite the scribe. She kept records of the weather, harvest yields, and even some gossip about the other nuns. Oh, and there is a self-portrait as well." She clicked her keyboard and spun her screen to Dani and Cable.

A stern-looking woman in a red-and-white nun's habit held a book and a staff.

"Not bad for a self-portrait," Cable said as he eyeballed the washed-out and cracked image.

"Wouldn't want to be on the receiving end of her wrath," Dani said.

"Sounds like a girl who went to Catholic school," Cable added.

"First communion and all," Dani said. "Sister Maria sounds like a social media influencer ahead of her time."

"About four hundred years ahead of her time," Celeste said as she spun the screen back around. "So Napoleon and his army come to town, and Sister Leticia has to evacuate. She takes what she can, and the rest is razed, including her convent, the Convent of San Norberto.

"So, what do you take with you when you have to get out fast?" Cable asked.

"Unfortunately, not a stone wing, but she did take three manuscripts with her and fled to Almonaster la Real."

Dani perked up. "They're here?"

"Let me show you. I pulled these out before you arrived." Celeste opened a drawer, pulled out three very old bound books with clear plastic protective covers, and carefully placed them on her desk. She donned white gloves and opened the one on top. About two-thirds of the way through was a slip of paper marking a page. She opened it to show them a hand-drawn recreation of the wing.

Even though the drawing was a bit rough, Cable knew he was looking at the right artifact immediately. "That's it."

"Incredible," Dani whispered.

The left wing filled half a page near the bottom right-hand side. Extremely neat Spanish handwriting filled the space around it. The drawing showed the carved feather relief and the perspective of a three-dimensional object.

"Is that the only drawing?" Dani asked.

"Yes."

"No view of the back of the wing," Cable asked.

"Not that I've seen," Celeste said.

Dani let a sigh slip out. "It is quite remarkable to find all three pieces of a sculpture made in the sixth century and separated by so much distance and time."

"Find 'em and lose 'em," Cable said, his voice betraying his disappointment.

Dani filled Celeste in on the theft of Cable's artifact and nothing more.

"Could we see what's on the next page?" Cable asked.

Celeste carefully flipped the page. It was filled with familiar, neat handwriting. With one exception. Near the top of the left-hand page were two lines of symbols. Symbols Dani and Cable recognized immediately.

Dani remained calm and casually asked if she could photograph the pages.

Celeste held the book open as Dani took several pictures of the symbols and the drawn wing.

They spent another few minutes chatting and invited Celeste to lunch. She took them to a local restaurant for tapas that were out of this world.

Eventually, they said their goodbyes, and Celeste headed back up the hill to her castle.

Cable and Dani checked into an Airbnb in the middle of the small town. It had clean white walls, Spanish tiled floors, and finally, two bedrooms.

Dani set up on the teal couch and placed her laptop on the hardwood coffee table. She connected to the Wi-Fi and opened her translation site. "This is gonna take some time. The symbols are hand transcribed from hand-carved symbols by a person that had no knowledge of the original language."

"So you're saying they are rough," Cable said.

"Very."

"Toss me the phone. While you're doing that, I'll get us tickets to the US. We can sort everything out once we get back."

"Sounds good," Dani said as she literally tossed the phone.

Celeste heard the footsteps before she saw the source. Two tourists had strayed beyond the chain and the No Pasar sign. One was built like a tank, and the other was not far behind.

"*Desculpe. No se puede pasar por aqui.*"

They looked at her curiously.

Celeste tried the only other language she spoke. "I'm sorry, but you are not allowed back here."

A pistol emerged from the pocket of the larger of the two men.

"How about now?" Luka asked.

Celeste's hands shot up in fear as she tried to focus on something. The gun, his face, or the other guy. "Wha..what are you doing?"

"I understand you have information on the statue of a stone wing from the Axum Empire," Luka said.

Celeste's mouth practically hit the floor.

The second man started searching the rooms behind Celeste. After a moment, he called out. "In here."

"After you," Luka said, using the barrel of his pistol to point the way.

Celeste stepped into her office, just ahead of Luka's gun. The ancient tomes she had shown Dani and Cable were still on her desk.

Tarik went right for them. "What do we have here?" he said as he collected them up.

"Be careful. Those are very old." She could have kicked herself for not putting them back under lock and key as soon as Dani had left.

"What is it you want to know?" She was starting to find her spine. This was her world, and she needed to defend it.

"See this?" Luka held up the pistol. "This means I ask the questions, and you answer them."

It sounded like a line from a movie, but she got the message.

"I want you to tell us everything you know about the stone-carved wing."

"I don't know——"

Luka interrupted. "Don't waste my time, Celeste. We've read your email to Dani."

"I was saying, I don't know much. Dani asked me to run a search for her, and I got a possible hit."

"What kind of hit?"

Celeste explained to the two men what she knew of the history of the wing.

She opened the book and showed them the drawing.

"That's it?"

Celeste nodded. "It's so weird. Those tomes sit on a shelf for most of their life, and today, they are the most sought-after item in this whole town."

"What are you talking about? The girl, Dani…was she already here?"

Celeste just realized she had said too much.

"How long ago?" Luka yelled at her.

"I, ah, two hours?"

"Where'd they go?"

"They took a picture of the wing and left. I don't know where. I swear."

Tarik collected the books off her desk and started for the door.

Celeste panicked at the thought of losing them. She stood and ran after the books. "You can't take those. They belong——"

Luka backhanded her with his pistol, and she flew backward, ricocheting off the corner of her desk. She dropped to the floor, unmoving. He used his foot to jostle her. Nothing, so he dropped to check her pulse. The girl was dead.

"That's on you," he said to the corpse as he stood back up and left the room.

CHAPTER TEN

J UNI STEPPED INTO THE LOBBY at the national police headquarters. She carried two cups of coffee. Well, one was a double espresso. Once past security, she took the elevator and headed straight for cyber.

Squirrel was not in. His desk looked like a real squirrel was living there, however. Wrappers, crumbs, and empty energy drinks, none of which had made it to the empty trash can just two feet away. She noticed that most of the letters had been worn off the keyboard as she set down the double espresso and scrawled a quick note.

Her office was a picture of contrasts. Even her pen and pencil were lined up perfectly on her overly organized desk. Juni sat and took a sip of her coffee as she logged in.

The entire floor was quiet, as most of the other staff were just waking up. The air smelled like fresh vacuuming over a dusty carpet.

Juni liked this time of day. There were no distractions, and she could let her mind focus. She flipped through her stack of folders, a ritual honed over time, reviewing the hot points of each active case. The morning's fresh perspective had helped make connections in the past that had closed many of her cases. Every day was a new day and a chance to look at a problem differently.

Eventually, she got around to her emails. The one from Squirrel got her immediate attention.

J.

Credit card search leads to Anker Hotel room in Oslo, then goes cold. There is a monitor attached to this number, but not from us or the police. That means someone had access to the card at some point. Further investigation has revealed a dark web asset dead end. Looks like somebody with some coin is either tracking or trying to find your suspects.

The *Arinna* was much easier. The yacht was indeed docked at Alvsborg on the day of the robbery. It left a short time later and stopped at La Rochelle two days ago for a quick load up or offload. Current location unknown, but it is leased by a shell corporation that is several layers deep. So, I did some serious digging. Cronus Logistics, out of Istanbul. They have popped up on our radar before. Stein Osman.

Attached are the emails for the last week on both suspects.

Oh, and you're welcome. S

Juni opened her file on Dani and Cable and looked it over. On the surface, they seemed clean, but they had fled the country and had managed to disappear off the grid.

"What have you gotten yourselves into?"

She did a police search for the Oslo Gardermoen Airport, using their names. Yesterday, two tickets to Seville, Spain.

Two Americans wanted in Sweden in connection to a museum heist of a very obscure artifact were on their way to Spain and not running for home. Something was up.

She opened the emails from Cable. Nothing stood out. In fact, it looked like it was hardly ever used.

Dani's, on the other hand, was very active. But in the last week, only one email caught her eye.

Dani, I think I have information on the wing you're looking for.

C.

A brief search revealed the sender, Celeste Navarro. Working for the UNESCO mosque preservation effort. She was currently based out of a small town northeast of Seville.

That couldn't be a coincidence.

Juni opened the file on Stein Osman. It was several pages long. She had tried and failed twice before to connect him to stolen artifacts. Interpol had worked a sting designed to purchase a carved funerary stone from ancient Greece, only he no-showed. Juni had heard rumors that the stone ended up somewhere in China, though she had no proof.

She flipped back to some basic history. He was born in Izmir along the west coast of Turkey. His father was British, and his mother was a local. Stein had spent his youth as a man of privilege and got good enough grades to attend the University of Cambridge in the UK.

After college, Stein worked at his father's import-export business and was on the fast track to take over as his father aged out. Then…nothing. She flipped the page. It picked up again years later with his name attached to a possible smuggling operation.

That's a big gap in your timeline, Stein. What happened?

Juni closed the file. If Stein was behind the theft of the wing, why? It was not like him to be so bold as to hit a museum in broad daylight. *What are you up to?*

He obviously had a buyer who wanted the piece. And how were the Americans involved?

Too many questions and not enough answers. Time to get more aggressive. She posted an Interpol red notice, last seen in Seville, for Dani and Cable. That would have every police force with an Interpol connection on the lookout for the two fugitives. It would also prevent them from leaving Spain. Next, she called travel. It was time to head south for some paella.

Dani looked at the row of letters she had translated and drew short vertical lines separating them into words. Cable leaned over and read aloud. "'Saint Georges has the path. A message only for the worthy.'"

He added it to the other translations they had gathered. Starting with the left wing, then the bird itself, and ending with the right wing. He read it all together. "'From the house made of one. A faithful pilgrimage begins. Saint Georges has the path. Wealth for the church and all. Pious and angels alike share. A message only for the worthy.'"

"That is a road map, and I know where to go," Cable said.

"You do?" Dani asked.

"Yeah, I've been to Saint Georges before."

A knock on the door grabbed their attention.

"Are you expecting anyone?" Cable asked.

"No. It might be Celeste."

"Did you tell her where we were staying?"

Dani shook her head.

Cable took the translation, wadded it up, and tossed it in the toilet. He pushed the handle and headed for the front door.

Dani wasn't sure that was necessary, but just in case, she turned off her laptop.

"Sí?" Cable said without opening it.

A squeaky young voice called out in Spanish. "I have kicked my fútball into your patio. Can I come and get it?"

Cable relaxed, feeling a bit silly for overreacting. He cracked the door open and confirmed it was a young girl about eight years old. She gave him a half-smile as Cable swung the door all the way open to let her in.

At that moment, she ran off, and a familiar face stepped into Cable's periphery. *The man from the museum.*

"Hello, Cable," Luka said, with a slight German accent.

"You don't know how many doors we have knocked on in the last hour. Even in a small town, you made yourselves hard to find, and I salute you for that." Luka spoke as he searched the home, looking for any second-wing clues.

Tarik stood off to the side with a subcompact pistol, ready to react at the first sign of trouble.

"We know you went to the monastery, and you had a look at the book. According to your friend, the wing was lost to time. Unfortunately, she had a terrible accident before she could tell us more, so we were forced to take the books."

A sudden shock coursed through Dani, and she wanted to scream and run to Celeste, but the gunman between her and the door prevented it.

"If you have the books, what do you need us for?" Cable said as he moved closer to Dani. "It is obviously a dead end."

"What I want is for you to tell me everything you know about the second wing, but first, I'm curious. Why did you flee Sweden and come all the way here?" Luka asked.

"Like you, we were curious. The goshawk, after all, has been in my family for a long time. I played with it as a kid."

"I understand that. Curiosity can be more powerful than knowing. It has sent many men to their deaths and fame. How do you say…'it killed the cat?'" Luka and Tarik shared a chuckle.

Dani spoke, barely containing her anger. "The wing was destroyed during the Napoleonic era. The books you stole after killing Celeste have nothing but a drawing of the wing and a brief mention of its origin. That is the dead end we discovered. There was no reason to kill her."

Luka looked at Dani for some sign of deceit but could only detect her anger. It radiated outward like heat waves in the desert.

"Your friend killed herself by thinking she had options," he began. "This might sound familiar because, once again, you both have options. The easy way or the hard way."

Juni trudged up the ramp that led to the ancient monastery. She had shed her coat at the car and was wearing navy slacks and a white blouse. She pulled her credentials from her purse and flashed them through several checkpoints as she moved closer to the building. First was the Policía Municipal, the local police. Next came the CNP, or Cuerpo Nacional Policía. Finally, once she got to the entrance, came the detectives. She was led inside, past the mosque's arched columns, into the *sacristia*. A covered body lay on the floor amid two crime scene investigators with cameras and swabs.

"Detective Eric Pérez?"

"Yes," said a man in a suit chatting with an officer in the corner.

"I'm agent Juni Eklund, Interpol."

"Right. Nice to meet you. Have a look. I'd like to get the body transferred as soon as possible. This room is starting to—"

"I'll be brief," Juni interjected.

Juni knelt and lifted the covering. A young woman with dark curly hair and a frozen look of shock lay in a dried pool of blood. There was a single cut on her face, and she was already starting to decompose. After a moment, she replaced the tarp and stood.

"Thank you for waiting for me, detective."

"Not a problem. Please call me Eric." The thirty-something detective with thick black hair turned to a man by the door. "Carlos, you can take the body." A ballet of sorts began as men with practiced habits collected up the corpse and carried it away.

"What can you tell me?"

"Celeste Navarro, age twenty-eight. Been working here for just over two months cataloging and preserving the site. She lived in an apartment in town, and she didn't slip and fall. You saw that gash on her cheek?"

"Yes. Looks like something hard but not sharp. Maybe the butt of a gun?"

"Could be. We'll know more once forensics has a look. It knocked her back into the desk corner. That caused traumatic brain injury, if I was a betting man."

"Are you?" Juni asked.

"What?"

"A betting man."

"Not really. I tend to favor facts over luck," Eric said.

Juni smiled for the first time since she got on a plane in Stockholm.

It made Eric smile, and before they knew it, they were both smiling at each other in an awkward display that caused them both to break eye contact.

"Anyway, I'll send you the autopsy and anything else that pops up. What makes you think this is linked to your case?" Eric asked.

"A single email from the deceased to one of my suspects. The suspect then travels to Seville."

"Presumably rented a car and drove here to kill a researcher? Some kind of love triangle?"

"It all seems to center around a stolen artifact. Currently, I'm pulling on a very small thread, but soon things will start to unravel."

"Small? It is practically nonexistent."

"Nature of our game."

"I suppose. Well, good luck to—"

His statement was cut short by a cry of anguish from the next room over.

Juni and Eric hurried to investigate.

An older bald man sat slumped in a chair, distraught.

"What is it?" Eric asked him.

"They're gone."

"What is?" Juni asked.

"*Los tres libros antiguos*." He gestured to the locked storage cabinet that lay open and mostly empty.

"Agent Juni Eklund, this is Professor Morales. He is overseeing the UNESCO mosque preservation effort."

The professor gave Juni a dismissive nod and turned back to the detective. "They have been taken," he said in English so everyone could understand.

"Three old books?" Juni asked for clarification.

"Not just any books. The last remaining history and journal of the abbess Sister Maria of the Convent of Saint Norberto. It was the jewel of this monastery, once a mosque."

Now, Juni had two stolen artifacts and a dead body. Her case was growing.

The drive to Málaga took six hours. Cable spent it tied into a ball and stuffed behind the rear seat with a tarp over him. Dani had been slightly better off sitting in the back seat with her hands cuffed behind her back.

Tarik took the first watch sitting across from her with his gun ready. Once they cleared Seville on the A-92, he switched with Luka.

They turned south on the A-45 and drove into the heart of Málaga. The Lancia Montecarlo stopped at a private dock as a quarter moon cleared the horizon, its meager light skipping off the harbor's calm water.

Cable could smell it before he could see anything. The ocean. His hands and feet had long gone numb. His shoulder and hip had been pounded against the metal floor for the last several hours and were severely bruised.

Even though it was dark outside, Cable squinted as the tarp was removed. He had to be dragged out of the vehicle and untied before he could even stand on shaky feet. Tarik grabbed his arm and forced him along as they moved to the waiting yacht, their movement in time to the clanging of loose halyards in the harbor.

The *Arinna* looked majestic and peaceful moored to the end of the dock, but Dani and Cable were filled with dread as they boarded the ship for the second time in a week.

Inside the salon, they were guided to a table. Cable sat next to Dani as Tarik and Luka grabbed a beer from the bar. An onboard guard took over the watch as the big diesel engines rumbled to life. The *Arinna* left the harbor, steering southeast.

It was the first time they had been able to talk since Cable had been hog-tied and thrown in the back of the car.

"You okay?" Dani asked.

Cable firmed his jaw. "I'll be okay, but I am pissed."

"How'd they find us?"

"I have no idea. These people have a pretty long reach."

"From Denver to Sweden."

"They are probably listening to us right now," Cable said.

"If we get out of this, no more side trips."

"Agreed. We take the first flight back to the US."

"I'd even take a flight to Cleveland at this point," Dani said.

"Cleveland? What's wrong with Cleveland?"

"My ex-stalker lives there."

"Okay," Cable said. "I'm just going to step away from that one."

"Thanks. It was not a big deal, just a coworker with an overactive imagination and sense of self. I seem to attract the—" Dani paused mid-sentence because she didn't want to put Cable in the same category she was about to verbalize, but mostly because Fannie entered the room.

Fannie wore her patented false smile as she approached in white shorts and a goldenrod V-neck blouse.

"Welcome back. I thought we'd seen the last of you two back at the museum in Sweden."

"That's funny," Cable said with an extra dose of sarcasm.

"You were quite predictable running off to the authorities. Trying to save the day. Just like you have been with Ms. Tran," Fannie said while looking at Cable. "I have to admit you did surprise us, though, when you changed countries without a trace and ended up in Spain." She now looked to Dani. "We might never have known about Almonaster la Real without your help."

Dani felt a sting of guilt but said nothing.

Cable tried to remain unfazed.

"It turns out we have another need for the two of you. I have to say, Dani, your translation skills of ancient Ge'ez are impressive. We thought we could do the same on our own, but it turns out you are most talented."

Luka returned carrying the three volumes of the old books taken from the monastery. He set them down on the table next to Dani, who shot him a look of disdain.

"How 'bout we make a deal," Cable said. "You drop us off at the nearest port, and we'll tell you everything we know."

"Two problems with that. There is now a red notice out on you both, so as soon as you set foot in Europe, you will be detained." Fannie paused to let the words sink in. "And we don't know what's ahead on this journey. We could very well need your services again. None of us wants to go through the trouble of springing you from jail when we already have you right here."

Fannie stepped over to the table and sat across from Cable and Dani.

"So, I have a one-time offer. Help us follow this puzzle to its conclusion, and we will send you home on a first-class ticket."

"Or don't, and we will send you home in a box," Luka added as he folded his arms.

"Luka, there is no need for that kind of talk…yet. Get the computer."

136

Luka stepped over and retrieved a laptop from the credenza. He placed it in front of Cable. "This laptop has a clone, so every keystroke you make will be seen. Try something stupid, and everything changes for you," Luka said.

"Cooperate, and you are free to move about the ship as before," Fannie added.

Dani looked at the books and the laptop. "So, specifically, what is it you want us to do?"

"Very simple," Fannie said. "Translate the entire message."

"We are missing a third of the message," Cable said.

"If the wing was important enough for it to be recorded in history, then so is the carved message. It will be in one of these books." She gestured. "Find it."

Fannie stood and left without waiting for a reply.

Luka lingered for a time before following his boss out of the salon.

Fannie entered the main berth one floor up and sat across from the desk. Stein looked back at her with his flat black-green eyes, confidence filling his face.

"You heard?"

He nodded as he leaned back in his chair.

"If the symbols are recorded in one of those books, they'll find them."

"Yes, I'm betting their lives on it," Stein said, with a slight upturn of his lips.

For the first forty-eight hours, Dani and Cable delayed as long as they could. Dani had initially retranslated the first wing's message from the translation Fannie had paid for.

From one mansion

Wealth for the church's own

Dani's retranslation was slightly different.

From the house made of one

Wealth for the church and all

It was a significant improvement and seemed to keep her happy.

They took their time looking through the book, Cable translating the Spanish writing into English, and Dani continuing to teach him how to use her site to translate ancient Ge'ez.

Finally, after three days, Fannie threatened to send the books to a contact she had and lock Dani and Cable in the hold.

A few hours later, Dani and Cable showed her the translation for the second wing.

The message was now complete.

> From the house made of one
>
> A faithful pilgrimage begins
>
> Saint Georges has the path to
>
> Wealth for the church and all
>
> Pious and angels alike share
>
> A message only for the worthy

After Fannie read through the message for the fourth time, she stood and left the salon.

Dani and Cable waited nervously, wondering what might happen next, now that they were of no further value.

"Cable, when I first translated the second wing, you said you knew where to go," Dani whispered.

"Yes. Saint Georges is a temple in Ethiopia."

Dani nodded to herself. It made perfect sense.

After a half-hour went by, they started to relax. Maybe Fannie was a woman of her word.

Cable stood and stepped through the slider. Dani followed. The aft deck had been their sanctuary over the last few days. A place where the engines and wind would hide their conversations, allowing them to speak freely and forget about their situation for a time.

"In case we don't make it to shore, I just wanted to say…this had been the best week of my life," Cable said.

"What?" Dani was a bit confused. "Getting kidnapped twice and falsely accused of a crime, then going on the lam?"

"No." Cable paused. "Getting to know you."

"Oh." Dani looked at her feet for a few seconds. "I've had a terrible time with trust and men…kinda sworn them off. You have surprised me, Cable, and that's not easy to do." Dani seemed to be building to something. Her voice was rising, and she was full of nervous energy. "If we're about to be tossed overboard for the sharks, we shouldn't waste what time we have left."

Her words seemed to fail her for a second. "This." She pointed back and forth between them. "This is not something that happens every day. We should—"

"Dani." Cable interrupted. "I just wanted to say that you are a wonderful woman, and I care a lot about you."

"Oh." Dani suddenly lost her nervous energy and seemed embarrassed.

Cable placed his hand on the back of her neck and looked her straight in her eyes. The corners of his lips moved slightly upward as his brown eyes sparkled, inviting.

Dani calmed, feeling comfortable in his presence. No. It was something more than that. She felt safe, maybe even loved.

Cable pulled her to him just as the slider opened and closed. Cable shifted his mouth to Dani's ear.

A guard stepped outside and watched them with interest.

He whispered to her. "I say we either plan an escape or maybe just go to the bedroom and see where this leads."

Dani cocked her head, trying to read Cable's real intention. "There is no escape. We're in the middle of the ocean."

"So, definitely the second one."

Dani punched him really hard and turned and walked away.

Cable laughed. It was worth it. He shrugged at the guard and followed her back inside.

CHAPTER ELEVEN

D INNER THAT NIGHT WAS DIFFERENT. First of all, a stranger sat at the head of the table. He was in his late forties with a trimmed beard and balding head. His eyes seemed dead like a doll, but he spoke with passion.

"I am so pleased to make both your acquaintances, Dani and Cable. Please, call me Stein." He shook both of their hands with vigor before returning to his seat. "Please sit."

They did.

Fannie joined them as plates of kebap were served, along with saffron rice and a small salad. A Vinkara Brut was poured after Stein approved it.

Stein raised his glass and looked across to Dani and Cable. "I am well aware of the machinations that have brought us to this point. So, let's dispense with the past, shall we?"

Fannie lifted her glass and took a sip in acknowledgment.

"I came across an obscure manuscript from the Axum Empire a couple of years back that mentioned your goshawk statue. It has been both intriguing and consuming for me," Stein continued.

"The scroll with the picture of the priest we were shown on our last voyage," Dani added.

"Yes," Stein answered. "Many men and women over the years have made their permanent mark in history by making a discovery that has inspired or redirected our current beliefs. Charles Darwin, Howard Carter, Mary Leakey, Marie Curie."

"Indiana Jones?" Cable added.

Stein paused. He was not used to being interrupted, but he would let it slide. "I suppose. These forward thinkers pushed themselves and seized the opportunity given to them. That same opportunity has come to me. A secret for the ages. Lost to time and now, in part, thanks to you two, I have a chance to place my name in the history books."

Cable stopped eating. "I don't recall any of the names you mentioned being connected to kidnapping."

"Now, now, Mr. Janson, I thought we had an agreement to leave the past out of our meal. Imagine finding King Solomon's mines or the Knights Templar treasure today. The value would be incalculable."

"King Solomon's mines played out three thousand years ago. There is nothing left to find but an empty hole, and the king of France helped himself to the Templar's treasure on Friday the 13th in 1307," Cable said.

"That's the difference between enlightened thinking and common— no imagination."

"Reality check. The scroll said, 'A pilgrimage for the worthy to unimaginable wealth.'" Dani added, "That could be anything, like a wealth of knowledge."

"Right. The fourth *Indiana Jones*. Not his best work," Cable added.

"Better than *Temple of Doom*," Dani added.

"True."

Stein was losing patience with his guests.

"The truth is, Mr. Osman, things of great value are rarely lost to time. People hang on to them, protect them," Dani said.

"Bury them," Fannie said.

"Sometimes. But take pirate treasure, for example. People love to imagine a chest full of gold buried and waiting to be found. In reality, most pirates divvied it up and went out and spent it." Dani finished by setting her fork down.

The chef brought out small plates with Turkish delight for dessert.

"Your points are well taken, and some even founded," Stein said. "If I were a realist, I would probably do just as you have said and find a reason not to push forward, but that is not my intention. The greats of the past all paid heed to their internal drive. It moved them forward, pushing to mark their place in history. I will go to the end of this mystery and discover what has been hidden so long ago. You two can serve a purpose along the way or get trampled. That is up to you."

Dani suddenly lost her appetite.

The dinner finished in silence and eventually, Stein excused himself and left the salon.

"You should be careful with your words to Mr. Osman," Fannie said.

"Why is that?" Cable asked.

"Because the last person who spoke to him in that manner had his tongue ripped out and fed to him."

Dani was escorted off the *Arinna* in the dark just before the sun crested the eastern horizon. Two white SUVs waited on the wharf, glowing orange from the sodium vapor streetlamp above. Men were loading the back of the vehicles with gear and arms. Even this early in the morning, it was still hot. Equator hot.

"Where's Cable?" Dani demanded, trying to resist.

"He is being held to make sure you cooperate, my dear. Anything stupid from you, and I can guarantee he will feel the consequences," Stein said as he climbed into the first SUV, dismissing any further conversation on the matter.

Dani was taken to the second vehicle, and they drove away. The city of Djibouti was a mixture of modern high-rises and crumbling shanties. The streets were relatively quiet as the two-car caravan sped through town. Within twenty minutes, they had left the city behind and were traveling west.

Luka drove the second vehicle, keeping a few car lengths behind as they merged onto the A-1 rutted highway. Fannie looked over from the passenger seat at Dani, sitting just behind Luka. Across from Dani was Tarik, always vigilant. His black eyes seemed to have but one focus. Dani.

"You look perplexed," Fannie said.

"Just trying to figure out where in the world we are," Dani replied.

"Djibouti."

Dani said nothing, but the fact that she was in Eastern Africa did little to calm her fears.

"Don't worry, we'll be in Ethiopia soon."

"Why didn't we just fly to Ethiopia?"

"Didn't want to leave a record of our entry. Plus, there is the *you* factor. The place we are crossing over has no border guards."

Great. She was in Eastern Africa with no trail or trace of how she'd got there. Dani suddenly came to terms with her fragile mortality. Her only hope now was that Cable was okay. She would do her part to help out, but if the opportunity arose, she would run. Her trust in their words was extremely low.

"Tarik, I think we can dispense with the cuffs for now. There's no place for her to run, and if she did, that would be the end of her *friend.*" Fannie said the last word with an added flourish.

As the sun's first rays appeared behind them, the lead vehicle turned off the highway and onto a dirt trail. It veered to the right, away from the highway and into an arid grassland. Dani sat transfixed as a herd of zebras ran past. A short time later, she spotted a lion partially hidden in the brown grass.

The vehicles turned left on a smaller trail and had to slow significantly as they bounced along. After about an hour of traveling, Luka announced from the driver's seat. "Welcome to Ethiopia. The birthplace of coffee."

Cable awoke. Everything hurt. He was lying on the floor, disoriented and confused. Dried blood stained the carpet, and his memory slowly returned.

It had been a rough night. Two guards with guns had come to his room. They had taken their time, tying Cable's hands behind his back. One held him upright while the other beat him with his fists. At one point, they switched positions, but Cable was losing consciousness by then. The memory was fuzzy. The last things he did remember were the words, "Compliments of Mr. Osman."

He tried to sit up. His abdomen screamed in protest, so he just lay on his back, staring at the ceiling. It took a moment before he realized the yacht was not moving.

He rolled over, crawled to the door, and reached up for the handle. It was locked, and he didn't have the strength to do anything about it. He collapsed back to the floor.

Boots pounded up the gangplank. Uniformed officers spread out and moved from room to room, clearing the *Arinna* as they went. There was no sign of the crew or the passengers. After the top floor was searched, they moved to the main cabins. One was locked and occupied.

Cable protested as the policeman roughed him up and dragged him to the deck. He was a mass of cuts and bruises and had a difficult time standing.

The Brigade Spéciale Recherché de la Gendarmerie had sent eight men to serve the Interpol red notice warrant, anonymously called in. The policemen in charge held a picture next to Cable's face. The match wasn't perfect, but close enough.

"Any sign of the woman?" the policeman asked.

"No, sir."

"Nothing."

The policeman nodded in understanding. "Take him."

They confiscated the yacht and hauled the prisoner off to the station.

The local jail cell consisted of cinderblock and metal bars. Three locals shared the cell with Cable, and the first thing they did was search him for anything valuable the police might have missed. Cable gave no resistance. He was spent. One of the men started to take his shirt, but when he saw the cuts and bruising on Cable's torso, he let him be. The younger of the three men helped Cable over to the cinderblock cot and laid him down.

Cable drifted in and out of his reality. The only constant was the residual rocking motion of Mal de Debarquement Syndrome and the pain. A lot of pain.

The first thing Juni noticed as she walked down the boarding stairs from the jet was the heat. It was oppressive. The next was the smell. She was not in Sweden anymore.

She waited close to forty-five minutes before her single piece of luggage appeared at baggage claim. Customs was slightly faster.

A rented Renault with several dings and a long scratch along the side came from the most reputable rental agency on site. She loaded her bag in the back and put Djibouti-Ambouli International Airport in her rear view. Following the turn-by-turn directions on her smartphone, she drove to the hotel. The sun was already getting low, and Juni didn't want to be out at night in a city she was unfamiliar with.

The city of Djibouti sits on the eastern shore of Africa along the Red Sea. With more than 600,000 inhabitants, it accounts for more than half the entire population of the country. Its main business was refueling the world's busiest shipping lanes. Once part of Ethiopia, the coastal country broke away in 1977.

Despite the intense tribalism in the region, Djibouti was currently a stable city with tourist-friendly shops and modern architecture.

The hotel was a three-story, slightly modern concrete rectangle with a variety of window shapes around the building like they had been gathered from leftover building sites and used as a style. It sat next to a dirt lot on one side and a walled field on the other. The cream-colored concrete walls did little to offset the glaring blue neon sign on the façade, Jano House. A street guard opened the gated passthrough for Juni's rental car, and she pulled into a secured parking structure.

A window air conditioner rattled full-time, trying to keep the reasonably clean room cool. White, orange, and yellow was the theme, and Juni pulled the bright bedspread down before testing the bed. It was very firm. She tried not to think about the microscopic critters that might live there. Instead, she let her mind review the details of the last two days as she tried to ignore the moldy smell in the air. Her stolen artifact case now included a possible murder. She would do everything in her power to prosecute the ones responsible. After settling in, she picked up her phone and sent a text to Squirrel requesting another search.

S

Need information on the location of Stein Osman

Thanks

J

She was tired of following a trail of crime across multiple countries. It was time to get ahead of her quarry.

The vehicles stopped and Dani woke with a start. They were inside the small courtyard of a boxy modern home. Fannie and Luka piled out while Tarik maintained his overwatch on Dani.

She was taken inside and allowed to use the restroom. As she exited, Stein was standing in the living room waiting for her.

"Where are we?" Dani asked.

"Addis Ababa. The Chinese capital of Ethiopia. I say that because China has spent billions getting their hooks into this country. I'm not judging, but Addis Ababa is one of the most modern cities in Africa. Chinese trains, roads, factories, and even the updated airport make it an Asian gem. A good example is the futuristic African Union headquarters. You won't find a building like it anywhere in Africa, but enough with the modern history lesson. I'm more curious about the past. Say, sixth century."

Dani watched as the three ancient books from Spain were brought in and set on the coffee table. Next came the goshawk and one wing. Finally, the drawing of the second wing was laid out.

Dani looked at the ancient sandstone carving. She was drawn to it like a magnet. "This is the first time these pieces have been back in this country in close to a hundred years."

"Yes, but my interests are more aligned with where we go next."

"Saint Georges," Dani said. "I thought that was clear."

Fannie sat on the leather couch and put her feet on the table. "The problem is there are eight churches here by that name."

Dani remembered Cable saying he knew where to go, but he managed to leave out the fact that there was more than one church called Saint Georges. "Okay. I'll need a computer and some water."

"That's my girl. Get her what she needs," Stein said as he left the room.

Dani set up in the theater room on one of the reclining chairs. The home was large and decorated in black and white, nothing more. Even the dining room table was checkerboard, surrounded by eight black chairs. Dani started digging into the history of the eight churches while two of the guards hung nearby, watching soccer on the enormous screen. Not surprisingly, a detailed history of Ethiopia in English was scarce. After a couple of hours, she had eliminated all but three.

Fannie and Stein were called in, and Dani gave them a report. "Okay, so I have narrowed it down to three and a half churches."

"Half?" Stein asked.

"The sacred city of Aksum was home to the Queen of Sheba. It supposedly holds the Ark of the Covenant safely tucked away in the Church of Mary of Zion. They have strict security there, and only the high priests can enter. Throughout the centuries, Aksum had been historically referred to as Saint Georges once or twice. So, it's a maybe."

"Makes sense," Fannie said.

"More promising is the Saint George Orthodox Church Summit here in town. It fits the timeline. Followed by the Saint George Monastery to the south. It is a neoclassical church, currently with a museum, but portions of the building also fit our timeline."

Stein moved over next to Dani and sat down.

Dani hesitated before continuing. "If I were to guess just one, it would be the Church of Saint George. It's located up north of here in a remote part of the country. It is built from a single piece of stone, carved from a huge chunk of granite."

"What do you recommend?" Stein asked.

Dani cleared her throat. She wished Cable had been more specific when he told her that the clue pointed to Saint Georges. "My thought would be to check out the closest sites first and then work north."

"Makes sense. Good work, Dani. What are we looking for?"

Dani passed out sheets of paper with her translation on each.

From the house made of one

A faithful pilgrimage begins

Saint Georges has the path

Wealth for the church and all

Pious and angels alike share

A message only for the worthy

"Whatever makes sense with these words."
They were still a long way from an answer.

The stench of the cage had long since faded from Cable's nostrils, though he supposed it was worse than ever, and he was now part of it. His pain level had subsided slightly, and he had found common ground with his cellmates. It helped that he spoke both French and Arabic. They shared stories and family interests, hoping to hide the slow passage of time.

Cable had lost track of the days as there were no windows, and the light in the cell never went off. His only clue was the two meals a day delivered by the worst waiter in the history of waiters.

He had asked the guards multiple times to speak with the US embassy or an attorney. It was a wasted effort. One day, the youngest cellmate was removed and never seen again. Finally, they came for Cable. He was escorted down a narrow hall and into an empty interview room. The bare concrete walls had yellowed over time. Two chairs and a small table helped hide a drain in the middle of the room. Dried blood on the table and floor was left there to help incentivize the unwilling. Cable sat with his cuffs on and closed his eyes, letting his mind go to more favorable memories. After an hour, a woman in a dark suit and blonde hair stepped into the room. She immediately reacted to the smell that was coming off Cable.

"I need to speak with my embassy," Cable said in Arabic.

The woman looked puzzled as she reached into her purse for something to cover her nose.

Cable tried the same words in French.

The woman perked up and replied in French. "I thought you were an American?"

"I am," Cable said in English.

"Ah, well, I'm Agent Eklund with Interpol. It's not every day that a red notice pays off, and yet here you are."

Cable stared back, giving her nothing.

"Okay, I was hoping to ask you a few questions."

"I'm Cable Janson, and I'd love to shower off before answering them."

"That would be preferable," Juni said as she stood and left the room. A few moments later, two guards came in and escorted Cable to an empty cell, where they uncuffed his hands and stripped him of his filthy clothes. They blasted him with water from a hose and sprayed Cable for lice. They gave him a faded, pre-used yellow prison jumpsuit before re-handcuffing and escorting Cable back to the interview room.

Forty minutes later, Juni returned. She took a tentative sniff and nodded as she sat back down.

She looked at the bruising on Cable's face. "They do that here?"

Cable shook his head. "That was a going away present from a man named Stein Osman."

The name caused Juni to sit up, an action that was not lost on Cable. "You worked for him?"

"I was kidnapped and framed by him. He didn't take too kindly to my insults."

Juni looked unconvinced. "And the girl?"

"Dani, is she okay?"

"Perhaps we should start at the beginning."

Cable leaned back. Not sure where to begin. So he decided to start with Dani. "I met Ms. Tran…"

He included every detail he felt was important and skipped the ones that made him look guilty or weak. After twenty minutes, he stopped.

A buzzing on Juni's phone grabbed her attention. It was a text from Squirrel.

J

Stein Osman's last location was pegged at the maritime customs in Djibouti.

He has gone dark from there.

S

Juni looked back up and tried to fit Cable's story into her version of the facts. It was a bit fantastical, but the pieces did line up, and now, with Stein in the wind, she just might need this interview to go her way.

"What is it about your goshawk that has Stein so consumed?"

"He thinks it leads to some long-lost treasure."

"And you?"

"I think it leads to something, but treasure is only one possibility."

"Explain," Juni asked.

Cable went on to explain his theory.

"Where do you think he is headed now?"

"I can take you there," Cable replied.

"That's not how this works." Juni leaned forward. "You tell me where he is heading, and I'll reach out to your embassy. I can even give them a recommendation as to your possible innocence."

Cable knew when he was being played. "Not interested. If my embassy finds out you ignored my request as an Interpol agent, that would not look so good for you. Especially when they find out I am the victim in all this."

Juni said nothing.

"Stein Osman is on a mission to retrieve whatever is at the end of these clues. Now, we can catch up to him, but only if we get a move on. I've been rotting in a cell while he is making progress."

Juni tapped her fingers on the battered table. Her mind flashed with scenarios. There was no way in hell she would take this man with her.

The drive to the Saint Georges Orthodox Church Summit took forty minutes. It was located east of the city along 5Q9 Street. The blue octagon with a green-, yellow-and-red-striped roof stood out on a lone hill. A large stone wall surrounded it, forcing them to drive to the back, where a dirt driveway allowed access. Hundreds of locals crowded the street, so Luka pulled to the side. Stein started to open the passenger door.

"Remember, you try anything, and your boy toy gets hurt," Luka said.

"Yeah, yeah," Dani muttered as she stepped from the rear of the car. The world beyond her bubble was not something she had experienced. Foreign culture was happening in all directions. It was breathtaking and alien all at once.

The locals were well-dressed, with pants and collared shirts for the men and white shawls over dresses for the women. A loud, distorted voice blasted through speakers from the entrance of the chapel, chanting in a language unknown to any of them. Colorful streamers, straight out of a used car lot, stretched across the sky.

Dani pushed through the crowd gathered to hear the speaker's message and stopped once inside the dirt courtyard. Many of the parishioners had brought umbrellas to guard against the intense morning sun, making it hard to see the speaker.

They patiently waited until a final prayer was given and the throng started to disperse.

Fannie led them toward the small chapel. Closer inspection showed murals painted on the outside walls. A young boy was in the process of dismantling the speakers stacked on the porch that circled the building. They stepped into the chapel to look around.

Stein immediately voiced his concern. "This is a waste of time."

"Welcome," said a voice with a very strong accent. A priest dressed in white approached. "You are welcome, but no shoes. Of course, generous donations are accepted here." He pointed to a wooden box with a slit on the top, showing his best missing-teeth smile.

Dani stepped up to the man and said, "We were hoping to find the oldest section of your church."

The priest hesitated, his eyes glancing among the group.

Stein slipped a 5,000 Ethiopian birr note into the slot.

The priest cocked his head for a beat before nodding. "Yes, right this way. This corner of the building is all that has survived the many centuries. You can see the stones here and here."

Dani inspected the two stones in the corner. They were well-worn with no carvings or marks. "This is it?"

"I'm afraid so. The church was ransacked and all but destroyed in the Italo-Ethiopian War."

"Well, thank you for your time. Your church is beautiful," Dani said.

The priest frowned as his newest patrons left.

The next stop was just north of the city off the A-3 highway. Saint Georges Cathedral was also an octagon made from carved stone. It was a fine example of ornate neoclassical and Ethiopian blended.

Inside, tourists milled about, and a French tour group off to the left focused on a stone effigy.

Dani looked up at the magnificent carvings and murals that filled the main chapel. "There was a time before banks when the church used vault churches to hide their wealth. Secret chambers that were only known to the highest priests. I could imagine an unexpected death might lead the vault to be lost to time and the valuables inside still waiting to be found."

Stein glanced over at Dani. "This is a bit different. We are following ancient clues."

"True, but these clues could lead to a hidden vault in a church."

"Yes, it's possible," Stein conceded.

"I'm curious, Dani, what made you follow your dream to become an insurance appraiser and not a field archaeologist?"

Dani hesitated. She was not excited to share anything personal with her kidnapper, but the truth was not that complicated. "The money is much better. I don't mind camping occasionally, but living in a tent for months isn't for me."

"I completely understand. Give me room service and a soft bed, any day."

Dani found herself wanting to laugh, but she suppressed the feeling. Instead, she found a priest who knew the building's history.

The structure had been rebuilt on the original foundation in the 1500s. The Italian Fascists burned it to the ground, and it was rebuilt in 1941. A familiar theme was emerging.

It was time to regroup and head north.

CHAPTER TWELVE

THE ALPI 300 BUCKED ACROSS hot air pockets as it flew west. It was a two-seater prop plane with a small cargo space in the rear that could be converted to a jump seat. Cable sat sideways with his knees to his chest, grateful to be out of the jail cell.

Up front to the right, the pilot focused on keeping them aloft. Juni sat across from him, splitting her time looking out across the Horn of Africa and eyeballing Cable, hopeful the stick for the co-pilot between her legs would not be needed.

"You're going to get a kink in your neck going back and forth like that," Cable called out over the noise in the cockpit. "I'm not going anywhere until we sort this out."

"So you've assured me multiple times."

"That doesn't make it any less true."

"No, it doesn't," Juni acknowledged. "You know, Stein Osman has a way of covering his tracks. That yacht we found you on? It was a lease that ended three days ago. The vessel was returned to the port in Málaga, Spain. The owners have no idea how it ended up in Djibouti."

"I'm a witness."

"One voice against?"

Cable realized what Juni was saying. "At least six, probably the captain and crew as well."

"If we don't catch him…" She spun her finger around the plane. "All this will be for nothing."

"I take it Interpol doesn't like its agents renting private planes and running all over the world."

"Interpol is a business just like any other. Spending $50,000 to solve a $20,000 heist doesn't work for them. The only reason I'm here is murder. We'll do anything it takes to bring a murderer to justice."

Cable understood her words, and he would do the same. Until Dani was safe again, he was committed.

The plane bounced on the dirt strip, leaving a dust trail behind. It came to a stop just outside a weathered hangar with a missing door.

Cable peeled himself out of the rear jump seat and hopped down. He rubbed his knees back to life and stood to look around. The air here was much drier than the coast, but the heat was just as oppressive.

It took twenty minutes before a dusty and battered cab arrived and drove them through the small town of Lalibela. The cab driver turned onto King Solomon's Road and then took a left onto a dirt path. Juni paid the driver and pulled out her handcuffs.

"You won't need those," Cable said.

"Until I meet our contact here, I will decide if they are needed or not."

Cable shook his head and held out his hands. They headed up the path to the right, with a magnificent view of the tree-covered rolling hills beyond and a clear blue sky above. The dirt path ended in granite, a flat exposed rock face about the size of a soccer field. Right in the middle of it sat the roof of a church. Hewn from the living rock was a three-story cross-shaped structure plunging downward.

Cable stepped to the edge of the hand-carved cliff and looked at the courtyard below. The Church of Saint Georges was one solid piece of carved stone, from the windows and design filigree outside to the rooms, alcoves, and stairs inside. It was one of the most amazing churches on the planet.

He moved down the ramp to the left that led to the courtyard below. The heat of the day waned as he reached the bottom of the pit, and the small-looking church from up top now seemed much larger.

Cable glanced around at the few tourists that had made this distant journey. He could make out several languages within the mix. His focus melted into a smile as he looked left. A tall Ethiopian man was grinning from ear to ear.

"Cable, my good friend. How are you?"

Cable and the man embraced as much as they could, with Cable's hands cuffed.

"It has been too long, my brother," Cable said.

"Yes, indeed." He stood back and eyed the cuffs on Cable's hands. "This is new."

"Kojo, I would like to introduce Agent Juni Eklund of Interpol."

Juni stepped forward and shook hands with the gangly man. He had a traditional yellow *dorze* cap on his head with a muted purple *dubaku* shirt over faded jeans, but the thing that stood out the most was his infectious smile, set against a bright orange beard and impossibly sky-blue eyes. An eye color that occurred in fewer than 8 percent of Ethiopians.

"So, how am I to be of service to Interpol Juni?"

Juni started to correct him but decided to let it go.

Cable answered, "Two things, Kojo. We are looking for clues to the start of a mysterious pilgrimage from around the sixth century, and we need to know if this woman has been through here yet?"

Juni showed Kojo a picture of Dani from the museum security camera. He nodded and took the picture.

"I can find this out." He said, holding up the picture. "But your quest is perhaps misguided."

"What do you mean?" Juni asked.

"You are talking of the pilgrimage of Akon, also known as the pilgrimage through the eye of faith, yes?" Kojo stated. "It is a well-known legend about a priest who hid the wealth of the church hundreds of years ago to save it from savages. Much like Prester John or King Solomon's mines, it is nothing but a fool's errand."

"Prester John?" Cable asked.

"A twelfth-century account of a descendant of the three Magi who became a Christian king of a wealthy land full of riches lost among the pagans and Muslims here in Africa."

"Was he ever found?"

"No, but a Portuguese cartographer did mention him on one of his maps from the late 1400s. Still, with many attempts to find the kingdom, nothing has ever come of it."

"I'm not interested in any quest," Juni said, very matter-of-fact.

"I hope you are wrong, Kojo," Cable said, pointing to the photo. "That girl's life depends on it."

"May the Nine Saints protect her," Kojo said before leaving with the picture to talk with the locals.

Colorful rugs were strewn about the floor, protecting the sacred site. Cable and Juni had removed their shoes, as was the custom, before entering the chapel. Huge stone arches supported the roof, all carved from the original stone. The faint wisp of incense wafted through the cool air.

"If you were leaving clues to a pilgrimage, where would you put them? Outside could be lost to the elements. Inside, the parishioners here can only visit the chapel, so unless it's meant for just the priests, it should be somewhere here in this chapel." Cable pulled a piece of paper from his pocket, which was no small feat with his hands still cuffed. He read the words one more time and then handed the paper to Juni.

"I told you, I am not interested in a quest. You promised me Stein Osman. Where is he?"

"For all we know, Stein has already been here. We need to solve this clue if we want any hope of knowing his next move."

"There is no next move. Do you think I'm stupid? Running around Ethiopia with a suspect chasing a phantom criminal? No. If they have beaten us here, so be it. We are done, and I'm taking you with me back to Sweden."

"Okay, but we both know Stein is real and here in Ethiopia," Cable said. "If Dani ends up dead because you did nothing, that's on you."

Juni slowly nodded as she let out an audible sigh and looked back at the paper.

From the house made of one

A faithful pilgrimage begins

Saint Georges has the path

Wealth for the church and all

Pious and angels alike share

A message only for the worthy

Cable stepped next to her. "Okay, so the first three lines got us here. Saint Georges, a house made from one piece of stone."

"The pilgrimage begins here, got it."

They concentrated on the next three lines.

"The first line is obvious. We are heading toward wealth," Juni said.

"It's the next two lines that have me flummoxed," Cable admitted.

Juni gave Cable a sideways glance at his word choice. "A message for the worthy. That speaks to me of a churchgoer."

"So, in the chapel, not hidden in one of the back rooms for just the priests."

"That's my take."

"And the middle line? Cable asked. "Pious and angels alike share."

"No clue."

"Thanks to Indiana Jones, we know that the pious man is a humble man. On his knees, head bowed. Look for an alcove, somewhere someone might pray."

"What are you going to do?" Juni asked, with a hint of distrust.

"Find the lowest place in the room and bow my head."

"My friends, I have the news you are seeking," Kojo said as he approached.

"What is it?" Juni asked.

"Your person has been here. Just yesterday"

"We are closing in, but only if we solve this and move out," Cable said as he looked to Juni.

Kojo did the same.

It took a moment, but eventually, Juni managed to move her head up and down, just barely.

Kojo and Juni moved to the walls, looking for alcoves that might hide a clue.

Cable moved to the center of the room and used his toes to feel for something other than a smooth floor under the rugs. His toes were rewarded with an uneven spot almost dead center of the room. Kneeling and bowing, he pulled the corner of the rug back to investigate.

A drain in the shape of a swastika appeared. Cable looked it over very carefully. He noticed two very small symbols side-by-side. "Juni, I need your phone," he called out in a loud whisper.

She walked over to Cable and handed him her phone. He took a few pictures of the symbols before replacing the rug.

"What have you found?" Kojo asked as he followed Juni.

"I'm not sure. Take a look."

Juni and Kojo looked at the phone while Cable stood back up and repeated a short mantra to himself. "Angels alike share," as he looked around the room. "I think the floor is only half the message…a shared message. Pious on the floor and angels…" He pointed up. All three squinted their eyes to the darkened ceiling above them. Because the chapel was carved from one chunk of stone, the windows were not very large. They were also the main source of lighting.

Kojo pulled out his flip phone and turned on the flashlight feature, pointing it up. Juni did the same.

"There. See that?" Cable said, pointing.

"Yes," Juni said as she zoomed in and took several pictures of three carved symbols above.

"What does it say?" Kojo asked.

"Dani showed me how to translate these symbols, but I'll need a computer and some time before I know."

"I have just the place," Kojo said with an ear-to-ear smile.

Juni didn't share his optimism.

Self-proclaimed president and rebel leader Dejin Kidane turned away as the young woman was dragged from her family's home. His soldiers began to beat her while her parents were forced to watch. He had seen it many times before and even participated occasionally. The screams were all the same, an aphrodisiac to his libido, but he had no time for that today.

Real terror was a message that moved through the masses faster than a bad flu. It made your opponent weak in the knees and did wonders to ease the efforts required to sack a town or garner information.

Axum was once the capital of a naval trading power that ruled the whole region from the fourth to the tenth century. Since then, its importance and population had decreased. Now, sixty-five thousand civilians still occupied the historic town, but that number didn't scare Dejin. Most were sheep that needed shearing.

The battle for Axum was bloody and, most importantly, successful, leaving thousands dead. As leader of the TPLF, the Tigray People's Liberation Front, Dejin knew a few would need to suffer before real change could take place. The kind of change that he truly believed this country needed. Though ethnic cleansing was considered a war crime, it was crucial to the New Jerusalem he was building here. A place where he would hold the power, and one day, the Prime Minister of Ethiopia would crawl to him, asking for his forgiveness. Until then, he would lay waste to his homeland with the hope of remaking it in his image.

Several gunshots were fired at once. Executions, Dejin surmised. Everything was going to plan. Today, thousands would fight, thousands would run, and thousands would be brutalized. It would be a massacre.

At fifty-six, Commander Dejin was a charismatic man with short-cropped hair and large ears. He wore his ubiquitous green fatigues and sunglasses, topped with a baseball-style hat with the symbol of his power. A flying goshawk.

Since first claiming independence from the capital, Dejin and his rebels had been forced to stay on the move. The Federal Police Commission issued an arrest warrant against him, and any foray too far south could be dangerous. The regular Ethiopian army had battled back and forth many times, ending in a stalemate, so hit-and-run tactics had become the norm. Today would be the first real strike into the heart of the enemy. The TPLF would swoop in and kill all undesirables, then take what they wanted and leave. Now was the time to rebuild and recruit.

One of his two MK1A tanks rolled ahead, clearing the way, while two Mi-17 helicopters fired sporadically from above at retreating forces.

The M462 Abir followed with Dejin in the back in the passenger seat. The Israeli military vehicle was favored by the leader for its durability and armor. The man next to him in the driver's seat was the closest thing he would ever have to a friend. Trust, in the revolution business, was needed but hard-fought. Colonel Haile was just as dedicated and certainly more vicious than Dejin, but he also had a great mind for operations and tactics. At forty-two, the colonel had operational control of the rebels. He used his position to push Dejin's agenda throughout the northern territory. He did all the hard work and let the adoring troops see Dejin as more of a messiah or figurehead. Colonel Haile was not built for politics. War was his companion and lover. He would live and die on the battlefield.

Haile adjusted his sunglasses, the one ode to his boss's effigy he boldly mimicked. Using his radio, he called the shots as the final mop-up of the city commenced. It was critical to gather as much money and supplies as possible and transport them back north to his base of operations. Taking a city was costly, and ROI was at the heart of every one of Colonel Haile's operations.

Commander Dejin waved, and his adoring troops shouted his name as they drove past. One soldier paused his hanging of an older woman to salute his leader. Dejin saluted back, giving the soldier one of his patented grins, a memory the soldier would always keep with him.

Dejin's smile, however, was only on the outside. Running a revolution was hard work. The Chinese had been a big help at first, providing money and a few arms. They liked the instability he provided the country. It created opportunities. The kind that allowed the Chinese to increase their grasp on the dark continent.

However, since the stalemate, the Chinese had lost faith in his effectiveness. That meant no more funds or support. Dejin needed money, and a failing civil war was not bolstering his perceived value. He needed a score, and soon. Hopefully, this brazen attack on Axum would boost his Q rating. Today's plunder would more than cover the costs. A scream to the left pulled his attention from his thoughts. A feisty young man was tied between two trees, being slowly flayed. Yes, today was a good day.

The white Land Cruiser had seen many good years of service, and some-how, it just kept going despite a very tired engine and almost useless suspension. Kojo pulled the vehicle to a stop after an arduous climb up the mountain. As the dust cleared, a dirt clearing with tents and several small *shantis* came into view. The tents surrounded a central building with a rusted tin roof and weathered wood walls. Beyond lay a spec-tacular view of the fertile valley below. Off to the right, a young woman squatted by a fire, flipping flatbread on a metal griddle.

Juni stepped from the Land Cruiser and rubbed her kidneys. "What is this place?"

Kojo smiled proudly. "My sister's place."

"See," Cable said, pointing to a crooked sign. Jegoley Family Eco Camp.

"How are we supposed to get computer access up here?" she asked.

"Oh, Zala is most ingenious. You will see." Kojo led them past the colorful tents toward the main structure. Before he could reach the door, a woman with braided hair and many woven necklaces emerged. She was tall like Kojo and had strong shoulders covered with a tattered black *dubaku*, or traditional African shirt. "Kojo! You are unexpected but most welcome. May God give you health," she said in Amharic. The two shared an embrace and the typical three-cheek kisses of the familiar.

Kojo turned and introduced Zala to Juni and Cable. Zala eyed Cable's handcuffs suspiciously. "Salam," she said.

Kojo explained the situation, and Zala took them inside the main house.

She tried out her burgeoning English. "Welcome Jegoley Family Eco Camp. We serve the forest, land, and you."

The home was spartan, with handmade furniture and a propane re-frigerator in the corner. A piece of plywood served as a kitchen counter, and a small sink provided warm running water from a tank outside. The ceiling was open-beam, exposing the tin roof, and the floor was compact dirt with a few rugs.

Zala showed them to a rough-hewn table to the right. It had a small laptop. "I use this to run the bookings. It is attached to a cellphone hotspot, and I have a boosting antenna outside that can get me up to two bars." She set everything up and then went outside to start up the generator.

A moment later, the small engine could be heard running. Cable sat at the laptop and held up his cuffed hands. "Surely these are no longer necessary."

Juni hesitated before finally relenting and removing the cuffs. "Just for this," she said as she pocketed the cuffs. She opened her phone and displayed the photos taken at the Church of Saint Georges.

Cable navigated to Dani's translation site and began the slow process. Eventually, Juni relaxed, lay back on a small cot, and drifted off. Kojo spent the time outside with his sister, catching up.

It took most of the afternoon for the message to clarify. The symbols on the floor represented the number nine, and the three symbols on the ceiling stood for 'true believer.' Cable leaned back and rubbed his eyes. He looked down at what he had written. *9 true believers.* It meant nothing to him.

Dani waited for the page to load. The Internet was dial-up speed at best. Tempers were starting to run short. It was like a thickness in the air, pressing down with no relief.

The ride from Lalibela to Bahir Dar had been bumpy and long. Located along the southeast shore of Lake Tana, Bahir Dar was the most popular tourist destination in Ethiopia, with a variety of attractions, including the lake, close access to the Blue Nile, and the majestic falls beyond.

They had pulled up to a small home along the shoreline of the lake. The home was clean, featuring local hardwoods and stone throughout. Dani was tired, but that would have to wait as her captors hovered while she connected to the Internet and finally to her site. Her heart soared when she saw the user logins. Someone else had been on the site— Cable. He must be free and coming for her. She would no longer let their threat of violence against him control her, and at the first opportunity, she would run.

"What is it?" Fannie asked, noting Dani's distracted look.

Dani shook off her thoughts and opened the translation page. "Nothing. It's just really slow Internet."

Eventually, Dani had the symbols translated for all to see. It was not what anyone expected.

"'Nine, true believer?' What does that stand for?" Stein asked no one in particular.

No answer was forthcoming.

Dani opened her computer back up and looked up synonyms for 'true believer.' A collection of words filled the page and she took her time considering each one.

Fannie picked up on her idea and began verbalizing each word or phrase, adding the number nine to the front and then the back. They hoped something would click or at least make more sense. For example, nine martyrs had possibilities, but a search revealed nothing conclusive. They continued doing searches for each word without success until they came to the *s*'s. "Saint...nine saint...saint nine," Fannie monotoned.

"Ninth saint," Dani said, her fingers suddenly clicking away. She pulled up a picture of an ancient, colorful tapestry depicting the Nine Saints of the Ethiopian Orthodox Church standing shoulder to shoulder. Each had their name in Amharic above them. Dani used Google Translate to get the name of the last one on the right. "The ninth saint is Abba Yemata. He was one of the nine original missionaries who started Christianity in this part of the world. It is disputed that Ethiopia was the first state to adopt the religion back around the third century."

"Nice history lesson. What about this Abba Yemata?" Stein said, suddenly interested now that they were making progress.

Dani typed some more. "Well, there is not a lot on him. He founded the Monastery of Ger'alta...and there is the Sky Church. or Abune Yemata. It is named after him. Both are from the right era."

"Monastery and church. Which one?" Stein asked.

"That's not something I can determine on a computer."

Stein stood from the reddish-brown couch and looked over Dani's shoulder. "Show me where they are located."

Dani pulled up a map. She could smell his aftershave, and it nearly gagged her. "Both are in the Semien Mountains." She pointed to the screen. "Here and here."

"Boss, the TPLF operates out of that area," Luka said.

Stein gave Luka a quizzical look.

"The Tigray People's Liberation Front. They were the ones responsible for the Axum massacre. Lately, they have been hitting villages along their proclaimed border. They're bad news."

"That's right between us and the churches," Fannie added.

"We'll need to be very careful if we are going in," Luka said.

"Oh, we are most definitely going in. So, check your gear and make sure we are ready. I don't want any rebels screwing this up, understand?"

Luka knew his boss better than most. He gave him a confident nod, even though he wasn't feeling it.

The single-engine SOCATA TBM 700C2 had flown in from Addis Ababa and transported Stein and his group north over the rebels' territory and into the small town of Wikro, along the A2 highway. The pilot made the rough dirt strip look easy and taxied the plane to the small metal shed at the end with a makeshift control tower. A local in a four-door Toyota Hilux pickup truck pulled alongside. Stein watched as their gear and personnel were loaded up.

It had been a long time since Dani had ridden in the back of a pickup truck. The hot wind kept the oven-like temperatures at bay as they followed a rutted path to a seemingly abandoned structure half-built into the side of a small cliff face. The Monastery of Ger'alta was unimpressive. A natural cave with a few additional openings carved in the stone. Adobe was used to fill in the gaps to make an arched doorway and three windows above. A single faded mural of a Coptic cross and a long-dead Saint Abba Yemata was done in shades of green above the entrance. Out front, a few stacked stone graves were overgrown. Even the dirt pathway they had arrived on looked lost to time.

The truck pulled to a stop, and the heat and black flies immediately started attacking. The driver led Stein, Fannie, and Dani toward the entrance. Luka and Tarik followed behind, their heads on a swivel.

Once inside the monastery, Dani calmed as cooler interior temperatures gave a reprieve. A narrow alcove was the first thing they discovered.

It led right and left, with several carved doorways along the way. Each doorway had teal wooden frames and hanging woven mats as doors. Stein pulled the mat back and used a small LED flashlight to illuminate the empty room carved in the stone. He repeated the process with each doorway until he found a much larger room. It had murals and an altar. The floor had rugs, and a warm glow came from several working lights hanging from the ceiling. A single occupant knelt at the altar, murmuring a chant no one understood. Dani removed her shoes and stepped inside.

The priest stopped and turned. He gave Dani a cautious smile and stood slowly on old knees. He wore a white *sticharion*, or robe, with loose-fitting green pants peeking out below it.

Stein called for the pickup driver, who spoke some English, to translate. Dani stepped next to the priest. "We are on a pilgrimage for the ninth saint, Saint Abba Yemata. Is this his monastery?"

The priest hesitated at the sight of armed individuals in the church.

Dani smiled nervously, and he slowly calmed and began a rapid-fire dialogue that even the driver had trouble translating. What they did understand was a basic history of the monastery.

Dani pressed the priest again about Saint Abba Yemata.

The priest nodded and took her to a mural above the altar.

In the meantime, Stein whispered to Fannie and Luka. "Check every inch of this place. We are looking for Ge'ez symbols or a swastika." They nodded and separated. "Tarik, get to the entrance and keep an eye out."

"On it, boss," Tarik said as he spun and left.

The mural depicted a gray-bearded man in a green tunic holding a Coptic cross and a wooden shaft. There was colorful filigree surrounding him and a far-off look that had been frozen in time. Dani stood close and checked the details and various patterns for any sign that might be a clue.

The priest watched with curiosity as Dani worked. His face took on a questioning expression that slowly turned to recognition. "You are looking for the pilgrimage through the eye of faith?" he asked.

The driver translated.

Dani paused, not understanding his question. "I know nothing of the pilgrimage through the eye of faith."

The driver didn't wait for the priest to explain. "It's a local legend about a young priest who hid the church's wealth to protect it from raiders. He established a pilgrimage only the most faithful could follow to a place of great wealth. Many have looked for it over the years, but it is just a legend."

The priest, who seemed to understand, nodded.

Dani paused. This changed everything in her mind. As an archeologist, she knew legends often contained morsels of fact. Could this journey actually be leading to a real place? She redoubled her efforts, searching the mural again even more carefully. Still, she came up empty.

Dani thanked the priest and called out to Stein. "Anything?"

"No. We need to move to the Sky Church."

"I'll need to arrange transport. There is no good place to land a plane there," Fannie said.

The driver listened to the banter back and forth before stepping outside. He dialed a number he had never used before and listened while it rang.

"Yes?" came a voice on the other end of the call.

The driver hesitated, then blurted out, "there is something you should know."

CHAPTER THIRTEEN

COLONEL HAILE HUNG UP AND took on a faraway stare, processing the conversation.

"What is it?" Dejin asked.

"Perhaps a solution to our problem," Haile said as he set his coffee mug down and moved to his computer.

Commander Dejin stood and followed his second-in-command.

The headquarters of the Tigray People's Liberation Front was an old warehouse with guard towers and razor wire around it. Inside, they kept their prized ground weapons. Two South African MK1A tanks and a collection of armored and armed vehicles. The soldiers slept outside in tents. A few mess hall tents and latrines were strategically placed, all within the fencing. Off to the right was a blacktop area with two older Mi-17 helicopters armed with rockets and machine guns and, most importantly, a mechanic who kept them in the air.

Dejin's second-floor office overlooked the warehouse. It had a row of windows along the back wall that also afforded a view of the training field beyond the fence.

Colonel Haile pulled out his chair and sat at a metal table off to the side of his commander's office. He typed as he spoke. "One of the locals we have used in the Mek'ele region just contacted me with some very interesting information. It seems there is a team with some specific clues to the Akan Pilgrimage."

The Internet had little to say about the pilgrimage other than what most locals in the area grew up with.

A young priest named Akan had laid out clues to be followed, but no one had ever found even one.

Dejin let the words saturate a bit before replying. "You believe they have found a treasure that has eluded mankind for over a thousand years?"

"Not yet, but they are definitely onto something," Haile replied.

Dejin turned to the window. Outside, some of his soldiers were doing drills. He loved watching the transformation from unskilled bush rube to fighting soldier that happened every day here at the camp, but without real funds, it would all come to a halt. He turned back to his second. "If there is even the slightest chance that these people are onto anything of value, I want it. Take three vehicles and a squad and get to the bottom of it. This is my country. That makes anything hidden here mine."

"Yes, of course," Haile replied.

"Did your contact say where they were headed?" Dejin asked.

"The Sky Church."

Kojo parked the Land Cruiser along the side of an old adobe farmhouse. "This is as far as we go," he said.

Cable exited with his hands back in cuffs. Two officers from the Federal Police Commission had joined the team in hopes of apprehending Stein Osman. As an Interpol agent, Juni was not able to serve a warrant without the help of the local police.

Officer Girma was a young man with dark, happy eyes and a scruffy beard that was two weeks old.

Officer Ruphal had a serious widow's peak and cold, calculating, narrow black eyes on a plump round face.

They rendezvoused with Juni just outside of Mek'ele, a desert city known for its political strife and modern Hyundai manufacturing plant.

Kojo was suspicious of the two newcomers and wasn't shy about it. He exited the vehicle and led the group around a dilapidated building to the weathered corrals behind. "My cousin Mesfin has assured me this is the safest route to the Sky Church. The Tigray rebels are very prevalent in this region. The main roads are not to be trusted. Plus, we can go in a straight line. The most direct road is a very big circle."

Cable paused. "Camels, Kojo? Really. You know, I hate camels."

"It is the camels who hate you, my friend. You must tell them who is boss."

Juni had just about had her fill of bouncing across the wilds of Ethiopia in search of her prey. The barren horizon held little interest for her. "This is the last step. If we don't find Stein at the church, I'm cutting my losses and hauling you back to stand trial."

Cable knew Juni was frustrated. She was out of her element and had nothing but failure and hardship so far to show for it.

"Juni. Did you ever have a case you couldn't solve, so you pinned an innocent to take the fall just to pad your closing rate?"

Juni stared back at Cable, ready to punch him in the face, but he was right. She had never done such a thing.

Cable continued, "A case takes what it takes to solve, you know that. Willing it to an end is just wishful thinking. We will find Stein. That I promise you. I won't stop until we do."

Juni stopped walking. She was a city cop, far removed from everything in her world. Spending the next few days on a beast in the desert was not even on her wildest bucket list. She battled briefly with her options and desires. Bringing Stein Osman in would be worth it. "Enough talk. Let's do this."

Cable held up his cuffed wrists and wiggled them with a wry smile.

"I suppose you have proven yourself, and there is nowhere you can really go out here," Juni said as she reluctantly removed his cuffs.

"Officer Girma. This is Inga. She is the strongest of all the camels and will carry our supplies, and though she likes to wander occasionally, she is a good girl," Kojo said.

"Kush," he encouraged Inga to sit.

She dropped down, and Officer Girma loaded their gear before mounting the camel.

"Interpol Juni, this is Zala. She is very friendly. Make sure you lean back when she stands," Kojo said.

Juni didn't understand why, then Zala started to stand by getting to her rear legs first and leveling out by including her front legs.

"Hut, hut," Kojo said, and his camel started walking. The others dutifully followed.

"What is my camel's name?" Cable asked.

Kojo replied, "Your camel has no name. He was found a few months back wandering in the Danakil Desert without a rider."

"You've given me a camel with no name?"

"You do not like camels. The two of you are a perfect fit."

Cable shook his head in disgust.

They left the small farm behind, heading west to the base of the Semien Mountains, Kojo and his orange beard leading the way.

The front-to-back rocking motion of a camel was unexpected for Juni. It took her a while before her white-knuckled grip relaxed, and she just let the beast do its thing.

The morning sun was still low on the horizon, and the worst heat of the day would soon be here.

The plain ahead stretched as far as the eye could see, broken up by hills that looked like hand-dribbled sandcastles and beyond that, just a shimmer of the Semien Mountains.

"And we couldn't drive over this perfectly flat plain because?" Cable asked.

"This entire area is a salt flat," Kojo said with a sweep of his arm. "The weight of a vehicle would burst through the salt crust on top, and we'd be stuck tight, tires spinning uselessly. Below us is a mixture of mud, salt, and water, depending on the time of year. The camels occasionally break through, but they can get back out. A car would be very stuck."

As if Mother Nature was listening, Inga, the pack camel, broke through the salt crust and stumbled before getting her leg free and continuing.

"Good to know," Cable said with intentional sarcasm. "*I've been through the desert on a camel with no name,*" he sang. "Doesn't have the same ring to it."

"No, but you have a lovely singing voice," Officer Ruphal said with a laugh in his words. The two officers chuckled.

Officer Girma added, "Are we there yet?" This made the two men laugh even harder. Soon Cable and Kojo joined in.

Juni shook her head. It was going to be a long trip.

On the horizon, a train of dots moved off through the undulating, distorted view.

Kojo pointed. "Caravans of camels come to this flat. The riders collect salt blocks to sell throughout the country. It is still chopped out by hand like it has been done for thousands of years."

After a few hours, their caravan passed a couple of rusted trucks that had long ago broken through the salt crust and been abandoned to the desert's whims.

Heatwaves obscured the horizon line as the sun beat down from its zenith.

"Is it just me, or do these camels stink," Juni said.

"We are coming up on the Danakil Depression. A very strange place. You are smelling the sulfur springs," Kojo said.

Cable added, "There are even naturally occurring sulfuric acid ponds, nasty stuff."

"You have been here before?" Juni asked.

"To the Danakil Depression, yes, but I took the long way in an air-conditioned car."

"No rebels back then," Kojo said. "The Danakil Depression is the hottest place on earth and one of the lowest, at over 300 feet below sea level. Three tectonic plates collide there to form some of the planet's most unique landscapes, including an active volcano with a glowing red lava lake."

The 119-degree temperature had Officer Ruphal guzzling from his canteen every few moments. He wiped his mouth with the back of his hand. "Many spirits live here. It is a place to visit, but not stay."

Juni looked over at what she considered foolish superstition from Ruphal, but in this remote part of the world, she had to agree with his second conclusion.

The sulfur smell intensified as the brown landscape transformed to lime green, royal blue, and cornflower yellow, all set against red and orange hills. The colors were spectacular, otherworldly. Bright ponds bubbled deadly toxins, and crystalline shapes grew from the ground in random patterns. Small geysers squirted liquid into the air, and sulfur springs flowed across white ribbons of minerals.

Juni pulled her camel next to Cable's. They rode in silence for a time.

"I'm curious. How did you two meet?"

"Kojo?"

She nodded.

"I was staying in a hostel in Bahir Dar, up by Lake Tana. It's a beautiful place. Anyway, there's a nice little bar down the street, and it all started with this girl."

Juni held up a hand. "Never mind, I don't think I want to hear it."

Kojo pulled his camel over to hear the story.

"Kojo thought she was a girl," Cable said.

"So did you," Kojo added.

"Yes, at first, but then a couple of things started to tell."

Kojo held his hands in front of his chest, making a boob-like gesticulation. "She looked like a girl."

"Yes, she looked a lot like a girl."

"I had too much Cheka to drink," Kojo said.

"You were very drunk, and you refused to listen to me."

Juni looked back and forth between Cable and Kojo, waiting for more.

"I must admit...I took her home."

"We have sworn a pact of secrecy beyond that moment," Cable said.

"Good, because I don't want to hear about it," Juni said.

Kojo had a face-wide smile. "Your Amharic was terrible back then."

"It's not much better now," Cable admitted.

Inga, the camel to Cable's right, suddenly let out a high-pitched grunt. The salt crust had given way, and she was sinking into the slurry below the crust. It was deeper here, and the camel was having trouble escaping. For every thrashing movement the animal made, it just sank deeper into the slush, and as it sank, the squeal grew in pitch.

Kojo spun and jumped from his ride. "Get a rope around her neck. She has all our supplies!" Kojo cried out as Inga thrashed. The weight of her pack was exacerbating the situation.

As soon as Officer Girma's camel sat, he grabbed a rope, hoping to use it to help pull Inga from her turmoil.

Cable was right behind the man, but he paused, sensing something was wrong. The camel was shrieking like something terrible was attacking it. And the smell of sulfur was intense.

"Girma, stop!" Cable cried.

But it was too late. Girma crashed through the salt crust into the slush below. He floundered for just a second before he, too, let out a blood-curdling cry.

The weight of Girma's torso drove him down before his arms arrested his fall on the surrounding surface. His first reaction was to gasp. Searing chemical fumes shot into his lungs, burning his trachea and diaphragm. Then, an equally intense pain covered his extremities as his skin started to burn away. The pain was so intense Girma lost all control, and panic consumed him, causing his body to thrash wildly.

"Girma, toss the rope!" Cable yelled out.

As Kojo arrived from the lead camel, he stopped next to Cable. "That's not salt water."

"It's acid. Help me form a chain," Cable said as he laid down on his stomach and slithered his way out to help Girma. Kojo joined him lying flat and taking second position behind Cable.

Girma realized, somewhere in his limbic system, what was happening and tossed the end of the rope in Cable's direction. The part of the brain responsible for survival was now operating at one hundred percent. He desperately tried to pull himself up onto the salt crust, like a breakthrough victim on a frozen pond.

Kojo grabbed Cable's ankles and supported him as Cable wormed as fast as he dared across the thin mineral crust out to help Girma. Fingertips finally reached the rope and Cable quickly took out the slack and pulled.

Officer Ruphal joined in to help, as did Juni, pulling Kojo, who was connected to Cable.

The salt around Cable cracked, but his spread-out weight seemed to do the trick.

Kojo held tight to Cable's ankles as Juni and Ruphal pulled the human chain back away from the danger.

Slowly, Girma was pulled from the slurry. He had succumbed to the high level of pain and was only mumbling now, half-conscious but still able to hold the rope that was his salvation.

As his torso started to pull free from the liquid death, a horrifying sight filled Juni's vision. The concentrated sulfuric acid had done its worst. Girma's lower extremities had been eaten away to nothing but bones, a few scraps of muscle, and gore.

Cable reactively let go of the rope connected to the now half-corpse he was pulling. Girma stared back at him with lifeless eyes and a contorted mouth. His skeleton trailed off from his remaining innards as he slowly sank back down and dissolved.

Juni looked away. "Oh no. That poor man."

Cable noticed that Inga was also no longer among the living. Her body was slowly dissolving as well, sinking into the caustic stew below, along with all their water and supplies.

"We have to go back," Cable voiced.

"To what purpose?" Juni deadpanned. "We are here, and nothing can change what has happened. Going back will only give Stein Osman more time to slip away. We owe it to Officer Girma to make his death count."

Cable realized she was right. Dani was in the hands of that madman, and Girma and Inga were gone. The only thing left was to catch Stein and save Dani.

"We must ration our water," Kojo said, holding up his half-empty personal canteen.

Officer Ruphal's canteen was almost empty, and a feeling of dread suddenly filled him.

Kojo moved his camel out, taking point again. "It is a day and a half to the Semien Mountains…and the next source of water."

They were in real trouble.

Colonel Haile sat in the front passenger seat of the lead SUV, followed by two technicals, each mounted with DShK belt-fed machine guns. A rutted and potholed-filled road known as the 830 highway pointed west, with just enough room for two cars to pass on the straightaways. It skirted around the Danakil Desert, an unforgiving place forgotten to time. His sunglasses cut the intense glare of the sun that bounced off the brown barren landscape that gave none who entered relief.

Haile had grown up not far from here in the small village of Gelebeda. He had played soccer in the dirt and chased butterflies. As a teenager, his life had taken a turn. His father, adamant about the lack of representation for the Northern Tigray people in the capital, had entered a most dangerous game. Politics. Men with guns started to hang around the house for protection. Haile's outdoor activities were curbed, and his time with friends dwindled.

As his father climbed the political ladder, they said goodbye to their rural home and moved to the city. Eventually, they made their way to the capital. It meant better schooling for young Haile but a loss of almost everything he loved. Resentment flared, and soon, he dedicated himself to anything that would go against his parents' wishes. He dropped out of college and joined an underground subversive group called the Fet'ani Ābiyoti, bent on change for change's sake.

Haile was smart and driven, two things that pushed him up the ladder of success in the group. He partook in several attacks and marches to further their message of chaos and became quite good at gathering intel. At one point, information he provided the group caused the deaths of his parents and several other serving politicians in an explosion that rocked the capital and his world.

Haile dropped out of the Fet'ani Ābiyoti and returned to his homeland, lost and listless. His parents had died without making one bit of difference in the North.

After circling the drain for several months, Haile crossed paths with another politically charged do-gooder, Dejin Kidane.

Haile had considered killing the man and saving the North a lot of pain and suffering. But the more time he spent around him, the more Haile realized this was a man who could instigate real change. A man who was willing and able to go all the way.

It pulled Haile from his slump, and he found a path that both inspired and suited him. Rebellion. A channel for Haile to focus his angst and the only way, in his mind, forward for Tigray and its people. He would commit his entire soul to achieving freedom from the tyranny in the South.

The driver called out over the sound of the six-cylinder diesel, "Do you think they are behind or in front of us?"

Colonel Haile pulled himself from his thoughts. "My focus is what to do once we find them. According to my contact, there is a girl with them who is the key to finding the treasure. She is my main concern. The others can bleed out in the sand for all I care."

Dani looked down at the two very battered-looking SUVs parked next to the dirt road. The SOCATA TBM 700C2 banked around and dropped into its final approach. Using a public road was risky, but this part of the desert allowed for a good view in both directions.

She had listened to the pilot argue with Fannie over his concern with taking the plane into the heart of rebel territory before they had left Wikro, but her ability to overpay and intimidate won the day.

Once they landed, the gear was offloaded and the two tired vehicles headed west as the plane hurried back into the safety of the air. The local drivers were being paid more than they would make in a year and had no such qualms about the rebels. They lived and worked among them every day.

After several miles along the main roadway, the vehicles turned off onto a trail. It would take longer to reach their destination, but the odds of getting there unmolested would increase significantly.

"You know the Sky Church is considered the most dangerous church in the world," Dani said, breaking the silence.

Stein looked over his shoulder from the passenger seat. "Human sacrifices?" he asked, with a bit of trepidation.

"No. Nothing of the sort. It's carved into a cliff face nearly 800 meters up. And the path to get there is very perilous."

Stein feigned a smile. "Good thing you are going first."

"What, and take a chance at losing your best clue finder?"

Stein's forced smile died instantly as his dull eyes processed her words.

"Not to worry, I will go first," Fannie said. "And you will be roped to me." She looked across at Dani in the seat next to her.

They rode in silence again for a time, the rough road creating a synchronized ballet of sorts as bodies bounced and swayed in unison. The sun had started its journey to the horizon and the promise of a cooler temperature to follow.

Stein looked across the never-ending sameness of the landscape.

His mind flashed back to a different time in his life. A time when he was content with everyday normalcy. It seemed like a lifetime ago. His father was a brusque man with a judgmental eye who only saw the flaws in his son. It had been an impossible barrier to overcome. Nothing seemed to please.

Stein had molded himself to fit the structure of his father's requirements in an attempt to avoid such scrutiny but had never truly been happy. College provided some reprieve, but spending summers working in the family business was unbearable.

One night, he had eavesdropped on his parents arguing about finances. It seemed their days of privilege were coming to an end. The business was more of an anchor than a cash cow. Stein took it upon himself to help his parents out. That night, he crept into the warehouse and set it ablaze. Surely, a nice insurance payout would right their ship. He remembered watching the flames consume his bane with zeal.

Unfortunately, his father had let their policy lapse, and Stein had done nothing more than put an end to their family's future.

After three months of struggling, his father took his own life.

His mother lost her way and ended up in a clinic before finally slipping away one night in her sleep.

The family estate was slowly sold off to pay debts until only the main house was left. Stein dropped out of college and struggled to find his path. As the world closed in around him, he became more desperate.

He grabbed two family heirlooms his father had been particularly proud of and walked away from the family home just before the bank's repossessors showed up. He found a buyer for the pieces, and with that transaction, an idea began to grow. *Find a niche and fill it.* They were his father's words, but now they became Stein's mission. Artifacts and antiquities were always going up in value. It was a growth industry. The

Gulf War provided an almost inexhaustible supply and the black market provided opportunities that could never be taken advantage of in legitimate business.

Stein evolved and flourished. He had found wealth and power to some degree but was anxious to prove himself and take his efforts to the next level. He needed a way to leave his mark on this world, something his father had failed to do. Now that he was free of his father's thumb, he would show the old man how things were really done. He would build a world of wealth and power beyond what his father could have imagined. Stein Osman would make a name for himself that lasted through the centuries. All that was now within reach. Wealth, power, and fame. He would have it all.

"What will you do with the treasure if we find it?" Dani asked.

The words pulled Stein back to the moment. He answered without looking back. "Treasure holds intrinsic value to the finder. Lost treasure holds a degree of fame along with that value. Long-lost ancient treasure holds fame and wealth that withstands the sands of time. I plan to leave my mark on this world by joining the ranks of the archaeologist elite who have changed what we know of history."

"Carve your name in stone," Dani said.

"What?"

"Carve your name in a prominent stone, and you will last through the centuries. The only thing keeping the centuries-old artists of cave paintings from fame is they forgot to sign their work."

Stein looked back over his shoulder at Dani with a restrained scowl.

"Just in case this whole treasure hunt is a bust," Dani added.

"I appreciate your concern, but we will get to the end of this journey, and I will have my day in the sun. The only way you will be a part of it is if you do everything in your power to make that happen."

Dani doubted Stein was the kind of man who would share anything, let alone an ounce of his yearned-for archaeology fame. For a man so consumed by the past, he seemed to sell artifacts off with little regard for anything but their monetary value.

Fannie cut off Dani's thoughts. "What do you hope to find at the Sky Church?"

"So far, the swastika, or symbol of truth here in Ethiopia, has been integral to this quest. So, I am hoping to find a swastika and an additional clue or the final resting place of whatever we are searching—"

Stein interrupted pointedly. "What we are searching for is a reason to keep you alive, Ms. Tran."

CHAPTER FOURTEEN

D ARKNESS ONLY EASED THE INTENSITY of the sun, not the radiation of heat from the ground. With no supplies and nothing to eat or drink, the caravan continued well past midnight before settling down for the evening at the base of Arta Ale. The active volcano glowed red-orange against the night sky. Small molten particles dispelled in the air like a dying Roman candle.

Here the sulfur smell had decreased as they started the gradual climb out of the depression.

Kojo had them circle the camels and huddle on the inside for the night. "Jackals roam this area, very dangerous."

Officer Ruphal had long since finished his water and was suffering from the effects of dehydration.

Everyone was exhausted, but sleep would be a hard-fought commodity.

Reaching temperatures over 120 degrees Fahrenheit during the day, the desert here would only drop to ninety-eight tonight. A person without water here would not last twenty-four hours. The Arta Ale basaltic shield volcano grumbled occasionally, and its persistent lava lake bubbled and popped inside the cauldron.

"I've never slept next to a volcano before," Juni said.

Cable turned her way. "Try not to think about it."

"Yes," Officer Ruphal mumbled in a gravelly voice, "it can generate quite terrifying thoughts."

"The odds of us being killed by lava tonight are very slight," Kojo said. "Now, being eaten by lions or jackals is much more likely. Also, getting mauled by a rhino or buffalo is common. The Bitis has been known to slither and curl up next to a person while they sleep. Envenomation is not a good way to die for sure, but the lowly mosquito is responsible for more deaths in Ethiopia than anything else, even war." As if on cue, a buzzing around Kojo grabbed his attention before he slapped the intruder into the next world.

Juni changed the subject. "How much longer?"

"We will see the Sky Church tomorrow afternoon," Kojo said.

The night dragged on. Cable couldn't find a comfortable position in which to sleep. The camel was too hot, and the warm ground was too hard. He finally nodded off just before the sky started to turn pink.

Kojo had the caravan up and running before sunrise.

Juni kept looking over her shoulder, afraid for the moment when the sun would clear the horizon and start to cook them all again. She had sipped her last drop of water, and her mouth was already dry again. It would be a long day.

The topography slowly changed back to a barren plain with patches of low grass as they left the black-rock volcano and the Danakil Depression behind.

Officer Ruphal was just hanging on as his body wobbled with the motion of his camel.

Cable cleared his dry throat. "Kojo, what are the chances we will—"

"Water, water," Officer Ruphal mumbled behind Cable. He spurred his camel into a gallop and sped past the riders.

It took Kojo a second to realize what was happening. He cried out to the policeman, "No!" before spurring his camel into a gallop to give chase.

Cable and Juni did their best to get their beasts in motion, but their lack of camel experience was working against them.

Officer Ruphal was driven by severe dehydration. His brain was foggy, as the blood that flowed through it was syrupy and thick. It affected his speed of thought and reaction time. As the beautiful lake in the distance grew closer, he could have sworn his mouth was starting to salivate, even though it was still dry as aged leather.

Ruphal jumped from his camel at the shoreline and pulled his shirt and gun belt away before running into the warm water. It was refreshing and magical. He sipped from the surface, hoping the sun had done its job of killing any bacteria within the first few inches of the lake. It was like he was being given the gift of life as the liquid poured down his throat. The water tasted like a penny on steroids with an extreme metallic twang. But just being in the water was a welcome respite. He laid back, closing his eyes. Someone from the shore was yelling at him, and he picked up his head to see Kojo gesticulating wildly. That's when the first twang of pain started to consume him. He didn't register the source at first because it was coming from everywhere.

Every molecule of moisture in his body was being pulled from his essence, and because he had consumed some of the caustic water, the same was happening on the inside as well.

As Cable galloped forward, a vast brown lake appeared. The waters called to him after being so dehydrated and thirsty.

Two camels stood by the shore. Kojo stood next to them, calling Officer Ruphal back from the water with great urgency.

Cable didn't wait for his camel to sit. He jumped down and ran to his friend. "What's wrong?"

"This lake is not as it looks."

Cable realized Officer Ruphal was not swimming in the water but flogging and writhing about.

"We must get him out." Cable started to run to the water.

Kojo grabbed his arm, stopping him. "No. It is too late."

Officer Ruphal had never felt such pain. Every pore in his body was burning, like ten thousand cuts. His stomach lurched, doubling him over, and he almost went underwater for good. Ruphal thrashed his way back to shore as the pain ratcheted up even higher.

Juni's camel finally arrived. "What's happening?"

Officer Ruphal's brain was completely misfiring as he swam-crawled into the shallows. Finally, it was too much, and he succumbed to his fatal mistake just as he was reaching an arm out for help that would never come. His face, a mask of horror frozen in time, sunken and hollow like he had suddenly aged 100 years. His skin crusted over with an uneven salt-like coating. Even his open eyes had the crystalline veneer.

"The lake here is supersaturated with sodium carbonite. It is a caustic alkaline brine that kills anything entering its waters. Even a small exposure can kill. Because it is alkaline instead of acidic, it fools many animals. I'm so sorry, but I was unable to help..." Kojo's words faded out.

Juni was aghast. Looking at her fellow officer's contorted pose did nothing to relieve her. The coating on his skin made the corpse look more like a stone statue than the man who had been part of their caravan just moments ago.

Cable turned away and encouraged his camel to sit before climbing on.

"We must press on, or we will be the next victims of this desert. Drinkable water is less than an hour from here...hut hut," Kojo said once he was back on his camel.

Juni picked up Officer Ruphal's gun and belt, adding the pistol to her own. From here on out, the more armed she was, the better she would feel.

The five camels and three riders pressed on. Water had suddenly become more important than this case or anything else.

As they moved along the water's edge, there was a macabre museum of displays. First, a bird sitting on a dead branch. It was crusted and dried out, its hollow eye sockets the only indicator of how long it had been perched there. Next, a water buffalo standing tall and proud but crusted over and frozen in time. A leathery fruit bat surrounded by a long-dead thorn bush. It still hung upside down, a grisly grimace hiding its torturous death. All victims of the lake that turned life to stone.

The spring sprang from the rock and then disappeared into the sand just a few feet beyond. If you didn't know where to look, you would die of thirst within feet of its lifesaving waters. The forlorn group filled their canteens and wet themselves down with the cool, refreshing liquid. The camels crowded in for their turn.

Juni could feel her body respond almost instantly. They stayed for a while, drinking and taking turns cooling off.

"Not much farther, maybe an hour," Kojo said as he remounted his camel.

The sun was just starting its descent, but the oppressive heat seemed almost normal after two days of cooking. The barren, flat landscape transformed into low rolling hills with sporadic bushes and trees. Up ahead grew a collection of sandstone monoliths stretching into the blue sky. To the left was an exceptionally tall finger, standing like a sentinel for all to see.

Cable was the first to notice it. A prominent hole carved about three-quarters of the way up the cliff face of the finger. "That is going to be a serious climb," he said.

"Yes, the Sky Church is not for the faint of heart," Kojo said.

"I don't see any signs of Stein and his merry band of thugs," Juni said.

"I think it's 'merry band of thieves.'"

"What?"

"Never mind," Cable mumbled.

"Does that mean he has come and gone while we were playing desert Russian roulette?"

"That, or we have beaten him here," Cable finished.

"I hope you are right, Cable."

Kojo stopped and dismounted his camel once it sat. "This is as far as our camels go."

Cable looked to Juni to see what she was thinking.

Juni scanned the vast horizon line, seeing nothing but emptiness. "Why on earth would you ever build a church here, let alone on the top of a cliff?"

"It is a very safe way to—"

"That was rhetorical, Kojo."

Kojo stopped explaining and tried not to look embarrassed.

Cable craned his neck up the face of the sandstone pinnacle. "I'm going to go up and see if Stein has already been here."

"Good, because high places are not a friend to me. I will not be joining you," Kojo said.

Juni pointed to a rock outcropping. "Kojo and I will post up here and wait for our guest to arrive or until you get back."

Cable nodded, collected his canteen, and reached a hand out to Juni. "I'll need your phone to take any pictures up there."

"Not a chance. In case you forgot, we are not here for a scavenger hunt, we are on a manhunt. My only concern is the capture of Stein Osman."

Cable dropped his hand and let out a sigh. *Some people would never change.*

"Cable," Kojo said as he tossed his flip phone to him. *And some could be depended on no matter the odds.*

"Thanks, brother," Cable said as he turned and started up the single-track trail. The narrow path meandered up toward the stone cliffs rising steeply ahead. Cable was greeted by a sign…of sorts. Two carved sandstone slabs held up by wires attached to a log set across two boulders. He couldn't read the Amharic writing, but he figured it said, 'Church This Way' or 'Kiss Your Butt Goodbye If You Pass Through Here.'

The path almost instantly grew steep as he worked his way up a slot between walls.

Juni had Kojo move the camels out of sight. She pulled out her two pistols and checked to make sure they were loaded. "You know how to use one of these?"

"I prefer something a bit more traditional in these parts." Kojo pulled an AK-47 from a hidden holster on his camel. He racked the slide and chambered a round.

Juni nodded, impressed. "We'll want the high ground. I'll take that boulder over there," she said, pointing.

Kojo moved up and to the right, selecting a spot of his own. "Okay, now what?" he called down to Juni.

"Now, we wait."

A few trees provided shade as Cable pulled hand over hand up the cliff wall. It had a couple of footholds carved in the stone and a permanent rope attached from above. He hauled and climbed his way to the top.

Once up, he found a narrow path that moved left along the steep face. It was barely two feet wide, with no safety rail or rope. He turned himself sideways and skirted along the smooth path. Cable could see that the peak he was climbing separated from the main rock that held the church. The thin trail ended, forcing Cable to climb upward again.

This time, a sun-dried log wedged in the sandstone was used to aid in his journey. As he reached the top, two rickety logs stretched across from his side of the rock to the other side, with a steep drop below. It was a good 600-foot express ride down on either side. Again, no safety rails or ropes of any kind. Cable put his hands out to his sides and tried not to look down. He focused on his feet as they stepped across the uneven bridge made from two tree trunks. A slight wobble had his hand fluttering to regain his balance. If Kojo didn't like heights, this part would have been too much for him. Cable jumped the last few feet and gripped the rock, thankful to be on solid ground again.

The trail moved upward across a couple of boulders and then turned left again. This narrow path was about three feet wide along the cliff's edge, but it was beveled downward like a ramp expediting your way to the promised land. A slip or misstep here would be fatal.

Cable finally released the breath he had been holding once he reached the level pad outside the church's entrance. He sat for a time, letting his heart slow as he removed his shoes and took a drink from his canteen. A warm breeze cooled the sweat on his face as he took in the view out across the valley. It was heavenly, not a building or human in sight. The doorway was a natural opening in the rock. Cable ducked his head and stepped inside.

It took a few moments before his eyes adjusted.

The church was hand-carved in the fifth century. Getting here and carving the rooms was a miracle in itself back then, but the colorful frescoes were truly breathtaking. Walls, columns, and vaulted ceilings were all covered with faces and patterns from the past. The dry air and lack of sunshine had preserved the artworks in their original perfection. Something very few historical sites can claim.

Stories from the Bible were painted in every direction Cable looked. One alcove held portraits of the Nine Saints who started the church here, while another had the twelve apostles. To the left, a horse galloped through the air, its rider regally seated. Cable took his time, not entirely sure what he was looking for.

From out of nowhere, a priest appeared. He was older, maybe sixty, wrapped in a white robe and turban. On closer inspection, Cable realized he was wearing a collared shirt and slacks under his robe. The priest gave him a gap-toothed smile. Cable bowed slightly, putting his hands together as he did. The priest started jabbering in Amharic, a language in which Cable was not well versed. He replied with one word, "*Memeliketi*." Cable moved his hand around as a gesture to his word, 'looking.'

The priest seemed to understand and stepped back to watch. His black eyes tracked Cable's every move.

Cable didn't mind. He figured an American all the way up here in the priest's church was not so common. He let his eyes scan the walls and ceiling. Nothing popped out. Was this another dry hole?

Dani leaned low to get a full view as they approached the majestic rock outcropping dominating the surrounding valley. The trip to get here had been laborious. The driver used every side road and gulch to stay off the main roads. It had cost them two tires and one radiator boil-over. Everything that broke could be repaired, but not the loss of time.

Stein understood logical delays, but after the second blowout he was starting to lose his cool.

Fannie leaned down and looked out the windshield. "We're going up that?"

Dani nodded. "Almost to the top."

Fannie sat back in her seat. She had been through some very extreme operations in her past but had never had a desire to rock climb. She pushed her mind to focus on anything but the upcoming ascent.

They pulled to a stop, and everyone got out into the blast furnace air. Dani stretched but stopped suddenly when she caught Stein admiring her form. *Could this trip get any worse?*

Fannie grabbed her Vektor R5 and racked a round in the chamber. She scanned the horizon, seeing nothing to concern her, but something had her senses on alert. It was as if she was being watched.

Luka picked up on his boss's vibe and grabbed his G36. Both weapons took the same ammunition, but professionals liked what they liked.

They spread out slightly and moved toward the trailhead. Dani looked up to the imposing sandstone walls ahead. After doing some research on the Sky Church, she was excited to see it for real. The Internet had done a good job showing the difficulty involved in the climb up, but the inside of the church was poorly documented. She felt confident this was the next stop on their quest.

"That's far enough. Drop your weapons or die where you stand," Juni shouted from behind her boulder. "Stein Osman, Agent Eklund of Interpol. You are under arrest."

"Cops?" Stein said to himself, mostly confused by this turn of events.

"I said drop your weapons. We have you surrounded, and I won't ask again."

Dani backed away slowly. She didn't want anyone to get the idea of grabbing her as a human shield.

"Blue," Fannie called out just loud enough for her team to hear. It was one of several code words they had practiced and trained for. "Okay, we are giving up don't shoot." She raised her weapon to make a big show of giving up. Meanwhile, Tarik and Luka moved their weapons in the direction of the voice. Automatic fire suddenly filled the space around Juni and she ducked just in time.

Stein dove to the ground, and the air around him exploded in gunfire. The team continued to fire while running for cover.

Kojo added his heavy 7.62x39mm bullets to the action and got the attention of several shooters for his troubles.

The driver from the lead SUV fell, unmoving.

Dani turned and sprinted away.

Luka took a round to his calf but managed to find cover. He ripped the bottom of his shirt and quickly stemmed the bleeding.

Fannie used her full-auto setting to spray bullets back at her targets as she pulled Stein behind one of the vehicles.

Once everyone had repositioned, the firing back and forth became more intermittent.

Luka yelled from his place of concealment. "I think there are only two shooters."

Stein edged his head up over the hood and took a quick look. "Agent Eklund. It seems you are the one who is surrounded and outgunned. I suggest you put your gun down and come out with your hands up."

A couple of shots from behind a boulder answered his suggestion.

"Don't do it, Interpol Juni, they will shoot you," Kojo called out as he poured a few more rounds down range.

A sort of stalemate ensued. Juni and Kojo's only advantage was the higher ground, but Stein's team had more guns and a lot more bullets.

Fannie used hand signals to get Tarik to work his way around to the right and try to get behind them. She fired off a fusillade of rounds as he sprinted right.

Cable moved to the priest and used the same word again. This time, he dipped his finger in his canteen and drew a swastika on the sandstone floor.

"Äwo, teketeli," he said, waving his hand for Cable to follow.

Äwo, Cable recognized. It meant 'yes.' He followed the priest to a far alcove where a crowned woman was riding a galloping horse and holding a sword above her head. She had large dark eyes and a serious expression. Her red cape flowed behind her in the wind as she raced forward. Below the mural was a border that framed it and hidden in the pattern was a lone swastika.

The priest pointed to the woman and said, "*Nigiiti Gudit.*"

Cable repeated the words, locking them in his brain, "*Nigiiti Gudit.*" He would have to ask Kojo what it meant once he got back down. He took a couple of pictures of the mural, amazed that it had lasted so many years in such pristine condition.

He felt small when he looked around. The majesty of this church made one feel their place in the universe—a grand design so big our existence had no bearing. Even though Cable was running against time, he felt peace here.

The priest looked at Cable and gave him a genuine smile. This was his favorite thing here in the chapel—watching as visitors connected with the spirit of the church and the history of his ancestors. It always reinforced his beliefs in an almighty and loving God.

Cable's experience with the big guy was not quite so black-and-white. The real world was filled with gray and it made it extremely difficult to find the peace and comfort of someone much greater than you, especially with the world's volume set so high.

You would literally have to find a cave far from the madding crowd to commune with such a person. In an instant, Cable knew why the elders of this church had gone to such extremes to place it here.

He smiled to himself and was grateful for the insight. As he reached his hand out to thank the priest, a barrage of gunfire down below interrupted.

The priest froze.

Cable moved quickly to the exit and looked down over the cliff. He could not see what was happening from his vantage point, plus there was nothing he could do to aid in a gun battle anyhow. Cable contemplated his options. He needed to get down the cliff and see what was going on. Then, he could make a proper decision.

He stepped back into the church to tell the priest, but there was no sign of the man. *Weird.*

The shooting down below had slowed, and he could hear nothing but unintelligible shouting from so high up.

Colonel Haile lifted his hand to stop the conversation that was happening between the men behind him. The diesel engine purred along. He waited and listened. Sure enough, there was gunfire in the distance. He strained to see what was up ahead, but they were still about five minutes out.

He picked up his radio. "Form a line and spread out. Be ready for a fight."

The SUV stayed on the road. The two technical pickups with heavy machine guns mounted in their beds separated left and right. The soldiers in the SUV started getting their rifles ready.

As they came around a corner, two older SUVs could be seen parked at the trailhead of the Sky Church. Shooters from two sides were taking potshots back and forth.

"Do you know who they are?" the driver asked.

"It doesn't matter. All that matters is we get the girl and the treasure. Everyone else is expendable." Colonel Haile issued more orders and checked his own weapon.

The two technicals came in firing from the left and right flanks, the .30 caliber rounds destroying everything they hit. Colonel Haile in the SUV followed slightly behind.

Guards dove for new cover, and Fannie spun at the new threat. It took her about two seconds to assess the situation. It was unattainable. She tossed Stein into the cab of the lead SUV and dove across him to the driver's seat. Fingering the key while staying low, she was relieved to hear the diesel come to life. She gunned the vehicle, heading away from the oncoming threat as bullets pinged and penetrated the metal skin. Luka limped out from behind cover, waving for them to pick him up, blood clearly soaking his left leg.

"We don't have time. Leave him!" Stein shouted to Fannie as the glass next to him shattered. She cringed as she went against her moral soldier's code and floored the vehicle past her colleague, leaving Luka exposed and behind. A bullet from one of the trucks found its mark, and Luka spun to the ground.

"Get that girl!" Colonel Haile shouted, seeing the lone female figure running from the gunfight.

The SUV turned from the road and quickly caught up to the woman.

Dani tried to keep running, but the vehicle just followed behind, waiting for her to tire. She finally stopped and put her hands on her knees, heaving in gulps of air as the vehicle pulled alongside. The colonel rolled down his window. He held his Colt Python .357 Magnum loosely in his hand, casually pointing in Dani's direction. "You are with us now, okay?" he said in broken English.

Dani nodded, knowing she had no other alternative.

The SUV returned to the trailhead where the technicals had the battle won. Colonel Haile exited the vehicle and looked around at the carnage.

Tarik lay sprawled on a nearby boulder with half his head missing. The remaining driver lay dead in the dirt, just out of reach of his driver's side door. The other guard was down, taking his last breath, and Juni and Kojo had surrendered.

Colonel Haile was still at a loss as to what was happening. He approached Juni and looked her over. Her hair was a mess, and her clothes were filthy. Sunburned skin glowed back at him.

One of his soldiers spoke softly to him and handed her badge over to Haile.

"Agent Eklund. You are far from home."

She had no reply.

"I am a curious man. Can you explain this?" He waved his hand around.

Dani sat in the back seat of the SUV next to an armed guard. She strained to hear what was being said outside.

"I am here to serve a warrant for a Stein Osman."

"And this Stein Osman is?" Haile prompted.

"He's the one that got away."

"I see…I'm guessing he didn't want to be arrested."

Juni put her head down in defeat. Ever since coming to Africa, she had continued to slip down the rabbit hole.

"And this is what, your police escort?"

"No. My guide."

"Kojo, Colonel Haile. Very nice to meet you," Kojo said with a bit too much enthusiasm. Kojo knew just how ruthless this man was and had no desire to share the fate of so many other countrymen.

"Your orange beard intrigues me, so I will not kill you."

Kojo visibly relaxed.

Haile rattled off something in Tigrinya, and two soldiers grabbed Kojo and hauled him off.

Kojo cried out, not fully understanding what Colonel Haile had said.

"Now. Hmm, what to do with you." Colonel Haile had turned his attention back to Juni. "Accidents happen all the time in this part of the world. No one will be surprised if they never hear from you again."

He pulled out his Colt Python.357 Magnum and looked at it, trying to decide. "On the other hand, as a burgeoning country, we need to play by the rules if we are to be accepted into the civilized world. A good faith gesture could help with that." He adjusted his sunglasses as he thought.

Juni stared the man down. "History won't be kind to you," she stood tall and unwavering.

Colonel Haile matched her gaze. They were both strong and determined, willing to do what it takes to get the job done. There were no future plans for a family, a vacation, or a retirement party. Just two soldiers from two very different wars, thrust into a life-and-death conflict in the middle of a forgotten land.

Colonel Haile didn't hate the woman, he just had no time for her. "Sometimes…you just gotta get your rocks off." He pointed his pistol and shot Juni in the head. She was dead before she hit the ground.

Haile turned to his men, switching back to his native tongue. "Okay, let's go check out this treasure. Bring the girl."

CHAPTER FIFTEEN

C ABLE SCRAMBLED DOWN THE CLIFF face, almost slipping and taking the shortcut to the bottom. He grabbed the rope and arrested his fall at the last second. His fingers burned from the friction, but he didn't let go.

Two bullets suddenly ricocheted next to him, and he ducked his head from the flying rock shards.

"Stop. We need him."

The voice came from below, and it was familiar. Dani. She was still alive, but who or why were they shooting at him? Stein must have lost his patience or his mind.

A voice he didn't recognize called up in broken English. "Cable, stay where you are. We are coming to you."

Cable hesitated. Who was Dani caught up with this time? He waited and watched as five soldiers with guns climbed into view.

Cable could see the look of terror on Dani's face. These men were not to be trifled with.

He led them back up the treacherous trail and into the chapel, his muscles burning from exhaustion.

Colonel Haile stepped inside to the cooler temperature and removed his sunglasses. He looked around. "Another useless distraction from our purpose. The people here put such great faith in these churches, but they are nothing but a physical history book. A reason to hope when the only hope is this." He held up his gun. "What you can do with this and this?" He pointed to his head with his free hand. "Now, where's the treasure?"

Dani looked to Cable, who nodded to the small alcove with the woman on horseback.

Dani's mouth nearly dropped to the floor. "The Warrior Queen," she said reverently.

Cable repeated the words the priest had told him, "*Nigiiti Gudit.*" He looked around, but there was still no sign of the priest.

"Queen Gudit was one of the most badass women in history."

Cable looked back at Dani, suddenly very interested. So did Colonel Haile.

"Legend has it that Gudit was a Beta Jew. She was persecuted for it in an almost all-Christian state. She suffered marginalization for not converting, so she pushed back. For her alleged blasphemy, her breasts were cut off, and she was sold into slavery. Well, skip forward a decade, and she had gone from slave to queen with a very big army and a whole lotta hate for the status quo here. She attacked the capital at Axum and decimated their army. To say she got revenge on the royal family would be underselling it. Each and every one of them suffered far worse than they had done to her. She ruled this kingdom for something like another forty years."

"I know of this bedtime story, but what does it have to do with the treasure?" Haile asked.

"First of all, we are not sure there is a treasure, but I truly believe there is a pilgrimage and we are following it to whatever is at the end. This right here is our next clue, but I will need some computer time to determine our next stop," Dani said.

"For your sake, I suggest you make sure there is a treasure. I am not here for a pilgrimage, nor am I a patient man."

Dani sighed. The colonel was no better than Stein. Just another impatient male with a god complex and a gun. This is why she had stopped dating.

Colonel Haile rattled off a few commands in Tigrinya and stepped back. One guard grabbed Dani and escorted her out of the church. "He will take you to a computer," Haile said.

"What about Cable? I need him," Dani called out.

"He will be along shortly."

Two other guards pointed their guns at Cable, daring him to speak. They pushed him to the floor and bound his hands and feet. Another guard went about attaching some C4 packets to the mural wall in the church with a Ramset, a gunpowder-actuated nail gun that can drive hardened nails into stone, concrete, and even steel.

Haile leaned down to Cable. "The trail ends here. A wise man once said, 'Three people can keep a secret if two are dead.'"

"Benjamin Franklin," Cable added.

"You can tell him hi from me when you see him." Haile turned and left the church.

The soldier who had set the explosives on the mural then used the Ramset to lock Cable's ropes into the stone floor. He took one last look around before setting the timer for five minutes and leaving.

Cable rocked back and forth. There was wiggle room, but no way he was going to pull free of the ropes with their anchors sunk into the stone floor. He tried to concentrate on the knots binding his hands behind his back. Beads of sweat almost instantly popped on his forehead as he looked over at the timer, clearly visible but out of reach. Three-twenty-five...three-twenty-four. Cable strained and fought, but whoever had tied the knots was a real pro. There was no way he was getting loose. Eventually, he let go and stopped fighting. He used the last seconds of his life to take in the holy feeling in this place. His eyes scanned from one mural to the next. They were amazing and beautiful. This was what he wanted to fill his head with before his number was called.

Dani looked up to the hole some 600 feet above her in the cliff face. She had hoped Cable would appear, scrambling down the stone, but instead, a violent explosion rocked the air, sending rocks and dust and much of the church out into the sky. Sixteen hundred years of history and tradition were gone in an instant, and the one man she had true feelings for with it. She dropped her head and sobbed softly, unaware of hands grabbing her in inappropriate places and pulling her along. In fact, it took nearly an hour before she came back to terms with her situation.

After another mindless passage of time, the convoy pulled to a stop next to a small house. It was made of adobe and tin. A guard went inside and came back out a few minutes later. He spoke with Colonel Haile.

Haile turned back to Dani. "Will a tablet work?"

"What?" Dani said, slowly coming out of her stupor.

"Will a tablet work? For the search?"

Dani nodded. "Yes."

She was escorted inside and a satellite phone was used with a data pack to connect her to the Internet. Over in the corner was a skinny man shaking in fear. He was lucky his wife and kids were off visiting her sister.

It took close to an hour before Dani paused and looked up.

"What is it?" Haile asked.

"Gudit Monastery."

"I know this place." He pulled his satellite phone from the tablet. "Come on, let's pack up," he said to the soldiers before pulling out his gun and ending the homeowner. Haile then dialed a number he was very familiar with. It was time to give an update.

Cable glanced one last time. The timer had slipped below one minute and he let out a guttural cry in frustration. There was no chance he was getting free without help or a knife.

A shadow to the left caught his eye, and he flipped over to get a better look. The priest from earlier had somehow returned. Cable called out in one of the few Amharic words he knew, "*Meriidati*." *Please*.

The priest stared at the man who he'd thought was a righteous man but instead had brought so much violence and disrespect to his doorstep. He was a deceiver, a blasphemer, and he was tied up for his crimes.

He then noticed the timer and the explosive charges set into the alcove of his church. Perhaps he had been rash. The priest made a snap decision and dashed over to untie the American.

The timer ticked down. Three...two...one. The ground shook violently as a shockwave blasted down the hidden tunnel.

Moments before, the priest had led Cable to a hidden passageway that exited out the back of the church. Cable dropped to the ground as debris shot past, and his ears shut down from the concussion. Silence followed as a slight ringing slowly grew in volume. Cable couldn't see anything in the tunnel that was just big enough to crawl through. He felt his way along until the glow of the sun ahead beckoned him.

The priest and Cable exited the tunnel, coughing and having nearly succumbed to the thick dust. The priest had tears streaming down his face, and Cable couldn't tell if it was from the loss of his precious church or the burning from the dust.

If the path to the main entrance of the Sky Church was perilous, the back door exit was terrifying.

Cable kept his face to the wall and inched along the six-inch shelf with a 600-foot drop beyond. His feet were longer than the path and it took everything he could muster to not make a misstep. He followed the mountain-goat priest, slowly but surely, step by step.

Cable was overjoyed when they finally merged with the original trail and moved down the mountain. If ever there was a savior living here as a mortal, this priest was it.

The trailhead was a mess. Bodies were lying about, and buzzards were already getting to work. Cable approached Juni and removed his shirt to place it over her frozen, surprised look. "You didn't deserve this. I'm sorry."

The priest was mumbling some sort of prayer for the dead, and Cable thought that would have to do for now.

He found a soldier who had a similar physique and stole his shirt, bullet holes and all.

A moan from behind a rock spun Cable around. He picked up a rifle and went to investigate.

Luka was lying with his head propped against the rock, holding pressure on his abdomen. Blood wept through his fingers. He looked up to see Cable. "You are like a bad penny," he said through gritted teeth.

Cable leaned down to investigate the wound. "Where did they take her?"

Luka grimaced. "Rebels came out of nowhere and took her. Fannie and Stein drove away...I'm sorry." Luka sounded truly sincere.

Cable nodded at the request for forgiveness. The priest came over and started up his prayer again. "Hang in there." Cable stood and ran to see if there was a medical kit in the old SUV left behind. Just inside the rear lift gate, he found a metal box with a red plus on it. He grabbed a shirt from another soldier and ripped it into strips as he hurried back to bind up Luka's wound. Cable came around the boulder to find Luka's still body. He had accepted the priest's words and moved on to the next life.

The priest bowed his head and said something Cable didn't understand, then turned back up the trailhead. He was going back to the only thing he knew, even if it was half destroyed.

Cable called out, and the priest turned.

"Thank you," Cable said as he waved.

The priest waved back with his gap-toothed smile before surefootedly ambling back up the dangerous trail.

The old SUV was pretty shot up. It had two flat tires, and something was dripping from under the hood. The camels had scattered with the first sounds of gunfire. They were trained to head back home, and Cable was sure he would never catch them. There were a few supplies in the back, even some ammunition and a couple of pistols. He chugged from a plastic gallon jug of warm water, then ate a granola bar. It was the ubiquitous snack for outdoorsmen on the go. He wiped his brow. The sun was only slightly cooler here than in the Danakil Depression.

A shimmer in the distance seemed like more than just a mirage, and Cable took a second glance. Was it moving? He decided to investigate.

The heat waves coming off the ground were heavy and thick, like an invisible jungle of vines, forcing Cable to push his way through them.

The image in the distance slowly resolved with every step forward. It was a man. Cable started to jog. He was tied to the ground spread-eagle, without his pants or shirt, just his skivvies.

As Cable grew closer, he could see the man squirm against his restraints staked into the ground. At one point, the man turned in Cable's direction, and everything changed. It was Kojo.

Cable sprinted up and then slowed as he realized the situation.

"Don't just stand there. Get me out of this."

"Why is there never a camera when you need one? Oh, wait, you gave me your flip phone. He pulled the phone out and took his time framing a shot. "Smile."

"I'm gonna kill you," Kojo called out in frustration.

"You might have to get in line."

"Do you know what that is?" He used his head to gesture to a jagged hole in the dry ground off to his right.

Cable looked over at it, but there was no movement. "An abandoned ant den?"

"No. A *siafu* den, a big one, and they are just waiting for the hottest part of the day to end. Then they will march out here, and as soon as one single ant finds me, a pheromone signal will have ten thousand of the little buggers feasting on my soon-to-be corpse."

"You must have really done something mean to piss someone off that bad."

"Colonel Haile. He is second-in-command of the Tigray People's Liberation Front, and he is a sadist just like his boss."

Cable bent down and started to untie Kojo's right hand. "I have never heard of *siafu* ants."

"The local name for army ants. Please hur—" Suddenly, Kojo let out a gasp. Then a yelp of pain and then another.

Cable looked over to see a small line of army ants heading toward them.

"Faster," Kojo said in terror.

Cable realized the true intent of this torture. The army ants had found Kojo, and it was time for an early dinner. He quickly moved to the other arm and untied it. The entrance to the den, silent only minutes ago, quite suddenly started to boil up as thousands of army ants swarmed for their prize.

Both men took an ankle, each one receiving bites from large mandibles and stings filled with burning formic acid.

Once Kojo was free, the two men ran from the den, doing a crazy dance to get the rest of the ants off them. Finally, the last ant was smashed.

"That was what I needed to video," Cable said.

"That was too close," Kojo said. "Thank you, brother."

Cable nodded as he looked back at a black stain that grew across the ground as the ants searched for their now-missing prey.

"What do you know about the Warrior Queen, Nigiiti Gudit?"

Kojo looked over to his friend. He pursed his lips in thought. "There is a monastery dedicated to her, mostly because she destroyed it, but it is not a place we can get to on foot from here."

"Come on, I need your help with a bullet-ridden SUV. If the rebels have Dani, then we are running out of time."

"What happened to my cousin's camels?" Kojo asked.

"I guess they ran off during the shooting."

"He will not be happy."

"That makes one of us," Cable said, happy not to be getting back on one of the fuzzy beasts.

"You are hoping to fix what is clearly beyond repair out here?" Kojo said as they approached the battered, shot-up vehicle.

"*Looks* beyond repair. I have no desire to walk out of here on foot."

"The nearest village is two days to the east," Kojo mumbled matter-of-factly.

Cable looked off in the direction Kojo had mentioned. It seemed like it would be a brutal walk. He dug around in the back of the SUV and pulled out a half roll of duct tape. He tossed it to Kojo. "See if you can fix the leaks."

Kojo opened the hood and wrapped the bullet hole in the radiator hose. He noticed a similar wound on the hydraulic hose. "There is no way this stuff will hold the pressure of the power steering line. We'll have to use brute strength to turn the car."

Cable found a tube of superglue in the first aid kit and used it to plug the least damaged tire. The spare was mounted up under the rear of the SUV, and it was still intact, so he swapped it out with the tire that had three bullet holes in it.

Kojo used most of their water to refill the radiator and closed the hood with his fingers crossed. He swept the broken glass off the front seats and reached for the key. Surprisingly, the old engine started right up. Now, all they had to do was fill up a flat tire with a superglued patch and no pump.

"That's disappointing." Kojo looked up to see Cable holding a can of Fix-A-Flat. It was empty.

"Why would they keep an empty can in the car?" Kojo asked.

Cable turned the can to reveal the bullet graze that had emptied the can. "Help me get this tire off. I have a plan B."

They jacked up the rear of the vehicle and pulled the tire and wheel off. Cable laid it flat on the ground and jumped on the rubber sidewall until it popped free from the rim, creating an open gap.

"Well, now we will never be using that tire."

Cable ignored Kojo's comment and siphoned off a cup of gas. He poured most of it into the open gap.

"Now what?" Kojo asked.

"Now, we wait for the gas fumes to fill the inside of the tire. I saw a guy nearly blow himself up doing this on YouTube."

Kojo stepped back a few paces.

Cable reached out and dribbled a trail from the tire to the ground—a liquid fuse. He pulled out a lighter, covered his head with his free arm, and ignited the gas trail. Flames shot toward the tire, ending in an explosion and flame burst that lifted the tire and wheel off the ground. Suddenly, the tire popped back on the rim, instantly extinguishing the explosion inside the now sealed and filled tire.

Cable slowly opened his eyes, wondering if he was missing any body parts.

The tire lay on the ground, filled and ready to go. He stood and smiled like he had planned it all along.

Kojo shook his head. "May God give us health," he whispered as he climbed into the SUV.

Stein Osman paced the small room like a hungry lion in a cage, puffing on a cigar like it was a pacifier. The disaster at the Sky Church weighed heavily. "Who were those bastards?"

Fannie looked up from the small kitchen island. It was covered with medical supplies, and she was just finishing up wrapping a bicep wound that she had cleaned and stitched up herself. She knew better than to feed his angst at times like these, so she changed the subject. "With Luka and Tarik down, we need to regroup."

Stein stopped mid-stride and spun in her direction, the anger on his face clear.

They had returned to their Vrbo along Lake Tana. It had taken most of the day and cost nearly double to get the pilot to come and pick them back up.

Fannie let Stein continue to fume for the moment. "I have reached out to Raven," Fannie said. "She pegs our unexpected guests as Ethiopian rebels, most likely from the Tigray People's Liberation Front. They tend to shoot first and make up their own answers after. How the TPLF got wind of what we were up to is beyond me, but they have a very good network in northern Ethiopia. It's very possible one of our locals made a call."

"I didn't come this far to quit now, but my desire to take on an entire rebel army is low," Stein said through gritted teeth.

"Not a chance we are going to quit," Fannie reassured him. "We now know what we are up against and what to expect."

Stein paused his pacing and looked Fannie's way.

"I know just the person to help us with our problem," she continued.

Stein tried to calm his demeanor. He knew anger would not help in this situation, but it came so naturally. "Person?" he asked, smashing out his cigar on the tabletop.

"Friend of a friend. Remember the guy that did the Ghana job?" Fannie asked.

"Philip, right?"

"Good memory. He owes me a favor," Fannie said as she pulled out her laptop. "Now, all we have to do is wait for Dani to give us our next stop."

Curiosity pulled Stein to Fannie. "What are you talking about?" He watched as she opened her computer and connected to a secure site.

"I still have a few friends in the SOG."

Stein gave her a curious look.

"Special Operations Group in South Africa. One of my former employers. The Dark Continent and all its little tribes are just one of the many things they keep tabs on."

The screen opened to a live satellite image of northern Ethiopia. She typed in a latitude and longitude provided to her by Raven. The image drilled down to a section of the country that looked just slightly less barren than the landscape around the Sky Church. It took some searching, but soon, she found the rebel caravan.

"You have a tracker on the girl," Stein realized.

Fannie didn't bother answering.

"There." Stein pointed to the three vehicles moving along the narrow road.

"The TPLF have strayed south of their usual border. Looks like they are heading to a place called..." She zoomed in even closer to the image. "Gudit Monastery." Fannie picked up her satellite phone and dialed.

Stein watched and listened to the one-sided conversation with interest.

"Colonel Hagos, I have that information I promised you...yes, that's right...I'm sending you the coordinates now. Remember, the girl is to be held for pickup...of course. Thank you, sir."

Stein's gruff expression melted away as he put all the pieces in place. He sat next to Fannie and reached out, placing his hand on hers.

She allowed the indiscretion.

"Did I ever tell you? You are very good at your job." He finished with a genuine smile that actually surprised Fannie.

Dani walked over the hard, barren landscape, wondering if this was the end of the line for her. The rebels seemed intent on eliminating anyone or any clue along their quest, and soon, that would include her. A prod in the back from an AK-47 pushed her forward toward the ruins of something up ahead. The Gudit Monastery looked like giant skeleton fingers reaching out of a grave. Legend had it that the Nubian Jewish Warrior Queen had destroyed this church with fire, but somehow, part of it had resisted the centuries and had yet to completely crumble to the ground. It had become a symbol of sorts to the people in the area. The church was originally a stone Gothic structure butted up against a natural cliff wall alcove, doubling its size from the outside.

Dani moved past a Tiya stele field off to the left. Nearly forty stone monolithic pillars stood in rows, still resisting time, like sentinels guarding history. Each one was slightly different from the next, with faded carvings and ancient lettering. She stepped over the crumbling stones that marked the entrance to the once-proud monastery. There was not much to look at or even make out. The alcove's frescoes were blackened from the queen's fire and had faded over time, leaving the images unreadable.

Dani's shoulders slumped as she desperately searched for a clue, anything. She could feel Colonel Haile's eyes drilling into the back of her head. If she didn't find something quick, soon it would be a lot more than just eyes.

"What is it?" His voice broke her fixation with her predicament.

"Fire and time have destroyed any chance at reading these," Dani said, pointing a finger.

"Are you telling me that I have spent money and time chasing a dead end?"

Dani didn't like his use of the words *dead end*, and the way he emphasized them left no doubt as to his intent.

"These things take time and sometimes a little luck." She looked around, her eyes not finding anything worth investigating. She could feel the panic building inside her.

"What is it you are looking for? Maybe we could help."

Good idea, Dani thought.

"We are looking for a swastika, either painted or carved." She drew the symbol in the soft earth for Haile.

He took one look and then rattled off orders to the twelve soldiers watching them from beyond the church.

The soldiers spread out and started their search.

Dani felt a lessening of her panic and continued her own search in the alcove with her newest helper and guard, Colonel Haile.

After nearly an hour, Dani began to feel helpless again. There was nothing left to find in the destroyed monastery. The lump in her throat seemed to weigh heavy.

Cable and Kojo crawled along the sandstone ridge that backed up to the destroyed monastery. Kojo carried the rifle they had collected back at the Sky Church. They dropped flat at the lip and looked down at the action taking place below. One SUV and two technicals were parked a ways off. Soldiers were spread out among the ruins and the nearby stele field, searching.

"See, I told you they would come here next."

"Good guess. Look, Dani's got everyone looking for her," Cable whispered.

The two had pushed their hastily repaired SUV to the limit getting here, and if they were honest, the vehicle, once turned off, would probably never start again.

"That's the guy who had me tied to an ant den," Kojo pointed as Haile stepped from the ruins, a gun pointed at Dani's back as he pushed her along.

"Looks like they didn't find anything in the chapel."

"That means we are out of time."

"What's our move here?" Kojo asked.

Cable looked at his friend. "Not sure we have one. We've got one gun between us with only six bullets against a squad of armed soldiers."

"Yes, but they are not expecting us," Kojo said with a smile.

"Suicide run? Okay, I like your thinking. Time for a little *Kojo mojo*. I'll make the run for Dani, and you can be the distraction. I mean, you are the one with the orange hair, after all."

"One six-bullet distraction coming up, but you better hurry."

Cable looked back down. Dani had been forced to her knees, and there was a gun pointed at the back of her head.

Cable stood and ran back down the cliff.

CHAPTER SIXTEEN

D ANI TRIED TO THINK OF anything to keep herself from shaking, but her mind was on overload. All her experience and education had never prepared her for this. She had never felt so helpless, and honestly, she was tired of being pushed around. A new strength filled her as she resolved that this was the end and crying on her knees was not how she was leaving this world.

"You have wasted my time, and that is unforgivable," Haile said as he pulled the hammer back on his chrome .357 Magnum.

Dani found her voice and steeled herself. "That wasn't my intention," she said, forcing herself up into a standing position and turning to face her executioner. "I have no wish to die today, but I won't grovel or beg. Do your worst."

The barrel of Haile's gun now rested right between her eyes. He looked impressed with the woman's boldness, but no quarter would be given. Haile squeezed on the trigger.

A voice called out from the left. Haile relaxed his finger and turned to see one of his soldiers waving. He lowered his pistol. "Don't ever waste my time. Your life is tied to my success."

Dani nodded as grateful tears flowed down. She had faced her mortality and proudly accepted it on her terms. She forced her legs forward as her racing heart started to slow. The soldier was standing in the Tiya stele field. As she neared, he pointed to one of the stones.

It was unremarkable—about five feet tall and in the shape of a distorted and pointy headstone. There were raised carvings on one side of a phallic-looking sword and a bird in flight. Below that was a swastika with a series of Ge'ez symbols.

The relief for Dani was palpable. "This is it," she hoarsely rasped. "I need a camera or a phone."

Haile reached into his pocket and produced his Thuraya X5 sat phone. He unlocked it with his face and opened the camera app before handing it to Dani.

Dani took several pictures of the symbols and made sure she could read them off the phone before passing it back to Colonel Haile.

"Let me guess, you need some computer time," he said, pocketing the phone.

Dani was about to affirm his question when bullets from the ridge above the monastery blasted to her right. Colonel Haile and Dani dropped to the ground. He pulled out his phone and hit the automated SOS button on the side. The satellite phone auto-dialed a preset number.

"What is it?" a voice said.

"We have the final clue to the treasure."

"I hear gunfire."

"Minor setback. I'll send you the coordinates as soon as the girl translates the symbols."

Soldiers returned withering fire back at the shooter.

Haile disconnected the call and put his phone away. He craned his neck around the stone to get an idea of where the shooting was coming from.

Kojo dropped his empty gun and slithered away from the edge of the cliff as shards of rock and ricocheting bullets filled the air around him. That was all the distraction he could give Cable.

After running back down the steep slope and around the sandstone formation, Cable was gassed. He hurriedly scanned for the place he had last seen Dani, kneeling on the ground about to be executed. His heart pounded for multiple reasons as he gulped for air. The sound of gunfire from Kojo gave him a small glimmer of hope that he might still have a chance to save her. His eyes darted left and right, trying to find her.

Gunfire from multiple soldiers blasted, and Cable dove for cover behind a carved stone. They weren't shooting at him yet, but instinct had taken over. As Cable looked up, he noticed a man pointing a shiny pistol in his direction. It was the man Kojo had pointed out. The one who had been about to shoot Dani. He raised his hands slowly, finally noticing Dani. His rescue had not quite gone to plan. Only the suicide part seemed to still be on the table.

"Please don't shoot him. He knows where the treasure is," Dani blurted out in desperation.

Once the shooting from the cliff top stopped, the soldiers slowly ceased fire.

Haile stood, keeping his gun on Cable. He threw out several orders, and soldiers responded.

Two of his men headed for the back of the sandstone cliff to search for the shooter. Two others took over guarding Cable while three men started digging up the Tiya stele with the Ge'ez symbols on it. Haile was covering every angle.

Cable mouthed the words, "You okay?" to Dani, and she gave a subtle nod.

Haile stepped over to Cable and looked him over. "So where is this treasure?"

"If I tell you that, you will just shoot me. I need assurances."

"I can assure you that I will shoot you right here and now if you don't."

Cable said nothing, and a moment of chicken passed between the two men.

Haile hated playing games, so he turned the gun on Dani. "Fine, I will start with her elbows and then her knees and work my way from there." He pulled and cocked his pistol.

Cable stopped stalling and quickly tried to think of something that would stop the maniac from shooting Dani. "I can get you there, but only Dani can get you in."

Haile was angry now, and he really just wanted to pull the trigger and be done with all this. He had convinced his boss he could deliver, and that was exactly what he was going to do. He vacillated on maybe still shooting one of them as the unmistakable thumping of multiple helicopters filled the air.

From around the sandstone mountain, the Ethiopian army appeared. Three gunships were flying low in attack formation. Haile called to his soldiers just as bullets started to spray. He dove for cover but hit the ground hard as a.30 caliber round found the back of his head and removed it.

Colonel Haile's dead, twitching body forced Cable into action. He grabbed Dani's arm and started to sprint for safety. Dani pulled free and reached into Haile's pocket, grabbing his cell phone.

Bullets ripped around them, destroying centuries-old carved Tiya stele and any soldiers using them for cover.

Dani quickly used Haile's remaining face to open his phone, then ran, leaving Cable to catch up. Bullets just missing them with every step. The gunplay seemed to be coming from everywhere as the two technicals nearby returned fire, and soldiers followed suit. Rockets from the helicopters quickly put an end to the machine guns mounted in the bed of the pickups.

Cable and Dani ran past the old monastery, just ahead of a line of machine-gun fire. They needed to put some distance between them and the fighting.

The back-and-forth combat lasted almost two minutes before Haile's six remaining soldiers surrendered. One helicopter landed and disgorged army regulars to mop up while the other two stayed in the air, guns pointed and ready. It was over.

Colonel Hagos stepped from the helicopter along with his Ethiopian army regulars. He looked over his victory. They had taken down a terrorist cell of the TPLF, including its number two. It was shaping up to be a great day. The information Fannie Müller had provided was solid intel. He would have to send her a bottle of Tella in thanks. Unfortunately, there was no sign of a woman among the dead or living.

Cable scampered behind the sandstone cliff, leading Dani out of sight of the military action going on behind them. Once they put enough distance behind their troubles, they slowed to catch their breath.

"How on earth did you find me?"

"Nigiiti Gudit. Kojo knew about the Warrior Queen's deeds."

"Isn't that a movie about a rabid dog?" Dani asked.

"Not Cujo, Kojo. He's a friend of mine that grew up around here. Been helping me. If he didn't get shot, he should be back at our car."

Cable led the way back to the old SUV they had hidden in a small box canyon. Kojo was sitting in the driver's seat, dabbing a rag to his bleeding forehead.

"You okay?"

"Just a graze." His eyes flicked over to Dani, and a smile grew across his face. "You must be Dani. Call me Kojo, delighted to make your acquaintance. You are even more beautiful than Cable has described. How marvelous."

Dani was slightly taken aback by the tall Ethiopian with orange hair and beard. But his infectious smile quickly won her over. She gave Kojo a hug, and he delivered three kisses to her cheeks.

They climbed into the vehicle.

Even with all the shot-out windows in the car, Dani wrinkled her nose. "I take it you two have been living in this car?"

"I wouldn't call it living," Kojo said with a broad smile. He turned the key. Nothing. As predicted, the vehicle had given its last to get them here.

They packed up a few supplies and started out on foot, leaving the battered SUV to the elements. Despite the skirmish, the old monastery was still standing.

The battle had been fought and finished with only the buzzards left to rule. They picked at the easily accessed and soft parts of their found meals: eyeballs and midsections. The bold birds were not afraid of a few humans walking past. Several corpses stared, eyeless and tongue-less. It was a macabre display.

Dani closed her eyes as they walked past the gore. The strong smell of urine, feces, and gunpowder mixed with the coppery twang of blood. It all threatened to overwhelm her, and her head felt woozy.

Cable hoped to find enough un-shot parts left behind by the rebels to cobble together a working vehicle. They had stayed in their box canyon a full hour after the sound of the retreating helicopters passed overhead. The rockets had done their job destroying the two technicals. The SUV, a Toyota Hilux Surf, however, didn't have a single bullet hole.

Kojo checked for a key. "Finally, something is going our way. Praise the saints."

They all climbed in and left the rotting soldiers to the buzzards. Hyenas wouldn't be far behind.

Kojo drove, and the three sat in silence for a time before Dani found her voice. "Check the glove box, there should be a tablet in there." Cable popped it open and handed her the small tablet the late Colonel Haile had taken from the cottage.

Dani held it in her hands just staring at it for a bit.

Cable watched her actions. "What is it?

"A man died over this."

Kojo looked back. "That's the kind of man Colonel Haile was. His death will be celebrated by many." He turned back to watch the road. "But I am afraid when his boss, Commander Kidane, finds out, it will not be good for the region. Death is the only currency left to many in this part of our country, and they will pay dearly.

"Lust for power is a sickness without a cure," Dani deadpanned. "We should just leave here. No treasure is worth a person's life," Dani said.

"I will not leave a means to power his brutality for another generation," Kojo said with resolve.

"The Akan Pilgrimage can stop with us. We are the only people on this earth with the final clue," Cable proposed.

"And if Commander Kidane knows this, we will be hunted to the ends of the earth. Right now, we have a window in which to operate freely before he points every soldier he has in our direction," Kojo said.

"He knows."

"What?" Cable and Kojo both spun in Dani's direction.

"Colonel Haile called someone right before the attack and gave him a full report."

"A *small* window."

Silence filled the vehicle.

"Maybe you're right. We can turn around and leave this place right now."

Kojo and Dani looked at each other, considering Cable's words.

"Kojo is right. We can't let a madman get access to this treasure. And if I'm being honest," Dani said, "I want to know what is at the end of this journey. After all we've been through, we have to finish this."

Kojo nodded his head in agreement.

"Okay. If that's the case, you'd best find us a direction to go, and soon," Cable beseeched.

"On it." Dani connected the Thuraya X5 satellite smartphone as a hotspot to the tablet. It took some time, but she navigated to her site and began the translation. After an hour, she spoke up. "'Great smoke.' Mean anything to either of you?"

Cable had no idea. "A historical wildfire of biblical proportions?" he ventured.

Kojo seemed to remember the words. "My mother used to tell me a folktale of the Great Smoke that guarded these lands and the mother spirit who dwelled there."

"That doesn't sound like Christian history," Dani said.

"It's not. It comes from centuries-old traditions. Long before Christianity came here, there was a folk religion that mixed nature with man. Bouda."

Kojo spun the vehicle around and headed in a new direction. "The Great Smoke she referred to was the billowing mist from the Blue Nile Falls."

"It looks like they are heading back toward us."

Stein and Fannie had been watching a small blinking red dot move slowly across a map overlay of the area just northwest of them.

"You mean her shoes are moving toward us."

"Correct." Fannie stood. She had spent the last two hours glued to a blinking dot on a map, and she needed a break. They had watched in amazement as the Ethiopian army attacked the rebels spread out by an old church. The satellite passed before the fight was over, leaving Stein and Fannie to guess at the outcome. It was the call from Fannie's contact, Colonel Hagos, that left them feeling anxious. The army had not seen a woman during or after the fight. Dani was in the wind, and when her tracker stopped moving somewhere north of the battle, they had given up hope.

Now, everything had changed with the movement of the tracker.

"If she's still alive, I'm betting she is still wearing her shoes." Fannie moved to her backpack and started repacking it. Reliable backup won't be here for another..." She glanced at her Apple Watch. "Twelve hours. I don't want to miss our window, so I say we go ahead, and they can catch up."

Stein helped her load the SUV, and they headed south out of Bahir Dar on the B31, the red dot on Fannie's laptop leading the way. After about five miles, they exited at the village of Sebatamit onto Tiss Abay Road, a narrow dirt road that skirted green pastures and fertile gardens.

Commander Dejin Kidane stepped out of his M462 Abir. The smell in the air was suffocating as the oppressive heat had kick-started his dead soldiers' decomposition. Four armored support vehicles with heavy machine guns, filled with soldiers, pulled to either side. The soldiers waited and watched as their leader walked the battlefield.

Bodies lay where they had fallen, many picked to ghouls by the buzzards and hyenas. Kidane fired off several rounds, chasing the opportunistic carnivores away for the moment. He raised his scarf as he moved through the tattered Tiya stele field. His foot shoved over the body of his number two, exposing a familiar face minus eyes. Kidane held back the bile. It would not look good to show weakness in front of his men.

He circled his hand in the air, and his soldiers moved out, searching the perimeter for survivors.

After a time, Major Lami stepped up to his commander and shook his head. "There is no one here left alive." Lami was a short, stout man with bug-like black eyes, a bushy mustache, and a round, balding head.

"Major, you will take Haile's place. Make sure these men get a proper burial."

"Yes, sir," Lami said as he saluted and started to execute the order.

"And, Major, we are not done. There is a small group of trespassers in our land. They have come to steal from us, to take our heritage away. I will not allow that to happen under any circumstances. We must find what it is they are after and possess it for ourselves."

"Understood. I'll put the word out."

"Whatever it takes," Kidane added.

The major turned away, rattling off orders as he walked.

Kidane looked back at Haile's desecrated body. He let his anger rise, filling his entire soul until there was no place left for it to go. He would use this anger to get what he wanted, no matter the cost.

The Blue Nile Falls sits in a valley next to the small village of Tissisat. The river is named after the Ethiopian silt it carries to the proper Nile. It is not blue, but under the right lighting and conditions, it can have a bluish cast. Kojo pulled the vehicle next to a small home along a rutted side road.

"Camels or on foot? We need to cross the old stone bridge at Nibret and it is too narrow for cars."

Cable was tempted to pass on the camels but understood the situation. "Fine. Camels. But I want one with a name this time."

Dani looked over curiously.

Kojo smiled. "Cable is a God and camel-fearing man."

"I don't fear them. I just had a bad experience on one once."

"Do tell," Dani chided.

Cable's ears reddened. "Alright. I was taking a self-tour in the Sahara on a camel named Maggie."

"Okay, that sounds foolish right there," Dani said.

"Actually, it was quite remarkable. The people that make their living in the desert there are fascinating. Anyway, a sandstorm came up when I was in between settlements. It was pretty intense, like hard-to-breath intense, even with a shirt over your face. So I pulled Maggie to the ground, and we hunkered down to weather it. The first chance she got, the dumb beast jumped up and ran off. Maggie had my water, rations, and compass."

"I take it you made it out," Dani prodded.

"Barely. Got lost for a bit, passed out at one point from exposure, and woke up in a Bedouin tent. The next day I step outside to find Maggie hanging with all the other camels. Turns out she was hanging at the oasis while I was eating sand."

"Okay, so I will make sure not to get you a Maggie," Kojo announced as he walked off to rent their rides.

Dani turned to Cable with a new respect for him. "I've never met someone quite so…adventurous as you."

Cable stared back, not sure how to respond. He never considered himself adventurous. It was more of a yearning to know what was around the bend or over the next hill. That was his driving force.

Once on the camels, it was Kojo who led the way. He heard the sound before he saw it. First, the mist hanging some 400 feet in the air, and then the white water cascading down 138 feet like an angry curtain.

Cable was bringing up the rear, struggling to show his camel who was boss.

The Blue Nile Falls is one of the earth's great wonders and was once Ethiopia's busiest tourist destination, but due to rebel activities and decreased water flow, fewer and fewer ventured to this part of the country.

They stepped off their camels and took in the majestic waterfall. Multiple falls cascaded over from the river above.

They took the trail over the old bridge and back to the far side of the falls, separating them from the everyday tourists. Most visitors drove to the main roadside pullout and snapped a few selfies with the falls in the background. The more adventurous hiked down the main trail to the west bank shoreline. Only a few put in the effort to cross the old bridge upriver and hike back down to the falls on the other side.

Dani held up the small piece of paper with translated notes on it from the Tiya stele back at the Warrior Queen's monastery. She read the words out loud for what seemed like the hundredth time.

"Great Smoke. 240 chains to the early summer sun to Rungu."

Cable had done a search during their drive, and *Rungu* or *knobkerry* was an Amharic name for a balled club head. A weapon usually made from a hardened ironwood tree root, like an Irish shillelagh. The African version had a distinctive oblong balled shape on the head, and the polished shaft was designed for easy holding and swinging.

It was historically interesting, but as a clue it had left the trio confused.

Chains were used in ancient Africa as a measurement and with a little research, Dani discovered a chain equaled around sixty-six feet.

"So, 240 chains is roughly three miles into the early summer sun." She pointed in an easterly direction. "Now the real trick is what to do with the rest of the information."

Cable stood and faced the falls. He held up the sat phone and did a geofencing from his location to the northeast between thirty and forty-five degrees on the compass. "That is approximately the direction of early summer sun from where we stand." His arm pointed more northward than Dani's had.

Kojo looked off in the direction Cable was pointing. Rolling hills built a wave-like swell on the horizon, leaving agriculture and civilization behind.

Cable then set a distance of three miles on the map displayed on the phone's screen. The resulting image was a pie-shaped grid over a section of the map. The pointy end represented their current location.

"We just need to search along this arc here." He indicated the curved section of the piece of pie. It was about five miles of rugged terrain.

"Let me see that," Dani asked.

Cable handed her the phone.

She changed the map to a topographical view and zoomed in along the curve, exploring with her eyes as her finger slid the image on the screen along the search parameters. At one point, she stopped, wrinkled her nose, and zoomed in.

"Take a look at this."

Cable shielded the screen from the sun's glare. Recognition slowly filled his face. "That looks a lot like a Rungu."

Kojo glanced over. "May the saints preserve us. You are right, a small box canyon in the shape of a knobkerry."

"I think we found it," Dani stated.

Smiles flashed across all three faces, and an excitement grew that couldn't be contained. A group hug was in order, and then the reality of their situation returned. Time mattered.

"Come on. I feel like we're being watched." Cable mounted his camel, and the others followed.

They left the majestic waterfall, the great billowing mist, and the roar of it all behind. Exiting off the trail, they picked their way up a narrow canyon that looked as if it had never been explored. Within a few minutes, the lush green of the Blue Nile valley faded away. Sandstone cliffs rose on either side of the caravan as they traversed the dry streambed at the bottom.

"There's a good chance this was an active stream during the Axum Empire," Kojo said.

"Like the Sahara Desert was once a tropical paradise," Dani added.

They continued on up the canyon, the slope intensifying with each step. The elevation leveled out again, and the canyon split in two directions.

"Which way?" Kojo asked.

"Give me a second." Cable powered up the smart sat phone and zoomed in to their position. "Left."

Kojo pushed his camel in that direction.

"It looks like our box canyon is another half mile on the left."

"Do you think this Commander Kidane is behind us?"

"Most assuredly, he is behind us and closing," Kojo said.

"We should assume that at the very least. Our best chance at doing this safely is doing it quickly."

Philip opened the door to the Vrbo and five mercenaries in civilian clothes followed him inside. Their military bearing and hard looks were a dead giveaway to their chosen profession. A handwritten welcome note on the island from Fannie told him he was in the right place.

"Thirty minutes. Make it count," Philip called out.

Gear was offloaded and weapons checked. The men took turns using the bathrooms and grabbed a quick bite.

The group had exfiltrated from a watchdog job in Syria a week ago, and Fannie's call came at the perfect time. They took the next flight to Addis Ababa and rented a truck. Through a local contact, they sourced weapons, ammunition, and additional gear.

It had taken almost fourteen hours to drive to the rented home on Lake Tana.

Philip pulled up a map on his tablet and dialed his sat phone.

It was answered on the second ring.

"Talk to me," Fannie said.

"We're here," Phillip countered.

"Good. I'll send our coordinates and we can rendezvous. We are about an hour south of your position."

"Give us a few to kit up, and we'll hit the road."

A dot appeared on his map showing Fannie's location. "Got your twenty," Philip said as he closed his tablet.

"Phillip."

"Yeah?"

"Thanks for coming so quickly."

There was a hesitation on the line. "Well, I do owe you one," Philip said just before hanging up.

A knock on the polished wood door was followed by, "Sir?"

Commander Dejin Kidane looked up from the speech he was going over. "Come."

Major Lami stepped into the spacious office appointed with exotic hardwoods and a trophy collection of animal heads of the big five—the five most dangerous African species. Lion, leopard, rhino, buffalo, and elephant. He navigated past two overstuffed chairs and a settee combination to the ornate desk in the back of the room.

"I have credible intel from one of our contacts in Addis Ababa. Six men, obviously ex-military, purchased weapons from him."

"You think this has something to do with our treasure hunters?"

"It is certainly possible. Haile intercepts the hunters at the Sky Church. Two of them get away, and now reinforcements arrive? I don't like coincidences, and this seems like one to me.

"Did your contact say where they were headed?"

"No, but he ID'd their vehicle, so I spread the word, and one of our scouts spotted them heading toward Bahir Dar."

Kidane tapped his finger on his desk. "Get me a dozen good men and warm up the Mi-17s. We'll need to link up with vehicles outside of Bahir Dar. Ones that blend in. I don't want to give our enemies a target like Haile did. If these thieves think they can pop into my land and take what they like, they are sorely mistaken."

Major Lami nodded and left the room. He quickly assembled the men and equipment.

Two Mi-17 Russian-made military helicopters lifted off from the safety of the compound. Lami chose to ride with his commander.

The older helicopters buffeted through the air, making it difficult to communicate without headsets, but only the pilots carried them.

"Where are they now?" Kidane yelled.

Lami had his phone propped up with a map program operating, but his main intelligence came from updated texts sent by the scout. "They've stopped at a vacation rental along Lake Tana. My scout is following them on a motorcycle, so he will blend in."

"You're sure these are the military men who bought the weapons?"

"To the best of our intel," Lami replied."

Kidane nodded. He had been getting anxious since the unprovoked attack that killed Colonel Haile and his soldiers. The Ethiopian National Defense Force had sent soldiers to kill his men. The government had deemed the TPLF a terrorist organization. Dejin Kidane a terrorist? It was apparently a crime against humanity that he and his people didn't see things the way the rest of Ethiopia did.

Kidane would make sure his soldiers taught any who dared to go against him a lesson the world would not soon forget. He tried to calm his ranting mind, but foreigners had come into his world and were trying to rob him. It had cost Haile his life, and he wanted the treasure and revenge.

Lami's smartphone trilled, and he answered it, keeping a finger in his opposite ear so he could hear. "Colonel Lami."

He listened for a moment. "What? Don't lose them." He hung up.

Kidane looked over at his second.

"They are leaving the house and they are no longer in civilian clothes. Armed and ready for a fight," Lami explained.

"Then it is a fight they shall have."

CHAPTER SEVENTEEN

FANNIE BOUNCED OVER THE ROUGH road, hands on the steering wheel with her eyes focused forward.

From the passenger seat, Stein kept his head on a swivel, not wanting a repeat of the surprise ambush at the Sky Church. "You mentioned Philip owes you a favor. What is it?"

Fannie pursed her lips, deciding just how much of that story she wanted to share with her partner. "I saved his life."

Stein glanced in her direction.

"We were doing a covert op along the Mozambique border. Small squad operation that got some bad intel on a local hot spot of rebels operating in the area. We went from observation to taking incoming rounds from a superior force in a matter of seconds. We returned fire as we tried to exfil. Everybody got shot up, even me." Fannie drove around an extra-large pothole. "By the time we got back across the border, I was the only one ambulatory, and Philip was the only other operator left alive. Drug his butt five miles before I passed out from loss of blood. Eventually, a rescue team showed up and patched us back up."

Fannie pulled the vehicle over behind several other rentals parked along the side of the road.

"Lost some good people that day."

Stein nodded slowly in understanding. "I'm sorry. But that's not gonna happen here. We get in and get out."

Fannie nodded before exiting the vehicle. She opened her laptop on the hood. The Blue Nile flowed nearby, and the sound of the falling water was thunderous. She took a second to admire the beauty of the waterfall before connecting to the cellphone hotspot. Tourists milled about taking pictures and talking loudly to be heard above the roar. Fannie navigated to the tracking map she had been using to follow Dani's progress. The red dot was no longer blinking. In fact, it was gone.

Stein was focused on the massive waterfall. He had been here once before on one of his original Ethiopian quests, but something this powerful always fascinated him. Like-minded souls, he surmised.

"Our tracking signal is down," Fannie called out.

"What does that mean?" Stein asked without looking back.

The ballooning mist was heavy in the air, cooling the intense sun's rays. Stein stepped next to Fannie to look at the screen.

"It means she is underwater, underground, or up in one of those slot canyons. It is also possible she found the tracker and destroyed it, or the battery died prematurely."

Stein turned back to Fannie. "Can you see where it last pinged?"

"Yeah, give me a second." After a few moments, Fannie looked up. "They went that way," she said, pointing toward the canyon and hills beyond. "We'll need to rent camels or horses to follow."

"Make it happen. How long until Philip and his men arrive?"

Fannie checked her watch. "We'll have backup in twenty minutes."

Stein considered the time. He looked back at the road to Lake Tana and then off to the rolling hills across the water. "I don't want the trail to go cold. Get two horses for us and enough for your team. They can catch up."

The two Mi-17s touched down in an empty field outside of Bahir Dar. They had flown southwest across Lake Tana to the southern tip. The soldiers began unloading their gear into three waiting SUVs. The pilots kept the rotors spinning, as they were no longer in the safety of the Tigray territory. As the last bag was pulled from the rear hatch, the helicopters lifted off and peeled back to a safe staging area north of the lake. From there, they could be called into action without too much delay.

Major Lami barked orders to the men and soon everything was loaded into the inconspicuous vehicles.

Lami checked in with his scout for an update before he climbed into the driver's seat of the lead vehicle across from Kidane.

"They are on the road to the Blue Nile Falls about twenty minutes ahead of us. We should be able to make up the distance if we push it," he said as he turned the key and started the vehicle.

"Try to close within a mile."

Lami nodded and stomped on the accelerator, leading the convoy south on the 831.

By the time they reached the outskirts of Tissisat, they had closed the distance.

Kidane held a tablet with a digital map of the area, trying to get a feel for where they were headed.

Major Lami's phone buzzed with an update. "They are stopping to pick up horses."

"Horses? That makes no sense. There are roads in almost every direction."

Lami did a quick inspection of the map. It showed a small village ahead, nestled in a valley with the Blue Nile flowing through it.

"Look, there are two bridges that cross the river here and here. Why horses?"

A voice from the back seat followed. "Those bridges cross only the outflow water coming from the Tisabay hydropower station upriver. I grew up nearby, sir. The only bridge that crosses the Blue Nile River here is the old Portuguese Bridge, and no cars can cross it. Too narrow and old."

"Show me," Kidane demanded.

The soldier in the back seat leaned forward and pointed to the old stone bridge north of town.

Kidane and Lami came to the same conclusion at almost the exact same time.

"We need to get to that bridge before they do, sir."

Kidane had made the right decision to appoint Major Lami as his new second-in-command after the unwarranted death of Colonel Haile. A rare smile showed his approval.

Kidane zoomed in on the other side of the Blue Nile. There were no roads and very few trails. This was a place you would need horses.

The three vehicles blasted through the village and its assortment of tourists and Ethiopian dust collectors for sale on every corner. Tissisat was the launching spot for the Blue Nile Falls tourists, one of the world's true wonders, but since the installation of the hydro plant, much of its majesty was now gone. Only during the rainy season did the falls come back to their full grandeur.

The convoy took the bridge across the power station's overflow and bounced past the circular Kidus Monastery on the right. The road turned into a trail and ended at a grove of trees along the gorge where the Blue Nile flowed below. Two obvious rental cars were parked nearby—tourists.

"The bridge leads to a trail that takes you to the other side of the falls. It is only for the more adventurous," the soldier added as they exited the vehicle.

Kidane quickly surveyed the area. A couple with day packs was crossing back in their direction. At the sight of armed soldiers, they ran to their car and quickly drove off.

"I'll take some men across the bridge and set up a crossfire," Commander Kidane said with a gesture. "The rest of you take cover here. Let them pass, and make sure to stay out of sight when they do. Once the target is on the bridge, there will be nowhere they can go. Call in air support and have them stack up. One here on station and one a few miles off with its eyes on the horizon. I don't want any unwelcome guests. Oh, and try not to kill the horses. We may need them."

Major Lami issued Kidane's orders, and soldiers moved out to take their positions.

The old stone bridge that crossed the Blue Nile was a Romanesque structure built by the Portuguese in 1626. It had one large arch over where the river had cut a deep gouge and several smaller arches designed to allow additional water through during the rainy season while still maintaining its strength. Due to its age and size, no modern vehicle could fit on it or cross it. Kidane led half his men down the trail and onto the bridge. It was just five feet wide, narrowing in some places. The side walls reached up three feet above the deck with slots every twenty feet to allow water to escape the deck during heavy rainfall.

Philip led his men on horseback at a trot, trying to catch up with Fannie and Stein, who had pinged him an update on their location. It was somewhere up one of the remote canyons on the other side of the river.

They rode past four vehicles parked at the trailhead and continued down to the old bridge. There, he pulled to a stop, letting his senses take in the surrounding area, just to be safe. He noticed nothing suspicious. Philip prodded his horse forward, and the others followed.

Soon, the sound of hooves on stone filled the air, competing with the distant roar of the waterfall downriver.

Philip was glad to leave the smell of the village behind. Being out in the wilderness like this always heightened his senses. He caught a brief reflection from an elevated two o'clock position and instinctively reached for his FN SCAR. "Heads up."

Barrel flashes ahead preceded bullets impacting all around him.

Phillip yelled to his men as he dropped from his horse and took cover behind the stone wall. His men followed suit just as effectively, returning fire.

They were mid-bridge with no cover other than the three-foot walls on either side or the horses.

Almost immediately, bullets started flying from behind them as well.

Three men broke off and covered the flank. "Sir, we're pretty pinned down here."

Philip called back. "We may be outgunned, but we are better trained. Make your shots count." Their more accurate fire held back the higher number of fighters for a time.

The spray of gunfire was interrupted as the thumping of rotors approached. A Mi-17 attack helicopter flew nap-of-the-earth right up the canyon floor. It hovered for the briefest moment before firing a single

S-8 rocket. The 1.5-meter weapon traveled at over 600 mph, which took the high explosive warhead exactly three seconds to reach its target.

"Incoming!" Philip yelled as he dove to the ground.

One of his men launched himself over the bridge and into the river below.

Just above the main arch of the bridge, the warhead exploded, sending stone shards and heat in every direction. The destruction caused the bridge to lose integrity, and a twenty-foot section collapsed into the water below. The rear horse, which had taken a round in its flank, lost its footing and followed the stones into the river with a high-pitched whinny.

The helicopter remained on station, hovering just over a kilometer away. The pilot kept one finger on the trigger for the next rocket.

Philip raised his hands to the sky, and the three men left alive followed suit.

Major Lami and his men moved down to the edge of the bridge, unable to cross.

Kidane and his soldiers quickly descended on their prisoners. Two soldiers took the men's weapons and emptied their pockets while four others held AK-47s pointing at their midsections.

"May I ask your purpose here?"

Philip took a half-step forward. "We were doing some boar hunting in the hills."

"With FN SCARs?" Kidane said while examining the high-end Belgian-made assault rifle.

"Our weapon of choice."

"Sir, I found this." A soldier handed a sat phone to Kidane with a map app on the screen.

A red dot flashed on one of the nearby canyons behind him. As if suddenly shy, the flashing dot blinked out and disappeared. Kidane used his fingers to zoom in on the area the dot had been in just a second before. It was a steep-walled canyon about five kilometers away.

He quickly realized the situation—he no longer needed to waste his time here with these men.

Philip could sense the change in the narrative almost instantly, but that was all it took for Kidane to point the man's own weapon back at him and eliminate Phillip and his three remaining mercenaries from his thoughts with a sustained burst.

"Toss them in the river."

He took the sat phone and mounted the lead horse. That left four horses and five men. The rest of his men saddled up, leaving one lone soldier to run on foot.

"Major!" Kidane shouted across the bridge. "Have the helo ferry you across the river and do your best to catch up. The canyon we are headed for is too steep and narrow for a helicopter to land."

Major Lami waved his hand in acknowledgment as Kidane spurred his horse across the remaining bridge and into a remote canyon beyond.

The sun was high overhead, making the narrow canyon a solar oven.

"If I never come back to this place, I will be just fine with that," Stein muttered as he wiped the sweat from his forehead.

"For me, it would depend on where. That waterfall was pretty spectacular," Fannie countered.

The two rode for a few more minutes before Stein posed a question. "What is it you want from this?"

Fannie looked over and realized he was serious. "This," she pointed between the two of them, "is what I want. We have built a successful business together. It is important to me. And if we find—"

Stein interrupted, "When."

"*When* we find this treasure, we will take our business to the next level."

"But what about for you, personally? There's more to life than business," Stein proposed.

"I used to believe that. I used to live it as well. All a relationship has ever done for me was bring disappointment. Business, on the other hand, when done right, has no emotions or mood swings. It is...pure, like a marriage between math, strategy, and hard work. I can get my head around that and don't have to worry about what you're up to behind my back because our concerns and plans are in alignment. If I feel the need for romance...that's easy enough to find for a night."

"Sounds lonely, but also like I have the best associate I could ask for." Stein suddenly pulled his horse to a stop. The sound of automatic gunfire ricocheted off the canyon walls. An explosion followed.

"I don't think we can count on our reinforcements."

Fannie was tempted to gallop back to the fighting to help out.

Stein picked up on her thoughts. "There is nothing we can do now but put ourselves in harm's way." He turned his horse back up the trail and coaxed more speed out of the animal. "Come. Our destiny awaits."

"Hang on. I'm going to disconnect our location sharing with Philip. I don't want any unexpected guests." Fannie shut down her sat phone's sharing feature, then hurried to catch back up to Stein.

Kojo tapped his camel with his crop. "Hut, hut," he said, trying to get the beast to pick up the pace. "We are getting close."

"So is whoever's following us," Dani added, referring to the distant gunfire.

As they came around a corner of the dry wash, the canyon split again in two directions.

"This must be it," Cable said.

A dribble of water flowed from the narrow gorge on the left and then dissipated back into the ground right in front of them. A huge bolder had fallen some years before from the canyon wall, blocking the way forward.

"We'll have to leave the camels here and go on foot," Kojo said as he lowered his camel and dismounted.

Dani and Cable followed. It took some effort, but all three made it over the bolder and back down to the spring trickling on the other side. They followed it back into a small box canyon. From the ground, the shape of the Rungu was unrecognizable.

"How anyone could find this place without the aid of modern tech is beyond me," Dani said as she stepped over a jagged rock.

"I think the original Pilgrimage of Akan required a little extra faith to make up the difference," Cable said.

"I have known of this pilgrimage for most of my life. It was a fantasy, a bedtime story that inspired young and old alike, but it was just that. A story." Kojo took a slight stumble over a rough section of the canyon floor. "To be here with you, actually following in Akan's footprints, goes beyond my wildest dreams."

"What do you suppose we'll find?" Dani asked.

Cable replied, "Enlightenment, knowledge, or maybe a giant diamond like the one in the tapestry Fannie showed us."

"A giant diamond?" Kojo said in surprise. "Ethiopia is known for her gold, not diamonds, but I would gladly accept a giant diamond for services rendered."

"Let's not count our diamonds too soon," Cable said as he looked up at the sun, just starting its journey back down for the day. "We still have to find this place and then get out of here in one piece."

"We have," Dani announced as she stopped walking. The box canyon ended in a sandstone cliff enclosure. There was nowhere left to walk. The only exit was back the way they had come. To her right was a natural arch leading down into a small alcove under the cliff. It was filled with blue water reflecting the time-carved sandstone all around it. To the left, a trickle of water flowed out of the pool and back down the canyon.

"Water?" Kojo asked. "Is this the treasure?"

"*Blue* water," Dani pointed out. "It's caused by calcium carbonate leaching through the limestone."

"It could have been revered hundreds of years ago," Cable said with no small amount of disappointment.

"No. There is something more here. Look at this."

Cable and Kojo turned to see Dani kneeling on the ground and pointing.

"There are depressions in the ground at regular intervals. Two here, two here, and two there." She dug at one of the depressions, and the loose soil revealed carbonized wood below. "There was a platform here at one time, and it ran across the water. These holes held the posts that supported it. Looks like someone burned it down."

"And it led that way." Cable gestured past the pool to the back of the alcove.

Beyond the water, they could see sandstone walls, etched and rippled from history, but nothing manmade.

Cable waded into the pool. "Okay, that's cold water." It was refreshing and shocking after the sweltering ride up the canyon. In a direct line with the indentations in the canyon floor, Cable crossed the water which slowly got deeper, forcing him to swim. The cliff on the far side was dominated by a wide natural column in the middle that looked like it was the last remaining support for the roof. Cable worked his way along the back wall, searching for anything that might look out of place. At the end of the wide support column, he found a hidden gap behind it.

"I've got an entrance," he called out. "It looks blocked off. I could use some help."

Behind the column, hidden from sight by all but the most curious, was a three-by-twelve-foot gap in the wall that led into the mountain. Unfortunately, man or nature had piled this entrance with a stack of rocks.

Cable and Kojo pulled rocks from the pile until a small opening at the top appeared.

Dani took a flashlight and led the way, up and over into the darkness beyond.

The room beyond was large and domed. Every surface, except the floor, was covered with paintings—artwork that hadn't been seen by human eyes for over 1,600 years. Dani was so taken aback she didn't even notice Cable and Kojo entering the ancient chapel.

"The Nine Saints," Kojo whispered as he pointed his flashlight up. "A church, God be praised."

Sure enough, the original Nine Saints who had started Christianity in Ethiopia were represented on the ceiling. There was a history of the religion all saved in paint. The baby Jesus in the manger, the Sermon on the Mount, and even the Crucifixion. The colors were bold and breathtaking.

"This is incredible," Dani said in reverence.

"My people's history," Kojo added. "Emperor Ezana. He made Christianity the state religion in the fourth century...this is truly a treasure to behold."

"We should take a look around in case there is something else," Cable said, pointing his headlamp back down where the walls met the floor.

"That's a good idea." The voice came from behind them, and all three spun to find Fannie and Stein pointing weapons their way.

Stein stepped forward. "And I suggest you get a move on. I dare say our time is short."

Cable started to take a step forward.

"I wouldn't," Fannie said, reinforcing the fact with her pistol.

Stein took a moment to look around the hidden chapel. "Quite remarkable." He then pointed his flashlight back down and pinned it on Cable. "Your life hangs on your actions, Mr. Janson. I suggest you act accordingly."

Cable and Dani moved right while Kojo went left. They used their lights to look for any detail that might be a clue or just out of place. The walls were smooth, arcing up to the ceiling with no alcoves or even an altar. There were no cracks or hidden doors.

"The *Garima Gospels*," Kojo muttered.

Dani turned to see what he was looking at.

"Only something is different here," Kojo said.

Dani and Cable stepped to the painting on the wall of the profile of a priest sitting in a leopard chair holding a crystal. He was surrounded by a dark filigree border like a hand-painted picture frame. The swastika on the bottom right corner caught Dani's eye.

"It's the same image as the tapestry you showed us on the yacht."

Stein and Fannie were fascinated but cautious as they approached.

"Very good, Ms. Tran. It does look the same." Stein unslung his backpack and pulled several items from it.

Cable watched as his goshawk statue and wing were set on the floor, followed by several printed images of the other wing and translations. Stein held up a picture of the tapestry and compared it to the one on the wall. It looked the same to him.

Fannie watched intently, keeping a safe distance from the group, as she covered them with her gun.

Kojo shook his head. "If I'm not mistaken, this is from the *Garima Gospels*. The earliest known illustrated Christian manuscript, but in the *Garima*, the priest holds a scroll."

"Was there a swastika?" Dani asked.

"I have no memory of that," Kojo admitted. "But I'm sure of the scroll."

"May I see that," Dani asked Stein for the picture.

He handed it to Dani and she did a very detailed evaluation. "They are nearly identical."

"Stein was quick to respond. "What do you mean, nearly?"

"I'd say as close as any hand-copied duplicate could be. The tapestry is the beginning of the pilgrimage. The goshawk and the swastikas were the clues, and this," she pointed to the painting on the wall, "is the end."

Cable moved forward and let his fingers move across the smooth surface of the painting. "There is an extremely faint seam here," he said while outlining the diamond in the priest's hand. He tried pressing on the diamond in the painting, but it wouldn't budge. "Little help?"

Dani, Kojo, and Cable all jammed together and pushed as hard as they could. The diamond slid back with a grating sound, and they heard a deep click within the wall.

CHAPTER EIGHTEEN

C ABLE STOOD BACK. OTHER THAN the sunken diamond in the wall, no other detail had changed. "Everyone heard that click, right?"

Dani nodded.

Cable used his shoulder to push on the side of the painting. A crack appeared right on the seam of the painted border. He pushed a bit harder, and the painting, now a door, rotated on a center pivot, revealing a black maw beyond.

Stein's mouth went dry. He was tempted to rush into the cavern beyond the door, but patience was a virtue that just might save his life. He had grown up watching booby traps take down even the most intrepid explorers in the cinema, and he would not make that mistake here. "You three go first," he demanded, holding his weapon.

Cable stepped into the space beyond. The tunnel was just slightly taller than he was and maybe twice as wide. He shined his headlamp on the natural sandstone as he wove his way deeper into the mountain. The composition of the stone grew darker and then lighter as he walked. Finally, the natural tunnel opened up, and something highly reflective caught Cable's attention. A room the size of a concert hall came into view, but it wasn't the size that impressed him. It was the shiny crystals that covered every square inch of the space, with the exception of a portion of the floor. It was like a giant diamond geode.

Dani was the first to speak. "They started mining here before it was closed off." She pointed to an assortment of ancient tools and boxes lying to the side, preserved in the dry air. There was an iron gad, stone wedges, and a couple of double-headed hammers, all in excellent condition. Dani noticed a stone shard with a handle attached. It was about the size of a small knife, and she covertly picked it up and held it out of sight as Stein and Fannie entered the chamber. They were too distracted by the glittering walls to notice.

"It is real…all of it," Stein said in hushed disbelief. "Raw diamonds as big as your fist in every direction." He stepped to the closest wall and put his pistol back in its holster. He let his fingers reverently play over a few of the crystalline baubles that covered the space.

"Truly remarkable," Fannie gasped.

Dani used her eyes to get Cable's attention and discreetly showed him her weapon. She then used her head to subtly point at the ancient pick-axe that was on a box to the right of him. Cable understood and slowly moved toward it until he was standing in front of the tool, blocking it from Fannie and Stein's view.

Fannie was the first to regain situational awareness and pulled her eyes from the diamonds to make sure her prisoners were still behaving.

"We have done everything you have asked. Now, let us go. We will not trouble you again," Cable said.

Stein pulled himself from his discovery. "Yes." His mouth was dry. "I suppose you have. I am not a cold-blooded killer, per se. Just a businessman."

"It's bad business to have witnesses," Fannie added, keeping her gun pointed at Cable.

"What are they going to do?" Stein postured.

"We won't tell anyone. I swear to it," Dani added.

A wicked smile formed on Stein's face. These were the kinds of games he loved to play and win.

"Dani, save your breath and your dignity," Cable said.

"Yes. Cable is right. Save your breath, you might need it." Stein pulled his gun back out and used it like a pointer. "Dani, Kojo. Nice and easy, over by Cable."

Dani and Kojo sidestepped over to Cable.

Cable willed his fingers to the pick just inches behind him, but he would never reach it before Fannie shot him.

A sinking feeling began to fill the air, and he considered just going for it anyhow. At least his actions might save the others.

"I hope you like the dark," Stein said, interrupting Cable's thoughts.

Once Dani and Kojo were next to Cable, Stein backtracked to the entrance of the chamber. "Fannie, it is time to say our goodbyes."

Fannie turned to the three captives but suddenly realized the intent in Stein's words. "You son of a—" She spun in his direction, re-aiming her gun just as a bullet impacted her torso, stopping her mid-sentence. Fannie managed to get a shot off but missed just to the left before she crumpled to the floor.

Out of panic, Dani chucked her knife at Stein, but it only grazed his cheek, causing him to rapidly fire back in their direction. Dani dropped to the floor. Kojo spun left, and Cable dove for Fannie's gun as bullets pinged all around.

Stein turned and moved down the tunnel, emptying his magazine back into the cavern.

In one move, Cable rolled next to Fannie, grabbed her gun, and took off down the tunnel to stop Stein before he could close the entrance door and lock them in.

A gunfight in a stone tunnel is one of the dumbest things you can do, as every bullet fired has the chance of pinging off walls and hitting someone, but Cable had no other options. He crouched low as he hurried up the tunnel, following the glow of Stein's flashlight. The distance closed with each step. Cable was gaining.

Dani dropped down to Fannie and inspected her wound. It was bad. She grimaced in pain and was having trouble breathing. "It looks like he punctured one of your lungs."

Fannie's lips grew more crimson with every breath. "He is a heartless bastard, but he was my bastard," she said between labored breaths. "I was a fool."

"Kojo, see if you can get me something to bind this wound."

"I will try," came a pained answer from the floor behind her.

Dani spun to see Kojo on the ground with a bullet wound of his own.

Stein reloaded and fired blindly back down the tunnel once he realized he was being followed.

Bullets bounced around as Cable ran, one so close he could feel it pass his face, his reaction to dodge coming way too late.

Like a lame game of Russian roulette, he never knew when a bullet might find its mark. He decided to stop being a target and fired a salvo back at the retreating flashlight.

The light fell to the floor, spinning its beam in all directions.

A muzzle flash to the right gave Cable some indication of his target's location.

Stein had taken cover behind a rock berm.

They traded shots until there was a telltale *click* from an empty magazine up ahead. Cable stood slowly, listening for the sound of a mag exchange, but instead, a pistol skidded past the flashlight on the ground.

"Okay, you got me. I give up. There is so much wealth here we can share it." Stein stepped out into Cable's headlamp, his empty hands out to his sides.

Dani ran to Kojo and lifted his shirt to inspect the damage. The sounds of gunfire in the tunnel made her nervous and jittery, but she could only deal with what was right in front of her for now. "Oh, thank God, it is just a graze."

"Yes, but it hurts like hell."

Dani ripped the bottom of his shirt and wrapped it around him tightly. She then spun back to Fannie, who was on her final breaths. Dani took the hand of the woman who had been nothing but a thorn in her side for the last two weeks. *No one should die alone*, she thought.

"You impressed me, Dani Tran, and that's not easy to do." She gave a weak, bloody smile and slipped to the other side.

Dani looked down at the dead opponent in front of her. She would not shed a tear for the woman, but she didn't deserve to die betrayed by the one she trusted most. She placed Fannie's hands to her side and slowly stood. "We need to get outta here."

Kojo managed to stand with Dani's help, and they started for the exit.

Cable slowly backed up, keeping the gun on Stein as he returned to check on the others.

Stein seemed to feel the need to talk, but Cable wasn't interested.

"Do you have any idea the kind of wealth this cavern holds? No government would idly sit by and let you take it from them. We have to do this way under the radar. And then there's the business of moving this kind of product. You have to have connections, and you have to do it right, or you could crash the market or even make yourself a target." As Stein spoke, he slowly lowered his hands.

"Keep your hands up," Cable ordered.

His hands moved back up as he continued. "We need to put together an operation that is shadow, unseen and unnoticed, as we carefully sell off a few pieces at a time. It will take planning and logistics. The first thing we do is purchase the land through a shell corporation. Do you even know how to set one up?"

Cable had heard enough. "None of this belongs to us. This historic site is the property of the Ethiopian people."

"Are you insane? Do you know what will happen if a corrupt government gets ahold of this kind of wealth?"

"I know what will happen if a person like you gets ahold of it, and that's never going to happen."

"Small minds think small deeds."

"Crazy minds think reckless deeds," Cable countered.

The rage that had built up in Stein overflowed, and he dove at Cable, unconcerned with the bullet that might come back his way, but all that happened was a *click*. Cable's pistol was also empty.

Both men fell to the floor in a pile of punching and kicking. They bounced off the walls until, finally, they separated.

Cable stood. His eyebrow was bleeding, and his ribs felt like a truck had run over them.

Stein had gotten a few good licks in, but he had a broken nose that gushed blood and forced him to breathe through his mouth. He grinned a bloody smile and launched himself back at Cable.

The two men scuffled, each giving as good as they got.

Cable used his Krav Maga, and Stein used Sayokan, a Turkish martial art with roots in karate.

Dani stopped as Cable flew past her, his headlamp flinging off his head.

Stein followed behind, shouldering Dani and Kojo out of his way and bulldozing back into the glittering chamber.

Cable rolled back to his feet and took a fighting stance, ready to counter Stein's next offensive. Now that they were out of the tunnel, they had room to move.

The two men faced off, testing their opponent for weakness and an opening to attack.

The attack came from Stein's right.

Dani had grabbed one of the ancient pickaxes and ran at Stein in anger.

He ducked at the last second, and the axe swung over his head and embedded into the diamond wall beyond.

Crystals disintegrated on impact, and Dani pulled her weapon back for another whack.

"Stop!" Stein shouted, his eyes drawn to the broken crystals on the ground. He knelt down and picked a few up in his hand. He rolled the crystals between his palms until they powdered to the floor. "The... they're not diamonds."

Dani used her pick to chip a chunk off into her hand and put it to her lips. "Halite."

Stein started to mutter in bewilderment. "All this for a bunch of worthless crystals. It can't be. Where's the treasure? There must be more..." He looked over at Cable, his anger building. "Look what you've done. I'll kill you for this!" Stein screamed as he charged at Cable.

Dani didn't hesitate. She swung her pick with all her might and made contact. Stein slumped to the floor mid-tantrum.

Cable knelt down and checked Stein's pulse. A hand grabbed his shirt as Stein battled to finish his attack and not pass out from the blow to his head. Cable pried Stein's hand away and stood. He gestured for Dani and Kojo to hurriedly take their leave while Stein tried and failed to stand.

Quickly, they moved up the tunnel and out into the magnificent chapel.

"What was that all about?" Kojo hissed.

"That cave is a giant geode of halite or rock salt," Dani answered.

Cable finally put the pieces together. "Of course, in ancient days, salt was used as a form of payment and at times was more valuable than gold."

"The priests that found that cavern must've thought they'd found the motherlode," Kojo added. "They put this chapel here to hide and protect it."

"Yeah, it *was* a motherlode back in 600 CE," Dani added.

Kojo gave a shining smile that practically lit up the whole church. "Too bad. I thought we were going to be rich."

"As long as we have each other, that's as rich as I'll ever need," Cable said as he paused to collect his goshawk statue and the wing. He stuffed them back into Stein's backpack and threw it over his shoulder. "Now, this place might bring in a few tourist dollars."

Dani moved for the exit. "Let's just make sure we're nowhere near this place when Stein comes to his senses."

"Dani, hang on a sec," Cable said, stepping next to her, still amped up. "If we run into rebels outside or whatever, I don't want to miss my chance. We almost died back there, and I'm not going to make that mistake again…" He took a deep breath and started back up. This time, much calmer. "Dani, I realize we have been through a lot, but I wanted to say that you are a remarkable woman. You're smart and independ—"

"Cable, sometimes you gotta just stop talking and go for it." She pulled Cable toward her and pressed her lips to his.

Cable pulled back slightly. "Did you just tell me to shut up?"

"No, I would never." Her smile suddenly betrayed her words.

She was dirty and basically a wreck, but Cable had never seen a more beautiful person in his life. He pulled her back, and they kissed again, only this time more aggressively.

Dani wrapped her arms around him in a solid embrace.

It was as if a thousand jolts of electricity and pent-up emotions had combined.

Kojo stood watching with a similar grin that filled his face. "*Fik'iri,*" he said. *Love.* "About friggin' time."

Eventually, they separated, though their eyes were still locked on each other.

"Okay, I needed that," Dani said with a genuine smile.

"Me too," was all Cable could manage.

"Can we go now, or do you two need some more time alone?" Kojo said.

Dani and Cable just stared at each other for another few seconds.

"Yeah, let's get outta here." She took Cable's hand and led him to the rock pile exit. The trio climbed up and out and swam across the small pool into the heat of the afternoon. A quick sprint back down the slot canyon to the camels followed, with Dani leading the way. Her smile never faded.

Cable and Kojo were slow to mount, as their injuries affected their mobility. Once the adrenaline wore off, they would both suffer.

Dani gathered a few additional supplies from the horses tied nearby before mounting her ride.

Kojo led them further up the canyon. "I think it is best we find another way out."

Dani and Cable couldn't agree more.

Stein's eyes blinked open. His head pounded from a combination of rage and a large bump on the side. He had never been good when it came to failure, but today had been one for the books. It took him a good twenty minutes of anger and self-accusation before he finally started to pack the destructive emotions away. He stood on shaky feet and picked up the headlamp that had fallen off Cable's head. He let it play around the huge, sparkling cavern one last time. He then took one of the ancient mining tools and began to smash it into the crystal wall. Powdering the rock salt with each blow. When he finally stopped, both hands were bleeding, and sweat poured off his brow.

He turned the beam to Fannie's lifeless stare. Regret flashed across his face. She had only been good to him and his greed had destroyed her. Pity.

He could not change the past, but from here on out, he could make up for this failure. It would start with hunting down and eliminating three meddling fools. They had swindled and tricked him. They were to blame. His aspirations and plans for the future would have to wait until he had recompense.

Stein turned from Fannie's body and walked to the exit. With each step, he became more self-assured and focused. He let an idea form in his mind. *Get back to the rental house and regroup. Then, hunt down Dani Tran and her two friends.* He would make them suffer for the nightmare they had subjected him to. For Fannie's death and for the loss of face he had endured.

He would relish in their screams and enjoy taking his time. Stein let his mind wander with enactments of their future torment.

As he entered the chapel, he looked for his backpack. It was gone. He dropped a few choice words in anger and started for the rock pile exit.

Stein slipped into the cool water and swam for the other side. Halfway across the hidden pool, he became very aware he had company.

Eight armed soldiers held rifles pointed his way.

Stein swam a bit slower, coming into the shallows until he could stand.

A man from the back stepped forward. He wore green fatigues and a matching hat with the emblem of a flying goshawk. He held his pistol at hip height, pointing it at Stein.

"I am Commander Dejin Kidane of the TPLF, and you have trespassed and tried to steal from me."

Stein raised his hands, preparing to disagree with the man.

"You've got it backward, sir."

Dejin was no fool to false words.

Stein continued. "I have been looking for you—"

A shot rang out, stopping Stein mid-lie. His face took on a perplexed look as he felt a burning sensation in his gut grow in intensity. A look down confirmed it. He was shot and bleeding out. How could this be? He had only wanted to prove himself, to make a mark on this world and show his father how things were really done. How had he harmed this man and his soldiers in any way?

Stein felt dizzy and weak. His wealth, power, and status flowed out through his fingers, pressed tightly to his midsection. He tried to say something that might make a difference, perhaps even save him, but nothing came out except a gurgle.

Stein Osman slipped back into the pool. His red blood mixed with the blue water, making purple swirls.

EPILOGUE

K OJO SPURRED HIS CAMEL UP the trail. They heard faint sounds of men and horses moving up the canyon behind them and had no desire to run afoul of the rebels again. Kojo could still feel the itch of ant stings and the horror of Interpol Juni's murder.

The canyon walls closed in and then widened as they moved further up in elevation. Near the top of the mountain range, the slot canyon fell away, and the landscape turned to rolling hills with forest.

Kojo pulled to a stop and the trio looked back down on the world below. Somewhere down there was a hidden chapel with exquisite art and a crystal salt cavern that, at one point in history, was a virtual gold mine, now all but worthless. The terrain bounced from green fields to red sandstone and back to forest. It was like a section of the mountain range was set aside just for that chapel.

"Where to next?" Dani asked.

"If we are being hunted, our best bet is to stay away from any roads or civilization. It is only a two-day ride to the Eritrean border," Kojo said. "Eritrea is a dictatorship, but at least they hate the Tigray rebels."

Dani stared at Cable, unconvinced of their destination.

Kojo walked his camel closer. "We can do this. I know the way."

Dani and Cable shared a nod. It made sense. "Okay, let's go to Eritrea," Dani conceded.

It took almost exactly forty-eight hours of crossing rugged terrain and avoiding any sign of civilization before their tiny caravan reached the Tekeze River, the border between northern Ethiopia and southern Eritrea.

Kojo had pushed them hard, and they never stayed in one place very long, the threat of another attack continually on their minds. They were exhausted and on edge, but they managed to avoid the rebels.

Kojo dismounted and inspected the slow-moving water for any signs of crocodiles or hippos. "We can cross here."

The three camels swam across with their riders doing the same alongside them. Once on the other side of the river, they took a moment to air dry. It was as if a heavy weight had been lifted from their shoulders when they realized they had left Tigray territory behind.

"We're going to make it," Dani said with a growing smile.

"Yes, we can say goodbye to the rebels for now."

"You mean forever," Dani added.

"Of course, but living in Ethiopia, one can never truly be free of some sort of rebellion."

Cable stepped up to Dani and held her in his arms. It was the first time they had not been in some kind of danger, and it was dreamlike. Eventually, they parted, and the euphoria slowly passed.

"How much further?" Dani asked.

"We will reach the village of Magala by noon tomorrow," Kojo said. "It's not much, but we should be able to get a ride to a bigger city."

"I'll be glad to say goodbye to camel riding," Cable said. "But I must admit, I'm very grateful and feel a lot safer to be on this side of the river." He took Dani's hand and they sat on a nearby boulder, taking in the beauty around them.

After a short rest, they remounted their camels and continued, no longer feeling the need to look over their shoulders.

"Wet camels. Now that's a whole new level of stink," Dani announced.

As the sun began to set, Kojo found a large tree next to a spring. They decided to set up camp there for the night. They had not seen a single human in nearly two days and based on their situation, that was fine by them.

Kojo gathered some wood and started a small fire.

Cable unloaded their meager food supplies. "We've got two cans of beans left."

"Beans and water, you sure know how to treat a gal," Dani said as she tied the camels near the spring so they could drink.

"Dani, see if you can find my knife so I can open these cans. It's in my pack," Cable asked as he hauled the cans and a skillet over to the campfire.

Dani stepped up on her tippytoes and reached into the pack still tied on the back of Cable's camel. As she dug through the main compartment, she dislodged something at the top. The goshawk statue dropped to the ground, hitting a small rock and breaking in two. "Oh my God. I'm so sorry, Cable."

"What is it?" he asked, walking over to the camels.

"Your statue. It fell. Your family heirloom, after all this."

He dropped down, and together, they picked up the two pieces. It was a jagged break that revealed a hollow center filled with halite crystals.

"Salt," Cable mumbled. "We should have done this two weeks ago. It would have saved us a lot of drama."

"I appraised that statue for 200 grand," Dani whispered.

"Two hundred thousand...dollars?" Kojo said, walking over to see what happened.

"Its value was never monetary to me," Cable said. "Childhood memories and my grandfather's legacy. A little glue will keep that alive for me just fine." He picked up the two pieces, put them back in his backpack, grabbed his knife, and headed back to make dinner.

As the beans started to heat up, Cable gave them a stir and a taste test. "These beans are pretty bad. You didn't see any herbs growing about while you were collecting firewood?"

Kojo was about to answer when Dani piped up. "What about the salt?"

It took Cable a few beats before he realized what she was talking about. "Salt would save the day."

Dani grabbed three crystals from the broken statue and tossed them into the pot.

Cable stirred them in and pulled the pan from the flames.

With the skillet balanced on a rock and their only flashlight illuminating the food, they all dug in. Dani with their only fork, Kojo with their only spoon, and Cable with his knife. It was bare bones, but any food tonight was welcome.

"I don't taste the salt," Cable said.

"Me either. Maybe I should get some more," Dani added.

"Augh," Kojo cried out. "That's not salt!" He took a crystal from the back of his mouth, along with some tooth fragments, and inspected it. "It's rock hard."

"Let me see that." Cable banged it on the edge of the metal skillet. "Quartz crystal, maybe?"

Dani held out her hand. "May I?" She took the flashlight and shined it on the crystal.

"I think I chipped my tooth," Kojo complained.

"This is not quartz." A confused look filled her face. "This is a raw diamond."

"Are you kidding me?" Kojo exclaimed.

"No. Find another one."

Cable and Kojo searched through the beans until they found another one, wiped it off, and handed it to Dani.

She inspected it as well. "So is this."

Silence filled the camp.

"We're rich!" Kojo said with renewed excitement, in spite of his tooth pain.

"Technically, these belong to Cable," Dani added.

"Technically, they belong to the church or person that hid them here, but I suppose no one is left to claim them. We should share them."

"Like I said. We're rich! May the Nine Saints be praised." Kojo jumped to his feet and started to dance around in excitement. It was contagious, and soon Dani and Cable joined in. They threw out some of pop culture's best on the theme.

"Diamonds are forever."

"Diamonds are a girl's best friend."

Even Kojo got in on it. "True friends are like diamonds, precious and rare."

"I wear diamonds."

"Like a diamond in the rough."

Grins and laughter filled the night until Kojo accidentally knocked over the pot of beans.

The dancing stopped.

"We are rich…but now we are hungry," he said without a care in the world.

IF YOU LIKED THIS BOOK

I would appreciate it if you would leave a review with your favorite retailer. An honest review helps me write better stories. Positive reviews help others find the book, fueling my ability to add more books to the series.

It only takes a moment, but it means everything.

Thanks in advance,

Brent Ladd

AUTHOR'S NOTE

This is a work of fiction. Any resemblance to persons living or dead, or actual events, is either coincidental or is used for fictive and storytelling purposes. Many elements of this story are inspired by true historical events. All aspects of the story are imaginative events inspired by conjecture. *The Eye of Faith* was a true labor of love. Like life, the writing process is a journey, one meant to be savored, and to me, it's more about the pilgrimage itself than the destination. I learned a ton while writing this book, and I hope it's reflected in the story and prose. Only you, the reader, can be the judge of the results. Drop me a line if you have feedback or just want to say hi.

Brent Ladd
BrentLaddBooks.com

ACKNOWLEDGMENTS

With deep appreciation to all those who encouraged me to write, and especially those who did not. I want to thank the following contributors for their efforts in doling out their opinions and helping to keep my punctuation honest: Jeff Klem, Carol Avellino, Hilary Glaholt, David Ihrig, Steven White, and Christy Monge. A host of family and friends who suffered through early drafts and were kind enough to share their thoughts: my incredible wife Leesa, who manages to put up with me and all my revisions. She is my first reader and best critic. And my editor, Cathy Hull.

A special thanks to my publisher, American Real Publishing, who helped make this all possible, as writing is only half the total equation. Finally, to Roger Harvey for the cover design.

As many concepts as possible are based on actual or historical details. Special thanks to the original action hero—my dad, Dr. Paul Loefke.

Lastly, writers live and die by their reviews, so if you liked my book, *please* review it!

More Cable Janson books coming soon!
– BrentLaddBooks.com

ABOUT THE AUTHOR

Writer-Director Brent Ladd has been a part of the Hollywood scene for almost three decades. His work has garnered awards and accolades all over the globe. Brent has been involved in the creation and completion of hundreds of commercials for clients large and small. He is an avid beach volleyball player and an adventurer at heart. He currently resides in Irvine, CA, with his wife and children.

Brent found his way into novel writing when his son Brady showed little interest in reading. He wrote his first book making Brady the main character—*The Adventures of Brady Ladd*. Enjoying that experience, Brent went on to concept and complete his first novel, *Terminal Pulse, A Codi Sanders Thriller*—the first in a series, and followed it up with *Blind Target, Cold Quarry, Time 2 Die,* and *Fatal Measure*, which takes our characters down many rabbit holes. *HU 2.0* is a near-future sci-fi thriller that is often too close to the truth of where we are heading as a planet. *The Eye of Faith* is a fun romp through history with some of his favorite characters.

Brent is a fan of a plot-driven story with strong, intelligent characters. So, if you're looking for a fast-paced escape, check out the Codi Sanders series, Jericho's journey in *HU 2.0*, or Cable Janson's search for missing treasure in *The Eye of Faith*.

You can also find out more about his next book, *Grain of Sand,* and when it will be available by visiting his website:

https://brentladdbooks.com/
https://www.facebook.com/brentladdauthor

GET READY TO PREORDER CABLE'S NEXT ADVENTURE!

SNEAK PEEK!
GRAIN OF SAND
WEST COAST OF AFRICA JUNE 570 BCE

B OAZ GRIPPED THE WICKER FENCE railing that skirted the perimeter of the Phoenician warship, with its round-bottomed cedarwood hull. A single mast held a large square-rigged, red and white-striped sail that slowly filled with air. He glanced at the large clay amphorae tied to the tall horsehead bowsprit, picturing the last few cups of fresh drinking water it contained. His orders to go ashore and restock dwindling supplies weighed heavy.

His rope-like muscles strained and his knuckles turned white as he processed his options. Risking his ship or crew was not an option. They needed to cut their losses and create some distance from this place.

He called out desperately to the other ships, hoping he wasn't too late. "Get clear; cut the lines. Row for your lives."

The incredibly tall African natives continued their attack from the shoreline with spears and arrows, some flaming.

One ship burned uncontrollably while another struggled to gain distance from the onslaught. Sailors pulled their oars for all they were worth, while others returned fire from the deck-arrows crossing in the air with no regard for one another.

A flaming arrow impaled just to the right of Boaz, and he plucked it from the hull and tossed it overboard like an unwanted stowaway. One of the sailors quickly extinguished the remaining flames with a bucket of ocean water.

The flotilla had stopped to gather supplies and fresh water from a small bay. A local tribe of warriors appeared as if by sleight of hand through the jungle and attacked without warning. It had been a monumental task to fight them off and get back to the ships, leaving a trail of bodies and supplies as they ran.

Three weeks back, they had lost a ship to an invisible reef that had taken the bottom out on a moonless night. Luckily, no lives were sacrificed to Yamm, the Sea God, but today would be an unmitigated disaster. Boaz's heart ached for his murdered men, like a burning arrow to the solar plexus. There would be time to mourn, just not now.

The next flaming arrow dropped into the ocean short of its target. Boaz allowed his shoulders to calm slightly, realizing they were out of range. Now it was up to the other ships to get free of the melee. He willed them to move faster. A useless pleading born of frustration and desperation.

Horror filled him as some of his Phoenician brothers, trying to escape the burning ship, were picked off one by one. His face filled with impotent rage as he watched the smallest ship in his fleet turn back to shore when the tillerman slumped over. Before the men could recover, they were cut down and flames slowly engulfed everything above the waterline.

Two ships were all that escaped, carrying forty-two sailors. In less than an hour, Boaz had lost more than half of his crew and fleet. The world was a dangerous yet curious place. Why the extra tall natives, dark as a moonless night, had taken offense to their stop-over would remain a mystery, but their prowess with fighting weapons was on par with any fighter he had ever encountered.

Boaz had seen the pillars of Hercules and sailed beyond the gates of the Mediterranean Sea. He had shaken hands with kings and killed off entire villages. Losing men and ships was not uncommon, both in conquest and to mother nature, but so many deaths over a few baskets of fruit and jugs of fresh water, that was a first. He considered returning in the night and teaching the savages a lesson, but his orders were clear and they did not include that type of action. This was strictly a fact-finding mission, but who would be the wiser if he did? Anger bubbled just below the surface like a waiting volcano.

He slammed his hand in frustration and turned to Tanith, the only female on this voyage. Her long, dark curly hair mirrored her eye color and accented an angled face that most men found attractive, but her determination and professionalism were too much for them to handle. Sailors said she could give and take as well as any of them, and they had made her a sort of mascot aboard the ship. Boaz treated her like a sister and counted on her skills with her parchment and ink to tell their story and to mark the way for those who would follow.

"Mark this cove as hostile. I don't want those sailors' sacrifice to be for naught."

A single tear was all that showed on Tanith's face as she nodded. "Of course." Then she collected her supplies and added details to her growing parchment map and lengthening journal.

Boaz watched from the stern as Adad, his number one, leaned into the rudder, pointing them south once again. The two remaining sister ships had almost identical features, including the clay amphoras with nearly empty drinking water and their limited food stores. They would need to stop at the next river that flowed into the ocean.

Boaz's parched lips pressed together as he remembered the day he left Carthage. Queen Dido herself had been present and presented him with a Tyrian purple cloak worth almost a year's pay. The send-off had been a grand affair. A limestone monument of the voyage was erected and a representative of the Pharaohs out of Egypt personally blessed their ships. There was more at stake here than any other voyage he had taken on. Two dynasties were counting on their success to open trade around the Mother of Mankind, also known as the continent of Alkebulan, *Africa*.

After five weeks of mostly uneventful sailing, they'd encountered many friendly and receptive villages along the coast, some with access to gold and other unique items that would make this trade route very profitable to the Phoenicians and the Egyptians. Boaz had been impressed with the people who lived here. Their dark skin and eyes held a genuine kindness and intelligence. They lived off the land in harmony with it rather than by consuming it like so many civilizations he had encountered, including his own.

One aggressive and deadly tribe could easily be avoided in the future. Boaz set his eyes on the upcoming horizon and let his anger slowly fade with the tide and distance.

After two more days skirting the coastline, the weather and seas changed, as did their heading. From south to southeast and finally, they were now traveling due east. They had come to the bottom of Africa. The end of the known world. Unprepared for cold weather, the white tunics worn by the men only covered from their waists to knees. The women had it slightly better as their garments wrapped from neck to ankles. The few horsehair blankets onboard were all they had to stave off the increasing low temperatures.

The real problem was the sea. Here, two oceans collided. It tossed and turned like two ragging rivers smashing together. This wasn't a storm, in fact, there wasn't a cloud in sight. It was a tempest born of nature and physics. The ship creaked out her protest as she bucked and healed with each swell. Waves came from the side while others blasted them bow and stern. Even the most hardened sailor found his legs weak and his stomach churning.

"We can't last much longer," a soggy and shivering Adad cried out to no one in particular. Even his usually perfectly groomed beard had lost its form.

"We are just passengers now my friend," Boaz called back.

"The bottom of the world is no place for us."

After nearly two days of hard sailing, the waters slowly mellowed and their course changed once again. Northerly. They had come through the worst of it and were heading into the unknown.

Boaz lifted his bearded face to the sun and let it warm him. He was beginning to believe that the cold in his bones would never leave. At five foot ten, he was taller than most men he knew. His years at sea had hardened his muscles and weathered his skin, making it bronze and lined. The salt-crusted hair on his head was dark and curly. He was a man of action, not words, but action without words only got you so far in this world. Boaz had forced himself to engage learned men whenever he was in port, making his weakness a strength. It had caught the eye of several noblemen and ultimately reached the queen's ears. That alone was enough to put him on the shortlist to lead this expedition. After bringing home three ships laden with Tyrian purple silks worth ten times their weight in gold, and through a massive storm that had been the doom of so many other sailors, his nomination was secured.

The next week pushed them farther north with fair seas and a brisk wind. The oars had been stored for the last few days as the sail did all the work. Morale had improved and thoughts of returning home soon were heavy in the air, like a draping wet blanket. Their course angled slightly more east and the temperature continued to warm.

Boaz stepped next to Adad, his arms locked on the tiller. The man's beard was once again trimmed and pointed. A fashion usually seen in court, not on a ship now entering its third month at sea. His red conical hat had lost most of its color but was still doing its job of hiding a large bald spot on the top of Adad's head. His serious unblinking eyes scanned ahead.

"We need to resupply soon. The water has turned, and the meat is white with mold."

Boaz looked across to Dagon, helming the sister ship just off his starboard side. The man was a beast of war, picked from Queen Dido's own personal guard. His dark braided beard and hair were colored almost white by salt. He wore his copper helmet despite the glaring sun and made a short lift of his hand for a greeting, and Boaz returned the gesture. They had been through the gates of Hades and somehow managed to persevere.

"What do you suppose awaits us?" Boaz said without looking back at Adad.

"The sea is fickle, and anyone who claims to know her is fooling himself."

"I suppose," Boaz replied, turning his attention back to Adad.

"Sea devils or perhaps safe passage only Yamm knows. But I tell you this, we are missing nothing."

"What do you mean?" Boaz asked.

Adad took a breath and pursed his lips before replying. "Carthage. She is still a glimmering pearl cast along the ocean's shore. The people there are still going about their daily lives and the market is still filled with the smells of coriander and roasting boar."

"Don't forget streets so foul they take your breath away, with thieves and cutthroats hiding in alleys."

"Ah, the good life," Adad said with fondness. "It hasn't changed since we've been gone, but the things we have seen and done..." He stared out at the sea. "We've changed."

Boaz nodded. "We have lived ten lifetimes compared to those in the city."

"Now, we just need to get home to tell our tale."

As Tanith approached, both men looked over. She was carrying an old scroll and a new parchment in her hand.

"I think we are getting close." She rolled out the scroll. Its edges were worn and corrupt. Then she held out the parchment next to it. "Take a look at this. Here is an old map drawn by an Egyptian expedition many years ago that journeyed down the eastern coast of Africa. They lasted about two months before giving up and heading back."

"So?" Adad said, leaning over the tiller to get a better look.

"So, look at the map. I have been recording the coast as we go. Along this portion here," she pointed, "the two images align."

"Yes... Incredible," Boaz said with punctuated excitement. "We are overlapping their original journey."

Tanith nodded.

"Now, all we have to do is retrace their steps back to Egypt. Present ourselves to Pharaoh Necho and we will be greeted as heroes," Adad said.

Boaz chuckled. "I guess the sea devils missed their turn."

As he said the words, there was a change in the wind and the sail pulled to starboard.

"Row for your lives," Boaz called,, now the second time he had used those words on this voyage.

Waves crashed over the deck as a howling wind drove them away from land. Sailors held on with grips of steel to anything that would prevent them from being washed overboard. A few had not been so lucky. Lightning randomly flashed from every direction, giving brief glimpses of their surrounding horror in the black night and then taking it way again as the bolt extinguished itself into the water. Oars dug into the turbulent sea, trying to make steerage at any cost. Should the boat get sideways, all would be lost. The mast had snapped sometime back, and their precious sail had washed away with it. The current and wind were in control, but Boaz and his sailors battled them for every inch. He held firm to the tiller, trying to keep the ship's nose pointed into the huge waves that pounded the ship. They had lost sight of their sister ship early in the battle with the elements. Now it was row or die, a concept simple sailors knew all too well. A large wave hit, and the ship shuttered before half the hull breached out of the water and then plunged back down.

The storm had been raging for more than fifteen hours, and the men had nothing left to give.

"Yamm preserve us," Adad cried out just before a wave pried him loose from his grip and washed him into the liquid melee.

Boaz was now alone on the tiller, forcing the ship's nose into the oncoming swells. "Keep fighting! It's our only chance!"

His words were drowned out, as a sudden scraping sound preceded a violent shaking of the boat, which came to an abrupt stop.

"We've run aground on the reef," someone shouted needlessly.

A wave pulled them off and nearly flipped the ship over. Sailors were flung from Boaz's sight as he shoved the tiller over to course correct their eminent destruction. A substantial hole in the bottom of the ship began taking on water, and she quickly grew heavy. Another wave hit and took more sailors with it. Once again, the ship ground to a stop.

"Every man for himself!" Boaz cried out.

Anyone left aboard made a hurried exit into the liquid cauldron of death.

As Boaz reached the hull, the ship twisted again and he was flung like a cartwheel into the black sea.

Dark eyes cracked and strained at the impossible brightness of the sun. Perfect white sand dotted with palm tree shadows came slowly into view. A curious-looking tan crab with white claws shuffled past, as a sudden bout of liquid coughing racked Boaz. He leaned over and vomited several times before, finally, sitting up and looking around. His body had somehow managed to find land and survive. Two miracles rolled into one.

In the shallows of a small natural lagoon were the remains of his ship, battered, beat-up, but mostly intact. It rocked gently on the easy swells that entered through the outlying reef.

"Oh, that's good news. I thought you were dead."

Boaz craned his head back in the other direction to find Tanith walking up the beach, carrying several coconuts. Her dress was ripped and rewrapped, only covering her chest and privates. Her hair was matted, and several obvious scrapes were visible across her smooth skin. Boaz had never seen her look more beautiful.

He watched her walk for a moment. "That's a good look for you," he called out.

Tanith nodded her head in exaggeration. "For you as well," she replied.

Boaz looked down, realizing his tunic was gone. "Apparently, God has seen fit to return me to this earth just as I was the first time I arrived."

He stood unfazed by his nakedness and took a coconut from Tanith. She used her knife to cut off the top, and Boaz guzzled the life-giving liquid inside.

"I think this is an island," Tanith said as she looked off down the beach. "I have seen no sign of habitation."

Boaz's eyes followed her stare. Off to his right, the beach intercepted with a rock face that jutted up into the air. The most curious-looking trees he had ever seen grew along the top. At the lagoon's edge, a large opening into the mountain allowed the tides to flow inside, like a giant rock mouth gulping the sea.

"The crew?"

Tanith's head dipped. "None that I've found."

Boaz nodded somberly.

She took a breath. "I was just about to swim out to the ship. Maybe there is a stray tunic aboard. Wouldn't want the sun to have its way with you," Tanith said as she put down the remaining coconuts and gave his manhood the slightest glance. She moved into the water and looked back, her eyes inviting.

Boaz let a small smile fill his face and then followed. "I'm more interested in the tools aboard. If we can't repair the ship, we can build a smaller one from its timbers.

Disappointment flashed across Tanith's face, then something pulled her gaze down into the hip-deep water. She froze. "Do you see what I see?"

Boaz paused and let his eyes search across the sea floor. The water was crystal clear, but it took a second before he realized what he was seeing. "Gods be praised. The treasure of a thousand kings."

Made in the USA
Las Vegas, NV
04 January 2025

15848147R00163